MW00491174

THE LIST
OF
ADRIAN
MESSENGER

THE LIST OF ADRIAN MESSENGER

PHILIP MacDONALD

VINTAGE BOOKS
A DIVISION OF RANDOM HOUSE
NEW YORK

First Vintage Books Edition, September 1983
Copyright © 1959 by Philip MacDonald
All rights reserved under International and Pan-American
Copyright Conventions. Published in the United States by
Random House, Inc., New York, and simultaneously in
Canada by Random House of Canada Limited, Toronto.
Originally published by Doubleday & Company, Inc.
in 1959.

Library of Congress Cataloging in Publication Data
MacDonald, Philip.
The list of Adrian Messenger.
Reprint. Originally published: 1st ed. Garden City, N. Y. :
Published for the Crime Club by Doubleday, 1959.
I. Title.
PR6025.A2218L5 1983   823'.912   83-5806
ISBN 0-394-71712-0

Manufactured in the United States of America

for MY SISTER MARY with love

THE LIST
OF
ADRIAN
MESSENGER

ADRIAN MESSENGER'S ORIGINAL LIST

P. BAINBRIDGE, *Insurance Agent*
14 Orme Terrace, Cardiff, Wales

JOSHUA BRADDOCK, *Farm Labourer*
Peterbury Old Farm, Moxdale, Yorkshire

IAN JAMES DALKEITH, *Lawyer*
27 Bothwell Square, Edinburgh, Scotland

JOHN MAXWELL DEVITT, *Physician*
113 Museum Street, London, S.W.

CHARLES McGOWAN, *Car Salesman*
18 Wellington Square, London, N.W.

R. F. MORETON, *Vet. Surgeon*
The Kennels, Little Madham, Hampshire

CLAUDE ORMISTON, *Lay Brother*
Retreat of St. Botolph, W. Polhead, Cornwall

A. T. PAXTON, *Shop Assistant*
18A Steelman Lane, Manchester

SIR FRANCIS POMFRET, *Landowner*
The Manor House, Mostyn-Underhill, Suffolk

J. SLATTERY, *Tobacconist*
12 Pope Terrace, Twickenham, Middlesex

CHAPTER ONE

For several years after it was all over, there was understandable resistance in high places to the public telling of this story, and even now the project is eyed askance. Grudging permission to publish has at last been received, however, provided first that certain changes, which are easy, are made to the names of people and places; and second, that no dates are specified, which is much more difficult.

But it can be done. By stating that the time is somewhere between the Second World-War-To-End-World-Wars and the yet-to-come Third which, by eliminating mankind altogether, will really do the trick . . .

The tale hinges, like so much in humanity's sorry history, on a piece of paper. In this case no broken treaty or injudicious epistle from one Personage to another, but a slip upon which Adrian Messenger wrote the names and addresses and occupations of ten men.

The list was the result of considerable thought and activity on Adrian's part, and he wrote it in his Mayfair flat on a cheerless November Wednesday. Other pieces of paper, which he had consulted as he wrote, he tore across and committed to the fire; then stood close to watch them shrivel to grey ash before crossing to the window and looking out—and shivering . . .

He picked up the telephone from the writing-table, and dialed, and when a voice said, "Scotland Yard," asked for General Firth and a moment or so later was saying, "George? This is Adrian Messenger——"

"For God's sake!" The telephone was astonished. "How *are* you, chum? Where've you been for the last six months?"

Adrian said, "Could you lunch with me on Friday?"

"Nothing I'd like better," said the telephone. "Where?"

"My club," Adrian said, and specified. "I'd make it tomorrow but I'm going out of town this evening. Get in a day's hunting before I take off for America."

The start of the day's hunting was a Meet of the Boileau Hounds at Deyming Abbey in Medeshire. Deyming Abbey was the Master's house, and the Master himself was Roderick Simon Fortescue Bruttenholm, Eighteenth Marquis of Gleneyre—who, despite his eighty-five years, was still a more or less active M.F.H.[*]

There was a frosty nip to the clear bright morning, and a pale November sun gilded the red brick of the old house and etched the bare beeches sharply black against the blending greens of turf and yew. In the forecourt and along the drive, overspilling onto the edges of the parkland, were horses, horses and more horses. The chink of bit and curb-chain, the rich crunch of hooves on gravel, mingled with the chatter of horsemen and the robot-sounds of the cars which had brought a crowd of watchers.

The terrace above the forecourt was thick with Hunt members who thronged around white-clothed tables, the scarlet of the men's coats punctuated by the somber black of the women's. Somewhere in the center, towering over a barrier of cronies, was the Master himself, smiling at everything and everyone, his white moustaches fierce against his tanned old face.

He drained his glass and looked all around him and said, "Pretty fair turnout. Glad to see it."

"Like old times, eh?" said the Oldest Crony, fifteen years the

[*] Master of Fox Hounds.

Marquis's junior. "Sort of—what's that damn word they're always usin' nowadays?——"

"Nostalgic," said Crony Number Two, a lad of fifty-five.

"And all your doing, Roddy?" Number Three slapped the Marquis on the shoulder. "You deserve a national vote of thanks, old boy." He included the whole scene in a gesture. "Look at it. Never know there'd been a war on, what?"

"No credit to me, my dear fellah." The Marquis smiled a deprecatory smile. "Just happen to have some money left. And if I hadn't, Mildred's got plenty, bless her!" He chuckled affectionately. "Moral: marry Americans."

There was a voice behind him and a small gloved hand on his arm, and he turned to beam approvingly at a dark-habited, top-hatted young matron who said, "Forgive me, Master—but my daughter's heard a rumor that grandson of yours is going to be out today in spite of school. What'll I tell her?"

Gleneyre smiled at her. "It's a true bill, Marian, m'dear; half-term holiday. Boy's around somewhere. Probably takin' the kinks out of that damn pony."

He was right. Some two hundred yards beyond the west wing of the house Christopher Derek Bruttenholm, Fifteenth Viscount Saltmarche, was walking the qualified pony in and out of the trees which lined the drive, keeping well away from the parked cars even though the once ominously arched back beneath him had slowly flattened out.

The pony was a grey, handsome and well turned out and seven years old. Which made him a bare five years younger than his rider, who had the fair skin and wide-set blue eyes of all the Bruttenholms and also, as his grandsire was wont to say out of his hearing, "The best damn seat on a horse of any kid you ever saw!"

He had good manners too. Which explains how it was that when a man climbed out of a sports-car and came toward him with the obvious intention of speaking, he drew rein and politely waited.

Somewhere in his mid-thirties, well-built and a trifle over middle height, the man was generally unremarkable. In the same way as the car he had stepped out of, which was neither old nor new, like his clothes. But there was something about him, in spite of his vaguely R.A.F. moustache, which made Derek think he was an American

13

even before he spoke. Perhaps it was the camera hanging around his neck.

He said, "Excuse me, but I've never seen a British fox hunt. I was wondering—where are the dogs?"

With some effort, Derek repressed a grin. "Hounds'll be here very soon," he said, and pointed. "You'll see them come out from behind the stables there."

The sun glittered on the man's tinted glasses as he turned his head to look. "Which way?" he said. "Would it be all right if I took a few pictures?" He lifted the camera on its strap and smiled at Derek.

Derek sort of liked him. "Of course it would," Derek said. "And here would be a good place. You see, we're drawing the home coverts first, and we'll be coming right by."

There was a clop-clip-clop of hooves on hard turf and an immaculate Adrian Messenger cantered by on a big, raking chestnut. He saw Derek and reined in, a wide smile brightening his usually saturnine face.

"Derek, you lady-killer!" he said. "Pamela Travers is looking for you all over the place. What you trying to do—break her heart?"

Derek flushed a hot twelve-year-old flush, and tried to cover it with a laugh. "Oh, come off it, Adrian!" he said, and looked sideways at the man he'd been talking with, to see whether he was listening.

But he wasn't. He had the camera up in front of his face, taking a picture of Adrian, and he didn't lower it until Adrian trotted the chestnut off. But then he said, "Who's that? Some big shot in the hunt?"

Relief led Derek into loquacity. "He's my cousin—Major Messenger. He's a Hunt Member, that's all. You see, all Members wear pink—"

"Pink?" the man said. "Looks more like red to me."

"I know it's sort of silly," Derek said. "But it's always called pink. And Members all wear toppers. The Master and the Secretary and the Huntsman and the Hunt servants wear hunting caps. That's how you can tell."

"What about you?" The man came nearer, laying a hand on the pony's neck. "Don't you belong to the Hunt?" His eyes swept Derek

14

from boots to bowler-crown, but he smiled as he spoke, and Derek still liked him in spite of the question.

"I—I'm not *quite* old enough to be a Member," said Derek, and couldn't restrain a downward look at his short black coat.

"*I* think you look great." The man stepped back. "Mind if I get a shot of you?" He raised the camera and sighted it and Derek noticed idly a little muscle twitching beside his right eye, under the corner of the dark glasses.

The camera clicked and the man lowered it. "Thanks," he said, and came nearer again and held out his hand. "My name's Lovett. From Canada—Toronto."

Derek shook hands. He thought Canadians must be like Americans, shaking hands all the time. He had ingrained dislike of sounding off with his title, so he said, "My name's Bruttenholm—Derek Bruttenholm."

He gave the name its traditional pronunciation, but it didn't make any difference. The man stared at him and said, "Hey! You must be some relation to the Marquis of Gleneyre?"

Derek said, "Well—yes. Matter of fact, I'm his grandson." He was so uncomfortable now that he wasn't sure he liked the man any more.

He looked over toward the house, and saw release. Hounds were coming out from behind the stables, boiling around the careful hooves of the Huntsman's big bay, so he said, "I'm sorry, I've got to go," and smiled at the man and forgot all about him as he cantered the pony away.

He had no idea—how could he have?—that within a few weeks the discovery and apprehension of the man would become a matter of paramount importance not only to Scotland Yard but to every police force in Great Britain and Ireland, to say nothing of the Dominion of Canada . . .

On the next day, which was Friday, Brigadier-General George Firth, D.S.O., etc., lunched as arranged with his old friend and fellow-campaigner, Adrian Messenger. Although in his late forties and some twelve years senior to his host, General Firth showed him a warm consideration which, in view of the differing years and rank of the pair, was quite remarkable. Quite remarkable until one took into consideration the fact—practically unknown except between the two—that not once but three times had the younger man saved the elder's life.

They sat in a bay window which looked directly out over the sleet-swept length of St. James's Street—and at last Adrian Messenger came to the point.

He said abruptly, breaking a cigar-and-coffee silence, "Look here, George, I'm embarrassed. So help me out, will you?"

"By all means, chum," said Firth. "But how?"

Adrian said, "It's a cad's trick, but I'm about to trade on auld lang syne and—er—and er——"

"And services rendered?" Firth said. "Well, trade away. It's about time."

"I know you're at Scotland Yard," Adrian said, "but I'm not too sure what the job is——"

Firth said, "How could you be? It's not listed, and it's not permanent. Sort of A.D.C. chore. Special assistant to the head of the C.I.D."

"That's Lucas,* isn't it?"

"Yes. Not at all a bad fellah. Very efficient." General Firth was just talking, watching his host's face.

Adrian said, "I want you to do something for me—without knowing why. If you can't, all you have to do is say so." He took his wallet from an inner pocket, and from the wallet the list he had so carefully compiled two days ago. He unfolded it, and looked at it, and handed it to his guest. He said, "Ten names; ten probable occupations; ten addresses. Scattered to hell and gone all over the kingdom——"

General Firth studied the slip, and looked up from it. "So what do I do?"

Adrian said, "Ask about them." Now it was he who was watching his companion's face. He seemed to expect the frown he saw there, and added quickly, "I know all about Scotland Yard only running London. But I also know they can get any information they want from any other police force. Anywhere."

Firth looked at the list again. "What d'you mean—ask about 'em?"

"Just that," Adrian said. "And do it *un*officially. I mean, I don't

---

* Sir Egbert Lucas, Assistant-Commissioner in charge of Scotland Yard's Criminal Investigation Department.

16

want their families worried by policemen . . ." He hesitated, picking his next words with care and leaning over the table to tap a forefinger on the list. "I'll put it like this: Are these men living at these addresses? . . . I think that ought to do it."

"Suppose they've moved?" Firth said. "Do you want to know where?"

"Well—if you like." Adrian didn't sound particularly interested.

Now Firth stared at him openly. "Let *me* talk a minute," he said. "In the first place, you know I'll do this for you, so that's that. But you also know I haven't any business to. Wasting the taxpayers' money on what looks like a private whim——"

"Whim!" Adrian laughed; a harsh sound with no mirth in it.

"I said 'looks like,' didn't I?" Firth wasn't disguising his own worry now. "But I flatter myself I know you well enough to be sure there's a good reason behind all this. Am I right?"

"Completely," said Adrian, and drained his brandy-glass.

"Then I've got a suggestion." Firth folded the slip and stowed it away in his own wallet. "I've been watching you, chum—and under that go-to-hell front of yours, you're taut as a bow-string. So why not tell me about it?" He hesitated, but his eyes never left Adrian's. "I have an idea this thing's big, whatever it is."

"Big!" said Adrian, on the same note that he'd said "whim." And then he said, "It's so big, and so—so *preposterous,* I daren't tell anyone yet." He looked steadily at Firth. "That's the truth, George. So help me!"

Firth said, "All right. Now tell me how soon you want this information? Might take a while to collect, you know. Especially the way you want it done."

"I'm leaving for America tomorrow," Adrian said. "Be back in about a fortnight. That too soon?"

"Sounds about right," said Firth, and made a business of knocking the ash from his cigar.

But he was thoughtful about it; so thoughtful that Adrian said, "It's no good theorizing, George. You'll only reach some utterly false conclusion. Like what you're thinking now—that I *imagine* I've uncovered some sort of Communist or Fascist or What-Have-You conspiracy." He smiled at Firth's expression, but the smile faded quickly.

17

"Believe me," he said, "there's nary conspiracy. And anyway, if I'm right about it, it's a far older sin than any politics . . ."

And that was all he would say. Over Firth's protests he ordered more brandy, and thereafter talked of this but never that until it was time for both of them to go.

They said good-bye on the steps of the Club, waiting for Firth's taxi. It came, and Firth told the driver, "New Scotland Yard," and opened the door—and then, for some inexplicable reason, found himself turning and going back to Adrian and shaking hands and saying, "Good trip, old boy—take care of yourself . . ."

Some twenty hours later and eighteen thousand feet above the Atlantic, the big Empire Air-Lanes plane flew serenely westward. It was several hours out from England, and the passengers had settled into after-luncheon placidity. Among them, the Chief Steward made one of his unobtrusive tours, and in the galley his two comely minions were relaxing over their first cup of tea since the take-off.

"Lousy load," complained the first Stewardess, a tall and notably curving redhead. "Just one attractive man in my lot—and he doesn't seem to know females exist!" She was talking about Adrian Messenger, who was staring unseeingly out the window beside him, lost in frowning thought.

"Too bad," said Stewardess number two, who was small and slim and dark-haired. "But there's something on my side, kid. Right up in front. French." And she was talking about Raoul Pierre Etien Anne-Marie St. Denis.

Who at this moment was lighting a cigarette and, as was his habit on air-trips, thinking about nothing in particular and everything in general. He was thirty-five if you measure age by time; much older if you take experience for a yardstick. He was a very big man, tall and wide-shouldered, with that lounging, slightly battered-looking elegance which only in fiction belongs solely to Englishmen. In repose, his face was gaunt and expressionless and faintly skull-like. But when he smiled, as he did now at some passing thought, it changed completely. Dangerously, many women thought.

For Raoul and Adrian and their fellow passengers, the plane was a fast and luxurious means of transportation; but from the bridge of the ocean freighter *Belle of Liverpool* it was a silver toy in the sky, tiny and temeritous.

"Lookatherel" said the *Belle's* Captain, pointing it out to his youthful third mate. "If you could of shown that to my old man, Mister, an' told him there was thirty-five or forty human bein's up there, he'd of said you was round the bendl"

"Know what you mean, sir," said the third mate. "Fantastical—that's what it is." He went on staring up—and then, as the Captain stumped back toward the companion and his cabin, suddenly shouted, "*Look!*" on a strange high note.

The Captain whipped around. His eye followed the youngster's upflung arm and he saw the plane again and said, "Oh, *Christ!*" and held his breath as he watched.

Instead of gliding smoothly, the silver toy was yawing in eccentric patterns. It jerked violently, first up and then down, as if some invisible hand had shaken it. And it began to fall, with a dreadful look of uncontrolled laziness, trailing behind it two black plumes of smoke . . .

The *Belle's* Captain jumped for the intercom. He roared orders, and the ship altered course. From her radio transmitter, messages started to pour, and she trembled under the full power of her engines . . .

Many sea-miles away, the aircraft was now only a couple of thousand feet above the ocean, and the horrible lazy-seeming fall was becoming a more horrible headlong plunge when, by some twist of fate or feat of pilotry, this turned into an angled dive . . .

Metal and water met with a hissing roar and a column of spray. A wing of the plane crumpled, and the whole battered craft slowly tilted toward it, revealing one gaping hole where the door of an escape-hatch had been torn away, and another, jagged-edged and cavernous, low in the fuselage.

Through the doorless hatch, an instant before it rolled down to the heaving level of the water, fell three human bodies, some freak of chance rolling them out like so many inanimate bundles.

Three. And then no more as the hole was sealed by the pressure of incalculable tons of water.

The hulk settled deeper, wallowing in the troughs of the grey swell—until some still unquenched flame inside it reached the fuel tanks.

There was a sound like muffled thunder, and a smoke-blackened column of debris-laden water reared fifty feet into the air . . .

Raoul St. Denis had come to consciousness and the surface some half-minute before. His mind whirled, and the water was so cold that for an instant he thought it was liquid flame. There was pain all through him, but he could breathe, and his legs and arms all worked. Instinctively he swam, instinctively forging away from the wreck.

His head struck something hard and unyielding, and he found himself clutching at the wooden slats of a sizeable, stoutly built crate —perhaps the one object that might have floated from the plane which would make a serviceable raft.

He found himself laughing, but it hurt him and he stopped. In his head he heard an echo of his mother's voice. It was reiterating, even as it had just before she died, her old and half-jocular belief that her son had the lives, not of one cat but of three . . .

He was hazily trying to figure out how many of the twenty-seven chances he'd exhausted in the past ten years, when the final explosion destroyed what was left of the plane. He and his crate rocked wildly on the edge of a maelstrom, and he watched in dazed horror as it died, taking with it every last trace of the great machine.

Every last trace—except two dark and sluggishly bobbing round-nesses he suddenly saw between him and where the plane had been.

He stared at the nearer—and saw it was a head. A woman's head. The woman was alive, because she was swimming. Swimming weakly, but swimming.

Pushing the crate, he kicked toward her. The swell lifted her out of his sight for a moment, but then she dropped down the next grey wall of water and he reached out a hand and clutched at her and caught her hair and pulled her to him just as it seemed she was sinking. He saw she was the little dark-haired Stewardess. Her eyes were closed and her face was dead white, with a huge bruise darkening on her temple. She was breathing, but there was no real consciousness in her, and he did the only thing he could. In a nightmare of struggle, he contrived to pull off his belt and slip it around her, under her arms, and then buckle it through two slats of the crate, so that he didn't have to support her to keep her head above the surface.

He thought he was exhausted when the job was done, but then he saw the other roundness again. It was another head—a man's. The man was swimming, too. But only by instinct, keeping afloat by scrabbling at the water like a dog.

Raoul forced himself away from the safety of his raft. He got an arm around the man and kicked out with one last ounce of effort and managed to grab the slats of the crate again. His fingers locked themselves like steel around the wood. He rested, until the weight on his other arm became almost insupportable and he knew he'd have to try and lash the man to the crate as he had lashed the girl.

The man's eyes were open, and his lips kept moving as if he were trying to speak. But he seemed incapable of any other exertion. His face was a strange bluish color and dark blood welled from a wound on his head.

Raoul's mind was spinning again, making thought as difficult as the pain in his side made physical effort. But he fought down a desperate wish just to let go of the man, and minutes or hours or aeons later had him, too, tied to the little raft.

The effort had been exhausting, and Raoul gripped the top of the crate with both hands, heaving himself up so that his body was supported on the top of it. His legs were numb from the fierce cold of the water, and his body felt as if a red-hot bayonet kept stabbing through it. And his brain seemed addled, filled with a ridiculous, whirling problem of language. He'd tied the man with his own *bretelles,* and now he couldn't remember what these should be called in England. *Braces* on one side of the Atlantic, *suspenders* on the other . . . But which was which? . . . Braces—suspenders . . . Suspenders—braces . . .

His mind whirled faster and faster, until there was no thought in it at all . . . His eyes closed . . .

When they opened again there was no trace of sun in the tilting grey sky, and the swell of the grey water was steeper as the crate swooped and climbed. On the one side of him the girl was silent, dead or still unconscious. On the other side, the man was talking, in a loud deep monotone.

". . . messenger," he kept saying, ". . . messenger . . . messenger . . ." And then, ". . . Jocelyn . . . got me . . . to tell . . . Jocelyn . . . got me to tell Jocelyn . . ." The words came out in unrelated, unpunctuated bursts, like bullets from a faulty machine gun. The voice rose. ". . . photograph . . . photograph . . ." it said. And then, more thickly of something which sounded like "Emma's book George Emma's book George Emma's book Emma's book Emma's book . . ."

It trailed off into silence after that. But the relief was short-lived, because within a few minutes it started on its nonsense again. Louder than ever. ". . . all the brooms," it shouted. ". . . clean sweep . . . only one . . . broom left . . . clean . . . sweep . . . clean . . ."

It stopped suddenly, drowned in an odd bubbling sound which might have been a cough.

But Raoul wasn't listening any more. As they had risen to the top of a high swell, he had seen something—

He had seen, not far away, the sleek giant bulk of a ship. Its bows cut through the water as if the heaving waste were a mill-pond, and it was heading toward them . . .

It was some four hours after the *Belle of Liverpool* had started the hunt, that a boat from the Southampton-bound Black Star liner *Carpathia* picked up the survivors. There were two of them—Raoul St. Denis and the girl. The *Carpathia's* doctor judged that the other man, who was Adrian Messenger, had been dead for perhaps an hour before the rescue . . .

Ever since the first reports of the crash, a large part of the so-called civilized world had been bombarded with the news—by television, by radio, and (a little behind, as they must be in these days) the newspapers. Which, however, made up for any lag in time by the bigness and blackness of their headlines, these running the gamut from the first "AIR DISASTER OVER ATLANTIC—ALL FEARED LOST," to the roaring, massive Clarendon cry, "*SURVIVORS FOUND!*"

Empire Air-Lanes being an English concern, the furore was possibly greatest in Britain. But France and the United States were tied a close second. France because Raoul St. Denis was not only the hero of the hour but also one of the most brilliant of current Parisian journalists; America because the passenger list of the plane had included two Senators and a movie star, to say nothing of Adrian Messenger. Who, although a British subject, was nevertheless a best-selling novelist and at least partial heir to the billions of that national monument to Big Business, "Messenger's Five-and-Dime."

Over the weekend more was learned and more still hypothesized, so that on Monday morning the headlines went on another rampage, ranging from the dignified, "PLANE DISASTER—BOMB POSSIBILITY BRUITED" of the *Times*, to the giant, hysterical "?? *S A B O T A G E* ??" of the *Express*.

But for the purposes of this history, it will be best to quote the *Morning Planet*. Then a comparative newcomer to the ranks of London's leading dailies, the *Planet* struck a happily median note between ponderous respectability and blatant sensationalism. Under appropriate headlines, and written by a female novelist considerably overpaid for her services, its special article ran as follows:

> As the Morning Planet's representative, I have been privileged, with certain other newspaper men and women, to interview the only man who can give first hand information about the terrible disaster which on Saturday morning last brought death to forty-one persons aboard the Empire Air-Lanes plane which crashed into the Atlantic.
>
> This man is Raoul Pierre Etien Anne-Marie St. Denis, himself a Parisian journalist well known in his native France for his brilliant interviews with, and analyses of, famous contemporary figures. Staying in London to write a series of these articles on English personalities, M. St. Denis was on a truly "flying" trip to New York, intending to return in a couple of days.
>
> Back with us again inside twenty-four hours, M. St. Denis —although he himself would be embarrassed by the term—is the hero of the day. By luck ejected from the plane into the sea; by luck finding a floating crate washed from the baggage compartment, M. St. Denis not only kept himself afloat for five hours in the freezing sea but, at what must have been tremendous peril to himself, rescued two other victims of the crash. Although in great shock and painfully injured (he has three fractured ribs) he somehow got these people to the frail raft and then, by efforts which must have been well nigh superhuman, lashed them to it in such a manner that

their heads would remain above water. These other victims were Miss Rose Matson, a crew member and stewardess; and the well-known war novelist, Adrian Messenger, co-heir to the fabulous Hiram Messenger fortune and great-nephew to the Marchioness of Gleneyre.

It is already a matter of tragic record that Major Messenger died from his injuries before the trio were picked up by the *Carpathia;* but I am happy to report that the Doctors give Miss Matson (who is still far too ill to be interviewed) more than an even chance of recovery . . .

Now we come to a revelation which must shock the world! It is already known to Officialdom, but is now revealed to the public for the first time.

The disaster may have been caused by an explosion in the baggage compartment of the giant aeroplane; an explosion which had nothing to do with the operation of the machine!

M. St. Denis, who holds a pilot's license himself, is not only an experienced air traveller, both civilian and military, but is also (by reason of his war service) something of an authority on explosives. So the gravest consideration must be given to his asserted belief that the disaster was no accident, but due to the planned detonation of some high-explosive material—IN OTHER WORDS, A BOMB!! . . .

Lest I be accused of sensationalism, let me quote M. St. Denis verbatim. He speaks English (as he does five other languages) fluently and with a charming accent. And here are his own words:

"You are asking me how it comes about," he said. "So I say this most carefully. As I have already said it to the Officials who made enquiry from me . . . We are flying along most calmly, at the elevation of a little something less than twenty thousand of your feet. There is nothing to suggest any wrongness in our progression. Then there is from under us an explosion! Not the explosion of *essence*—of petrol—but of some high-explosive . . . The explosion is of considerable proportion. Extremely considerable. A hole is in the floor, and fire. There are persons dead, and others injured. The aeroplane herself is falling, but myself I am in high luck. I am down among my seat and the next seat, with every one of my senses and some rib-cracks only. But everything is now Hades as we plummet. Once, perhaps twice, we turn over . . .

"If the aeroplane had stricken the sea in fall, I should not be here. But *something* takes place before the strike. It is a miracle? Or the pilot has contrived to obtain control? . . . There is no way to answer . . . But for the last perhaps

24

six hundred meters, the aeroplane is gliding. Steeply, but gliding.

"The impact with the water is all the same one hell of a bang! Everything and every person tumbles forward. There is a hole where was a door, and I am in some way through it. My head comes crack against the side, and I am kayoed. I recover, and I am in the water. It is cold. I am swimming, and I find this crate of wood—another miracle! The aeroplane now explodes itself, I think from fire meeting at last with the *essence*.

"I then find there are two more persons also in the water," concluded M. St. Denis. "And after this——? You know as much as myself."

And that was all I or any of my colleagues could get out of him. A newspaperman himself, M. St. Denis had been prepared to make a statement, but this was all of it. As I suggested before, he is extremely averse to being treated as a hero—and, we also gathered, is not in any event given to talking about himself. We did try to get the answers to a few questions, particularly what he himself thought might be the *origin* of the bomb. But he refused to speculate, saying this was a matter for the authorities to decide.

As of course it is—although it immediately occurs to me, as it will I am sure to thousands of readers, to ask how anyone can decide anything, or come to any conclusion at all, when every trace of the plane and all its contents, including the bodies of the other passengers, are now spread about upon the bottom of the Atlantic, in a region where the tremendous depth obviates any possibility of salvage?

That, if I may use the phrase, is indeed the question . . .

And it can also be the signal for me to stop trying to write about the important things, like a real reporter, and concentrate on those trivia which—let us face it?—interest a great majority of my sex . . .

I will start with the crate. This homely article has fascinated me from the beginning: it seemed to me such an unlikely, not to say fortuitous, thing to find upon an airliner. And when I heard M. St. Denis himself use the word "miracle" in connection with it, I became so curious that I pestered Empire Air-Lanes officials until I found out all about it.

In the first place it *was* an unusual object to find upon this airliner, even in the baggage compartment. Secondly, it has an odd little history. Specially made in London by expert carpenters, it was being shipped to New York for the air-transportation, to England, of a prize-winning poodle recently purchased in America by the wife of an Empire Air-Lanes director. And when one considers not only that such an object has never before been carried by Empire Air-Lanes, *and* that it somehow escaped disintegration by the bomb, and *then* that it was actually washed out of the wreckage in time to be used as a raft—well, it is clear that M. St. Denis's use of the word "miracle," was no mere figure of speech . . .

And so on went the article—and on. With all the other disaster-stories in all the other papers, it was read by hundreds of thousands of persons in London; read in houses and offices, on trains and buses, in tea-shops and restaurants and bars.

One of the bars was in Wardlaw's Hotel in South Kensington. Quiet, comfortable and of impregnable correctitude, Wardlaw's has for fifty years been a haven for retired officers, visiting clergy and a sprinkling of business and professional men who know a good thing when they find one. The bar is small and a little on the dark side, but the liquor served at it is good, and it is never over-crowded.

On this Monday morning, in fact, the bartender had only one customer, although it was nearly noon. The customer was a new visitor to Wardlaw's; an American, registered as Charles K. Hoag of Detroit. Mr. Hoag, it was understood, was combining a business trip to London with a certain amount of sightseeing. In his middle thirties, clean-shaven, well-built and a trifle over middle height, Mr. Hoag was quiet-mannered, conservatively clad and generally unremarkable.

But all the Hotel servants liked him very much, particularly the bartender, whose improbable name was Kidgery. A gregarious Cockney, Kidgery's only complaint about his job was that the clientele of Wardlaw's was not generally of the type which chats with the man who mixes its drinks, and Mr. Hoag was proving a pleasant exception to this rule. Mr. Hoag, it seemed, was always ready for an interchange of time-wiling generalities.

This morning, over his Amontillado, Mr. Hoag was reading the special air-disaster article in the *Morning Planet,* and when he'd finished and put the paper down, Kidgery saw an opening and jumped into it.

"Terrible thing, that plane, Mr. 'Oag!" said Kidgery.

"Certainly is," Mr. Hoag assented. "I may be old-fashioned, but give me ocean travel every time."

"I see as 'ow they're sayin' it was a bomb," said Kidgery. "Meself, I wonder."

"Could be, I suppose," Mr. Hoag said. "But they'll say anything in the papers."

"You're right enough there, sir." Kidgery gave weighty assent. "But 'owever it come about, it was certainly 'orrible! Forty-three livin' souls on that aircraft—an' on'y two of 'em left!" He regarded Mr. Hoag's empty glass with an enquiring tilt of his eyebrows.

Mr. Hoag nodded, and Kidgery refilled the glass with care. "This 'ere Frenchman done all right, though," he said. "Like you'd say in America, sir, 'Quite a guy!'"

Mr. Hoag nodded. "*And* lucky," he said.

"Can't 'elp feelin' sorry for that other chap, though." Kidgery shook his head. "The one what died on that raft-like. Name o' Messenger, was it? So near and yet so far, if y'know what I mean, sir."

Mr. Hoag sipped at his wine. "Yes," he said. "Too bad."

He set down his glass and put a hand up to his forehead, rubbing casually at a spot by his right eye, where a little muscle had begun to twitch . . .

CHAPTER TWO

By the following Thursday, although mention of the crash was still to be found on front pages, the space devoted to it in the Press had shrunk by some ninety percent. Enquiries were in full swing; by the Airline itself, by a Committee of the House of Commons, by the Special Branch of the C.I.D. But until any or all of these more-or-less august bodies came to some conclusion, there was little or nothing with which to tickle the public news-palate. It might have been different had there been any possibility of communication with either of the survivors, but Miss Rose Matson was still hovering incommunicado between life and death,* while Raoul St. Denis had been

---

* Miss Matson died two days later, never having recovered consciousness sufficiently to be questioned.

spirited away to a private Nursing Home into which not even the most resourceful reporter had so far been able to thrust himself.

This Thursday was the same day on which Anthony Gethryn returned to London from Rome, where for three interminable weeks he had been engaged, *sub rosa,* upon a diplomatic mission of great delicacy and abysmal lack of interest.

Except for the reports he must make, the mission was over. He was heartily glad of that, but not so glad to be back. In Rome there had at least been sun, but London was chill and dirty under a dun-colored pall which couldn't decide whether to be a fog or not. Also, to make things worse, the city didn't contain the only two people he really wanted to see. For his son was away at school, and his wife was in Switzerland, where it was impossible for him to join her until the aforesaid reports had been made.

White* brought the new Voisin down to the airport to meet him, and all the way back from Hounslow to Knightsbridge and 19 Stukeley Gardens, Anthony's depression increased. Even in his own house, warming his long legs in front of a blazing fire in his own study, his mood refused to lighten. Which may explain his alacrity in accepting the invitation which came with his first phone call.

The caller was Lucas. And Lucas, it seemed, would be glad if Anthony could dine with him that night.

"Delighted," said Anthony. "Where?"

"My club," said the telephone, and Anthony said only, "What time?" Which, considering he has always thought this institution the dreariest in London, was true revelation of his state of mind.

"I thought about seven." Lucas hesitated, and a barely perceptible difference came to his tone. "George Firth will be with me."

"Good," said Anthony. "Like to meet him." And then he said, "There was something in your voice, my friend. What is this—a problem?"

"That," said Lucas cryptically, "is what Firth wants to find out."

Lucas's club was the Chatham, but in spite of what Anthony had always called its necrobiotic atmosphere, he found himself enjoying the dinner. The food was edible if unimaginative, the wines were

* Anthony's *fidus Achates,* his servant for many years.

excellent, and the man Firth had turned out to be good company. Also, of course, there was the real purpose of the occasion to whet his appetite; the Problem so intriguingly described as being the problem of deciding whether some unknown quantity were indeed a problem or not.

Lucas didn't mention it through the meal, but over coffee suddenly looked at Anthony and said, "Firth's got something on his mind he wants to consult you about. Personally, I take the view there's nothing in it except coincidence. However, if by some remote chance there is, I don't know anyone who'd be more likely to make sense out of the whole business than you."

Anthony grinned. "Praise from Sir Egbert is praise indeed!"

He drew no answering smile. "There's one question I'll ask you," Lucas said. "And after that I'll turn you over to Firth. Did you, by any chance, know Adrian Messenger?"

Anthony shook his head. "Only one of the family I ever met was his brother Bernard. Why?"

"Firth'll tell you." Lucas looked at his other guest. "Take over," he said, and retreated behind his cigar.

Firth said, "Bernard was killed at Alamein. The only way he could be connected with this at all is through his marriage . . ." He seemed to hesitate. "To Jocelyn Quist," he said, and stopped.

"If that's the miniaturist," Anthony said, "my wife knows her. I met her once for a couple of minutes. On the heroic scale. Cable address, Valhalla."

Firth said, "Yes. Yes, I know what you mean. Adrian was hopelessly in love with her. For years. From before Bernard even knew her."

Lucas emerged from a screen of cigar smoke. "First I've heard of any Norse goddesses in this affair," he said. "Or any brother of Messenger's. May I suggest that if they aren't obviously involved, they're misleading."

Firth's laugh was embarrassed. "I was just warming up," he said. "Sorry." He looked at Anthony. "All right, Gethryn, here goes: Adrian Messenger was a friend of mine. In the fullest sense of the word. He served with me in France and Libya. Three times he saved my life. I *knew* the man, outside and in. So if I tell you later I could read more into what he said than appeared on the surface—well, I have some justification for saying it. I won't just be letting imagination run away with me. See what I mean?"

"Why shouldn't I?" said Anthony.

"I don't really know." Firth lifted square shoulders, and shot a sidelong glance at Lucas. "Except it isn't everyone who does."

Lucas said, "Get to the point, man."

"Right," Firth said, and then to Anthony, "In '42 I caught a packet and Adrian and I got separated for the rest of the War, and didn't see much of each other afterwards. So I was delighted when he phoned me at the Yard last week and asked me to lunch. It didn't make any difference to me that he somehow sounded as if he wanted something from me. I was glad to be seeing him again, for whatever reason."

He reached into his breast-pocket and pulled out a wallet. He didn't open it, just held it in his fingers. "So I went to lunch," he said. "And after an hour's worth of bush-beating, Adrian got to the point. He did want something from me, and he knew that strictly speaking I shouldn't agree to do it without more information than he was prepared to give me. But he also knew that if *he* asked me I'd break most of the rules in the book."

He opened the wallet and took from it a folded slip of paper which he handed to Anthony across the table. It was Adrian Messenger's list.

"He gave me this," Firth said. "What he wanted was information, which I was to obtain from the local Police Forces concerned, about the men whose names he'd written on that paper. He wouldn't tell me why he wanted it, though I pressed him. But he did admit that whatever-it-was was 'big.' That was the word he used. And it was about all I could get out of him about it verbally. But as I said just now, I *knew* the man. So I could see he was strung too tight, really worried about something. Up to the point, I'd say, of finding it difficult to sleep." He stopped abruptly, seeing that Anthony had unfolded the slip of paper and was studying it.

Anthony looked up. "Go on," he said.

Firth said, "Well, I promised to do what he wanted——"

"Which was?" Anthony interrupted. "Exactly, I mean. You told me he wanted information about these men, but you didn't specify what he asked for."

"Sorry," Firth said. "I can quote you his words—which he chose very carefully. Too carefully, if you know what I mean. What he said was, 'Are these men living at these addresses?' Before that, I should tell you, he'd insisted the enquiries were to be discreet; he didn't want the men's families 'worried by policemen.' He also hinted that when he came back from America in about a fortnight, and got the answers, he might be in a position to tell me more."

Anthony was frowning at the list. "Odd sort of job-lot," he said. "Unless it's meant to be a cross-section of Homo Britannicus, *circa* 1950."

"I don't know who the men are," Firth said. "Or what made Adrian link them together." He paused. "But I do know something which might link some of them with him."

He opened the wallet again and took out another folded paper, larger. It showed typescript as he unfolded it. "Here's a précis of the reports on six of 'em, if you want to check the names from Adrian's own list. The others aren't in yet." He read, slowly, "*Joshua Braddock . . . John Maxwell Devitt . . . Charles McGowan . . . Robert F. Moreton . . . Arthur Thomas Paxton . . . Sir Francis Pomfret.*"

He stopped there, and Anthony smiled. "You don't have to drag it out, you know. I'm on the hook already."

"Nearly there." Firth's answering smile was transitory. "It was last Friday I lunched with Adrian. I put the enquiries in train the same afternoon." He was talking very slowly, picking his words. "The next day, Saturday, Adrian died. And bomb or no bomb, I think you'll agree his death is listable in the column '*Accidental.*'"

He stopped again, and this time Anthony said, "So——?"

"That's the column," Firth said, "where you can find every one of those names I just read to you." He drew a deep breath. "In other words, Gethryn, all six are dead. Each having met, separately, with a death put down to accident!"

There was silence for a long moment after that.

Until Anthony said to Lucas, "Do I sleep, do I dream—or did you say *coincidence?*"

"You don't agree?" Lucas was expressionless.

"My dear fellow, how could I? Reduce the thing to its basic terms,

31

and look at it: *An intelligent man, troubled by or about ten other men, asks a friendly police official to enquire about them. The next day he qualifies for a Death-by-Accident headstone, leaving said F.P.O. to discover that six out of the ten enquirees have also met the same sort of end.*" Anthony shook his head. "Six out of ten, Lucas! Three out of five! It's too high a proportion for Chance. So vastly improbable that we have to behave as if it were impossible."

Firth smiled to himself, settling back in his chair.

But Lucas wasn't smiling. "Very neat," he said to Anthony. "Very tidy. But there's another point of view. Firth: tell him what the accidents were, and where."

Firth unfolded his paper again. He read:

> "Braddock—Cycling accident—Yorkshire.
> Devitt—Accident with lift—London.
> McGowan—Car smash—Kingston-on-Thames.
> Moreton—Fall from railway bridge—Hampshire.
> Paxton—Traffic accident—Birmingham.
> Pomfret—Drowned while sailing—Yarmouth."

"Thank you." Lucas spoke to Firth, but kept his eyes on Anthony. "Now as to dates; I believe the last of these six deaths was about seven months ago——"

"Eight," said Firth. "Robert Moreton."

"And the first was four *years* ago——"

"Almost five," said Firth. "Sir Francis Pomfret."

Lucas put down his cigar, carefully. "Now listen to me, Gethryn," he said. "In the first place, statistics play hell with your theories. These six deaths cover a period of five years, and an area which includes most of the United Kingdom. As a percentage of the total deaths by accident for that time, over that range, they'd work out to something like point-o-to-the-tenth-four-three! In a word, infinitesimal!"

He seemed to expect some reply, but didn't get any. He said, "Secondly, although you haven't had the temerity to say so, what you're asking me to believe in would have to be a mass-murder plot of such motiveless magnitude that Hollywood wouldn't accept it! Not even if the villains were Communists or Murder, Incorporated!"

Firth shifted in his chair. "Funny you should say that. Because Adrian mentioned Communists, too. When I was trying to pump

32

him, he told me not to run away with any ridiculous notions about any sort of conspiracy—Red or Fascist or What-Have-You."

"He did, eh?" Anthony's tone was sharp. "Anything else like that?"

"I've told you he said it was 'big.' But he also used the word 'preposterous.' It seemed to me he thought nobody would believe him until he had more—what shall I say?—data."

"The poor devil foreshadowed you, Lucas," said Anthony. "You and your statistics and your motiveless magnitudes! All you mean is you can't find any explanation——"

"Can you?" Lucas cut him short.

"How do I know yet? But I don't mind trying. Personally, I like to close stable doors before *all* the horses have gone."

"Spare me!" Lucas groaned. "If I've heard your True-Function-of-the-Police lecture once, I've heard it a hundred times!"

Firth said suddenly, "Oh, Gethryn, there was one other thing Adrian said. After he'd told me this wasn't any conspiracy, Communist or otherwise, he made a rather strange remark. He said, 'It's a far older sin than politics.'"

Lucas picked up his cigar. "Isn't it possible Messenger was letting his imagination run riot?"

"Instead of stifling it with statistics?" Anthony grinned. "However, since you like figures so much, I'm going to throw you some more. Add Messenger himself, and we have seven men out of eleven who've met with these *accidental* deaths. That's a little over sixty-three percent, my boy! I could bear to know how much more you'd want before you take this seriously. Suppose, for instance, that when Firth gets the rest of the reports, we find a couple *more* of the men have died from *accidents?* How would you feel then? Or are you a whole-hogging diehard—a hundred percent or nothing?"

Firth started to laugh; then checked himself as he saw with some astonishment that Sir Egbert Lucas, K.C.B. had actually flushed. From imperturbable chin to grey-flecked Olympian temples.

"Let me see," said Sir Egbert Lucas slowly. "One more would make it about seventy-three percent . . ." He was silent a moment. "I don't think we're going to get one more, mind you, but if we do"—he hesitated again—"if we do, I suppose I'd have to jump over the fence to your side . . ."

He drew on the cigar and wreathed himself in smoke once more and pushed back his chair. "Let's have a change of topic," he said. "And scene. The brandy'll be just as good upstairs."

They traversed the cavernous length of the Chatham's dining-room and made their way to the lobby. They were taking the necessary detour around the monstrous bronze of William Pitt the Younger when Firth muttered, "You fellows go on. With you in a second," and disappeared.

It was a full five minutes, however, before he joined them in the big bay window of what is still called the Melville room. He slid into a chair and accepted brandy and waited quietly enough until Lucas had finished an anecdote. And then he said:

"I called the Yard just now. I remembered the reports from Scotland always come in about nine at night."

"Scotland?" said Lucas.

"I thought," said Firth, "there might be something from Edinburgh."

"Edinburgh?" Now Lucas sounded wary.

Anthony said, "It may be *lèse-majesté*, but sometimes I'd like to kick you in the seat! . . . He means something on Ian Dalkeith, Sir Egbert. Number Three on Adrian Messenger's list——"

Firth said, "Exactly," and turned a deliberately blank eye on Lucas. "You might like to know," he said, "that Ian Dalkeith is dead."

And then he said, "You may remember reading about a railway accident in the West Highlands a couple of years ago. When one of those little Scottish branch-line trains went off the rails. Fifteen people were killed—and Dalkeith was one of them . . ."

So what had begun as an academic Discussion of Probabilities ended as a conference of Ways and Means; not at the Chatham Club but at Scotland Yard. To give Lucas credit, when he jumped the fence he jumped it whole-heartedly, at least for the time being; even going to the length of allowing himself to be transported to Whitehall in the new Voisin with its owner at the wheel . . .

In the headquarters of London's Metropolitan Police there is little difference between day and night, and the sudden arrival of the Chief of the Criminal Investigation Department, accompanied by his new aide and by the lean familiar figure of Anthony Ruthven

Gethryn, caused no noticeable stir except within the ranks of the C.I.D. itself, where men girded metaphoric loins and sat a little lighter on their chairs.

But Lucas sat heavily in his, frowning down at the top of his desk, at nothing in particular.

"Well," he said, "what's our first move in this weird business?"

"Get a real policeman," said Anthony. He had pulled back the window curtains and was looking thoughtfully out over the dark river.

Frowning, Lucas picked up one of his telephones. "Lucas here," he said into it. "Does Superintendent Pike happen to be in tonight? . . . Oh, good. Ask him to step along and see me, will you?"

Anthony turned. "How much does Pike know about this, if anything?"

"As much as I did when we started dinner tonight. He discussed it with me and Firth before I phoned you this morning."

"And what did he think?"

Lucas shrugged, and Firth said, "He wouldn't give an opinion." He came from the hearth where he'd been standing and sat on the arm of a chair near the desk. "Said he'd wait to hear what *you* thought."

Lucas smiled, a trifle wryly. "Gethryn and Pike are a sort of mutual admiration society, Firth——"

And then there was a knock on the door and Pike himself. He said to Lucas, "You wanted to see me, sir?" and nodded to Firth and shook hands with Anthony, a wide smile creasing his lantern-shaped face.

Lucas said, "This Adrian Messenger business, Pike: we've got to do something about it."

"Yes, sir." Pike was placid. "I guessed that was what you wanted to see me about."

"You did, eh?" Lucas stared at him sourly. "May I ask if you've also guessed Mr. Gethryn would agree with General Firth? And that I'd have to go over to their side?"

"Well yes, sir. Especially after I happened to see the reply from Edinburgh. I thought seventy-five percent was coming a bit high for coincidence."

"Seventy-*three*, dammit!" Lucas snapped; and then, as Anthony laughed and Firth discreetly hid a grin, managed a smile himself.

"All right," he said. "All right! . . . Take a chair, Pike, and join the conference." He picked up a pencil and began to draw aimlessly on his blotter. "Anyone any idea of where to start?" He looked across the room at Anthony, now sitting on the window-sill. "And *don't* say 'the beginning,' for God's sake. Because from our point of view there isn't one!"

Pike cleared his throat. "I know something we ought to do, sir. Right away. We ought to check on the other three men on that list. Because if any of 'em are still alive, they're in danger. They've got to be warned. And protected." He looked at Firth. "You see, General, we can't afford to be diplomatic any more, the way you had to be."

Firth nodded. "You're absolutely right, Superintendent."

"Yes indeed!" Lucas's frown had disappeared. "And isn't there another thing, Pike? As well as warning and protecting any survivors of the ten, we must question them. Ask 'em what the link is between them and the rest of the names. Then we'll have a starting-point, at least."

"Yes, sir. Though that might have to come a little later." Pike started to his feet; then subsided as he looked across the room and met a doubtful eye.

"Just a minute." It was Anthony who was frowning now. "I think there's something we're missing." He stood up and came over to the desk. "Owing to the fact—forgive me, Firth!—that the C.I.D was left in ignorance of Messenger's reason for making enquiries about the ten men on his list, we're in the dark on a most important point. If any or all of the three remaining men are still alive, we can't be sure that one of them isn't responsible for the removal of the others."

He waited, flicking a glance around at his listeners. Scowling, Lucas had gone back to his drawing as he pondered. Pike was rubbing thoughtfully at his chin. Firth's eyes had widened and he said suddenly, "My God—I never thought of that!"

"You see the corollaries?" Anthony dropped into a chair. "*If* any of the three are alive, the one thing we mustn't do now is show them even the shadow of a policeman! We can watch them, certainly; guard 'em too. But only from a discreet distance. None of 'em must get the idea that the multiple *accidents* have come under any sort of suspicion. Because, if one of 'em *is* guilty, suspicion would warn him. And then all he'd have to do would be what the Americans call 'clam up,' and we'd never get anywhere!"

Lucas threw down his pencil. "I suppose I see what you mean. But I see a lot of other things too. Mostly negative." He sounded bitter. "How the hell can we ever find out what links these ten men together if we can't ask any survivors? And if we can't find out what links 'em, we'll never find a motive for the killings. And if we don't find a motive——"

Anthony cut in on him. "Hold your horses! I didn't say we'd *never* be able to ask 'em. I said we couldn't do it *now*." Seeing Pike shift restlessly, he suddenly laughed. "The old pro," he said. "Right as usual."

Lucas glared. "What the devil are you talking about now? And what's so damn funny?"

"We are. Pike's wondering why we don't find out if any of the three *are* still alive. Before we scratch each other's little eyes out."

Lucas muttered, "See what you mean . . . All right, Pike."

Smiling, Pike got to his feet. He said to Anthony, "Don't worry, sir—we won't show 'em any shadows," and was gone.

He left a silence behind him. Anthony lit a cigarette, and Firth began to pace. Lucas picked up the discarded pencil and stared at the ceiling . . .

Between his fingers the pencil snapped suddenly in half, and he sat up, flinging the pieces into a wastebasket with a violent clatter.

"Even now, I can't swallow this!" he said. "I don't care about the Law of Average, I can't swallow it! I don't see how you fellows can accept it so completely. Do you realize you're asking me to believe that some human being, or combination of human beings, has not only spent brains, money and five years of time in murdering eight men, but has cold-bloodedly killed at least fifty others in the process! Why, assuming it had a foothold here, which it hasn't, even the Mafia would blench at the idea!"

"It's no combination, Lucas." Anthony was still infuriatingly placid. "It's not even a partnership. As you'd know if you'd read either of Messenger's books."

"I have." Lucas stared. "Both of them, as a matter of fact." He was far from soothed. "But what the devil have they got to do with what you're saying?"

"They show he was highly intelligent, far from hysterical, and a man who respected our language. So we add these three facts to three things he said to Firth." Anthony ticked the items off on his fingers. "He said this was 'big.' He said it was 'preposterous,' implying it was hard to believe. And finally he said it wasn't any kind of 'conspiracy.'" He looked at Firth. "Am I right?"

"Completely." Firth's nod was decisive.

"I suggest you look up the word *conspiracy*, Lucas." Anthony was pressing now. "You'll see it's defined something like this: 'An agreement, a plotting, between *two or more* persons to commit some unlawful act.' A man as careful of words as Messenger couldn't use it to mean anything else. So when he said this was *no conspiracy of any kind*, he meant exactly that!"

"Meaning this alleged holocaust was the work of one man?" Lucas's honeyed restraint was ominous.

"Or woman," Anthony said. "Though vastly improbable, she's within the bounds of possibility."

"One *person*, then?" The restraint was cracking already. "Have you considered where that leaves us? Face to face with that ultimate incredibility, the Napoleon of Crime!" Lucas was in full blást again. "Meet Professor or Mrs. Moriarty? Shake hands with Doctor or Mrs. Fu Manchu!"

Anthony smiled; but the smile faded quickly. "I sympathize," he said. "But I don't agree . . ." He got to his feet and wandered to the window and back again, shoulders hunched, hands deep in pockets. In his lean face, the green eyes seemed unusually dark.

"It seems to me," he said slowly, "that we're up against something a lot tougher than any paper-back Arch-villain. And a lot more dangerous . . . I give you Mr. Smith Brown-Jones. An unrecorded, unknown, and to the public eye unremarkable, member of our population."

Watching Anthony's face, Lucas didn't speak. But Firth said, "Does that mean you've dropped your first theory, Gethryn? About the three men left on the list?"

"Hardly a theory, was it? I was in the conditional mood, if you remember." Anthony was back at the window now. "I said *if* any of the three were alive, we had to be careful because one of 'em *might* be our man." He stared out at the Thames again. "But I think it's highly improbable. A murder-list three-quarters victim *could* contain the murderer's name in the last quarter. But the odds must be a hundred to one against it."

"Which leaves us where?" Lucas was surprisingly mild.

"In suspension." Anthony wandered back to his chair and dropped into it. "Also serving. Sitting and waiting."

The waiting, which *in toto* lasted until after midnight, was punctuated by two visits from Superintendent Arnold Pike.

On the first, which was at eleven-fifteen, he reported that according to his friend Chief Inspector Evans of the Cardiff police, Percy Bainbridge had been absent from his home in that city for almost a year. His present whereabouts were unknown, but further details would follow.

"Well, well!" Lucas was thoughtful. "That's one who's not definitely defunct, anyway."

"The first out of eight," said Anthony. "Or nine, if you count Messenger."

And then they waited some more. Until, at ten to twelve, Pike appeared for the second time.

Now J. Slattery, of 12 Pope Terrace, Twickenham, was his subject. And J. Slattery, it seemed, was safely at home, safely in bed, and presumably in untroubled slumber . . .

Lucas sat straight. His eyebrows went up and he said, "That's *two!*"

Anthony regarded him with a weary eye. "A rip-roaring eighteen percent!" he said. "Living like flies, aren't they!"

Which, except for desultory remarks unworthy of record, lasted them until Pike came back at twenty-five past midnight.

He brought with him a report on the last man of the ten, Claude Ormiston, a lay Brother of the Order of St. Botolph.

A few months ago, it appeared, Ormiston had been transferred from the Brotherhood's Retreat in Cornwall to a newly established one in the Cumberland fells. Sent out on an errand of mercy one day about six weeks after his arrival, Ormiston had failed to return, and a search-party had found his body just after dawn; on the outskirts of a lonely hill farm. He had been crushed under the wheels of a huge hay lorry which by some tragic mischance had rolled down a steep slope from the spot where it had been left for the night . . .

This time Lucas was mute, and it was Anthony who broke the silence.

"Bringing the death toll to nine," he said. "Nine out of eleven, Lucas! A percentage, if you work it out, of eighty-one point eighty-one recurring . . ."

That was at twenty-seven minutes past twelve, and by the time Big Ben tolled the half-hour from across the street, Lucas had capitulated. This time completely.

He sighed. "Let's get started," he said. "What first?"

"The old pro, surely." Anthony looked at Pike. "Tell us what *you* want to do."

"A lot of things, sir." Pike glanced unhappily at Lucas. "This is going to take work."

"And men." Lucas was unhappy too. "And money."

"'Fraid so, sir," said Pike, and got down to business. "In a way, the most important thing is Slattery. But I'm going to talk about him later, if you'll forgive me." He paused for a reflective moment. "Apart from him, there are three main steps I want to take, and the sooner the better. First, I want to request full reports on all these 'accidents' from all the local police forces concerned, together with the personal opinions of the Chief Constables concerned. Then, in regard to Percy Bainbridge, who's disappeared from his home, I want to get Evans to make a full enquiry so we can possibly trace what's happened to the man. And then I want particulars, again from the local police forces, of *all* living relatives of *all* the deceased men, so we can ask 'em if they know anything at all about any of the other men on the list. Or about Major Messenger."

Pike stopped there, abruptly. He looked at Lucas. "Doesn't take long to *say*"—he smiled ruefully—"but it means work. Believe me!"

"The old story." Lucas sighed. "Too few men. Too little money." He looked at Anthony. "Any remarks?"

"One—but it's probably superfluous . . . Pike, when you talk about getting 'full reports' on all the deaths, I asssume you mean that, in

40

the more recent cases, you'll also try and inspire more investigation? To see if we can't get *some* line on the killer that way."

"Naturally, sir." Pike was reproachful. "Goes without saying, if you know what I mean."

"*Mea culpa!*" Anthony grinned. "Sorry . . . However, in connection with those same reports, there's something I want; something you haven't even hinted at so far. I want to know whether any or all of the ten served with our armed forces during the recent global fracas. And I want to know, specifically, what units of what forces. Also, *where* the services were given, geographically. If one's looking for a link between eleven widely differentiated men, it seems to me that in these days——"

He didn't get any further. Because Pike slapped a loud hand on a knee; Firth said, "Of *course!*" in hushed amazement; and Lucas asked, "Doesn't it ever pall, Gethryn, being right *all* the time?"

"You'd all have seen it." Anthony laughed. "Sooner or later."

"Don't rub salt in the wounds," Lucas said. "All right, Pike'll look after it. Anything else?"

"Several things. First, I could bear to know anything the Special Branch has found out about the alleged bomb on that plane——"

"*You* say 'alleged'!" Lucas was pained. "Of all people, you should be the first to say a bomb was certain."

"Not *certain.*" Anthony shook his head. "Merely ninety-nine percent probable! Now you're completely satisfied there's a killer at work, I can point out that one, or perhaps even a couple, of the deaths *could* have been due to genuine accident. Satan, as it were, helping his own."

"*No!*" Lucas clapped a hand to his forehead. "For God's sake, man, have pity! . . . Just let me tell you about the bomb! The Special Branch, *and* E.A.L., *and* the House committee—they're all convinced there was one. They believe the man St. Denis."

"They do?" Anthony was attentive. "I was wondering about him."

"I enjoy that puzzled look on you!" Lucas rubbed his hands. "But I suppose I'll have to tell you. Raoul St. Denis is quite well-known to the Special Branch. And better to the War Office, especially your old branch in Intelligence."

He waited, and Anthony said, "All right, I grovel. Who is Raoul, what is he, that all Whitehall believes him?"

"Today, he's a journalist of some reputation on the Continent, as you probably know." Lucas was still enjoying himself. "But a few years ago he was high up in the French Resistance forces; their top man on explosives. I think it's quite likely you've corresponded with him in your time. His *nom-de-guerre* was Ajax."

"Well I'll be damned!" Anthony nodded in memory. "I've not only corresponded with him, I've spoken to him. On short wave. Several times . . ."

"That's confidential, of course." Lucas was official again. "I merely mentioned it to show why his statement about a bomb was accepted so readily . . . But as to who planted the thing, or how, there's no further information."

"No," said Anthony. "No, there wouldn't be. That's up to us now."

He relapsed into silence, and after a moment Lucas said, "Next please?"

"Slattery, J." Anthony glanced at Pike. "We didn't give you time to come back to him."

"Thank you, sir." Pike sat forward. "Slattery's got to be approached directly, of course, so's he can be asked about the other men on the list. But"—he smiled at Anthony—"the approach musn't be by anyone he'd spot as a policeman. So we'll have to send a good man, with a good story——" His glance at Lucas was half humorous, half apprehensive.

"No!" Lucas slapped a palm sharply on the desk. "You know better than that, Pike! Great heavens, man—we can't go round just *ignoring* Regulations!"

"No, sir." Pike was dutiful—but one bright eye was cocked at Anthony.

Who said, "So you want me to supply the *agent provocateur?* Don't listen, Lucas. How about Flood,* Pike? Or Dyson?"

Pike nodded happily. "I think Mr. Flood, sir."

"All right." Anthony glanced at his watch. "We can't do anything tonight, anyway. But I'll get onto it first thing in the morning."

"I didn't hear that." Lucas looked at his watch too. "You finished, Gethryn?"

---

* Flood is a newspaperman who, together with his friend Dyson, has worked on many of Anthony's cases, particularly on jobs which could not, or should not, be carried out by official detectives.

"With you and Pike, yes." Anthony got to his feet and looked around the somber room. "And if you'll forgive me, with these none too joyous surroundings." He looked at Firth. "I want three or four more things. In this order: two or three drinks, *and* all the *personal* information I can get on Adrian Messenger——"

In his study at Stukeley Gardens, Anthony provided the drinks and questions, Firth the information.

Which, reduced to its essentials, was that Adrian Messenger had always been, if not secretive, at least a notable keeper of his own counsel; that he was a man of few, if any, confidants, but that in all probability Jocelyn Messenger, his widowed sister-in-law, was the most likely to have filled the role; that he had possibly known, when he gave Firth the list, that at least some of the men on it had been killed, as witness his disinterest when Firth had asked him if he wanted new addresses should any of the men have moved their habitations; that the ostensible reason for his intended visit to America had been "family business": and, finally, that he had been at work for nearly a year upon a new book, but had as usual refused to discuss with anyone even its subject . . .

It was after two-thirty when they finished, and Anthony, overriding his guest's protests that he could find a taxi, drove him back to his bachelor quarters in South Kensington. Which, it turned out, were a suite in the Wardlaw, characterized by its lessee as fairly cheap, very comfortable and near enough to everything.

The streets were almost deserted, and the Voisin made the short trip from Knightsbridge in a time too shocking to be recorded, ending in a noble sweep around the Gloucester Road Underground station which brought them up to the hotel entrance just behind a newly-arrived taxi whose passenger was paying his fare.

Firth climbed out and shut the Voisin's door and stooped to look back through the open window. He said: "Thanks very much," and smiled. "I mean for everything. Mainly for making them take this seriously." He started to turn away, then ducked back for a last remark. "I'll phone you those addresses in the morning," he said. "About ten."

Pulling out the key the Wardlaw gave its more permanent residents, he mounted the steps behind the passenger from the taxi. He saw the man looking for the Night Porter's bell-push, and recognized him as the pleasant American on the third floor. He said, "It's all right, I've got a key," and came up beside the man and opened the door into the dimly lighted lobby.

"Oh, thanks," the man said. "Thanks a lot." He had a pleasant smile. "Not often I'm this late."

They entered the lift together, and Firth, who was nearer the controls, said, "Let's see—you're third floor, aren't you?"

The man smiled again, and nodded without speaking. Firth was favorably impressed; here was an American who didn't spray one with unnecessary words all the time. He gave the man a "good night" as he got out, and forgot him. Forgot him forever; because he never saw him again.

Because this was the last night Mr. Hoag from Detroit had allowed himself at the Wardlaw. Tomorrow, in Birmingham, he would become Mr. Bronson from Vancouver. He didn't know—and it wouldn't have worried him particularly if he had known—that a few hours earlier, in one of the *sancta sanctorum* of Scotland Yard, he had been renamed Smith Brown-Jones . . .

CHAPTER THREE

Raoul Pierre Etien Anne-Marie St. Denis was bored. Abysmally.

He sat, uncomfortably because of the broken ribs and the sheathing of tape around them, on a very comfortable chair in a very comfortable room on the second floor of the Burton-Maxwell Nursing Home in Welbeck Street. And he contemplated, with complete lack of interest, the writing on the pages propped on the ingenious contraption in front of him. The contraption which was fixed to the arms of his chair and reared in front of him like a malicious robot.

He disliked the contraption with an almost personal dislike. Admitted that it had helped him to use a pen without undue reminders from the ribs; admitted that without it he would have been unable to finish the final draft of his *Portrait d'un Brandon Anglais* (subtitle: *La Panachure d'Ethelred Devvins*) and would then have been more bored than ever; everything admitted, and handsomely, he still disliked the thing.

And he disliked being in hospital; even in this luxurious one. Which led him to dislike of his own craft and fellow craftsmen. Because if it hadn't been for the persistent pestering of his English *confrères*, he could have gone back to the Chelsea flat which was his for another two months and let the ribs mend in decent solitude.

But most of all he disliked the officials he called to himself *Les Inquisiteurs*. He couldn't get away from them, anywhere. Knowing it wasn't their fault that they came so often to ask him the same questions, he still disliked them . . . "You say this was high explosive, monsieur. Now *why* do you say that?" . . . "You say the explosion was in the baggage compartment. Do you know where the baggage compartment is located in this make of aeroplane?" . . . "Monsieur, could you hazard a guess as to the *type* of explosive which was used?" . . . "Monsieur, are you sure? Monsieur, can you tell us? Monsieur, did you see? Monsieur, did you hear? Monsieur, did you feel?"

Aloud and *con fuoco*, he expressed himself and his feelings with his country's favorite five-letter word. He unscrewed one side of the robot and swung it clear of his body and with due caution in movement got to his feet. He crossed to the window and stood looking down at the ineffable smugness of Welbeck Street, more than usually depressing in the cold, mud-colored absence of darkness which only a November London can produce as daylight. With his left hand—because moving the right might draw protest from the ribs—he found a pack of Caporals in the pocket of his robe, and a lighter.

He stood and smoked, and surveyed Welbeck Street with disfavor. A big man—a very big man—in a handsome robe of white silk over pyjamas. A robe with a scarlet dragon embroidered on the back of it. A robe from Saigon, which (more because he liked it than in memory of its donor) he had been using in preference to all others since he had first acquired it.

He heard the door open behind him, and knew who had entered by the sounds; a deft, quick turn of the handle, followed by a starched and scratchy rustling. With care for the ribs, he turned to see the day nurse. As expected.

Her name was Bottsford, an ugly sound. But she herself was the

45

reverse of ill-favored, having those clear-skinned and vaguely equine good looks possessed by so many Englishwomen; especially by those of the dark-haired Celtic type. However, she was also comfortably married, completely humorless and suffering from the persistent Anglo-Saxon belief that all Gauls are undivided in their determination to seduce and/or ravish every woman they meet; a hope-fear which, try as she would to conceal it, colored her every word and action whenever she was in Raoul's presence.

He had found relief from boredom, and a mildly malicious pleasure, in fostering the myth. So now he smiled and came away from the window toward her. He said, "It is an impossible thing, Gwendolyn, but every day you are seeming more beautiful——"

The "Gwendolyn" was new: purely by chance, he had heard another nurse address her like that only yesterday. He watched the effect as he took her hand and carried it to his lips, and had the grace to feel slightly ashamed of himself. She flushed (hope), and her lips tightened to a thin line (fear), and she snatched her hand away.

"Don't be silly, m'sool" she said. And then, "There's a visitor to see you."

"*One* Torquemada only?" Raoul was genuinely surprised. Hitherto the Inquisitors had come always in bunches of two and three.

"I don't know what you mean," she said. "This is a lady. A Mrs. Messenger."

Raoul frowned. Although he had as much as possible avoided reading the newspapers, he knew that Messenger was the name of the man he had tied to the crate with his own *bretelles*. So this was probably the widow. In all decency, he supposed he must see her. He sighed and said, "Very well. Okay—okay," and went to the table near his chair and crushed out the stub of the Caporal.

When he turned, he was alone. So he waited, rehearsing phrases of condolence in his head, and a not-too-gory description of the man Messenger as he had seen him before he died.

The wait seemed like ten minutes, but was probably three. And then there was a tap at the door, and the glimpse of a starched cuff, and the voice of the Gwendolyn, "Mrs. Messenger——"

In the small fraction of time before his visitor appeared, a strange thing happened to Raoul, in his mind. A premonition. Something

46

was looming, something of vital importance to him. A fantastic sensation, and the reverse of comfortable . . .

And then she was in the room, the door closing behind her. She was very tall, almost as tall as he. But the tallness didn't matter; it vanished in its perfect proportion with the magnificent rest of her.

He knew he ought to go forward and greet her, but he couldn't move. It was extraordinary, and a little ridiculous—but he couldn't move. He started to say something, but felt it coming out in French and stopped before he knew what it was. Her hair looked like spun white gold, and one knew it was this way by nature. Her eyes were deeply blue under darker brows. And somewhere, not long ago, her skin had trapped the sun which wouldn't shine on London. It was the color of honey, and he knew it was thick and smooth and cool, with warmness tingling deep beneath.

She came toward him. He thought she was going to hold out her hand, but then she didn't. She said something with the names "Jocelyn" and "Messenger" in it, and then his own name.

Some English came back to him and he said, "How do you do?" Ridiculous sounds. Like a small dog barking in the night.

She said, "It's kind of you to see me." Her voice was deep and soft, and there seemed to be a faintly breathless quality in it.

"Thank you," he said. "Not at the least." It didn't sound quite right, but it was the best he could do. He made a gesture toward the easy chair without the robot on it. "Please, if you will sit——"

She walked past him and took the chair. He saw without seeing that she wore a tweed coat and skirt not at all new but of beautiful cut, with a silk handkerchief almost the color of her eyes knotted around her throat. There was perhaps some small sort of beret-like hat on the shining hair. But he wasn't sure, then or afterwards.

She looked up at him, her eyes fixed on his with an oddly unwinking concentration. She said, "I—I'm a sort of ambassador from Adrian Messenger's family, M. St. Denis." She pronounced his name carefully, with an almost flawless accent.

He didn't want to look down at her. He reached out his right hand and picked up a small straight chair—and the ribs retaliated with their red-hot bayonet stab.

A small sound, instantly repressed, burst from his lips. A ridiculous sound, half-squeal and half-groan. He felt extraordinarily foolish, and

47

set the chair down to face hers and hoped fervently she would make no *bruit* of sympathy.

She didn't. She gave no sign she had heard; she sat and waited, looking at him with that odd determination. It began to worry him, in case it meant that only civility made her look at him at all.

He sat on the straight chair, carefully. "An ambassador?" he said. "From the family?"

"Yes. Principally his mother in America, of course. Then his great-aunt over here. And his cousins."

"Then you are not—not——" Raoul couldn't think of the English word for *veuve*. "You were not the wife of M. Messenger?"

"Oh, no. I'm sorry, I should have explained myself better." The blue eyes still held on his. "Adrian Messenger wasn't married. I'm his sister-in-law, his brother's widow. My husband was Bernard Messenger. He was killed in Libya."

"I understand, madame." With difficulty, Raoul kept his voice decently grave. "My sympathies, if I may offer them——"

She murmured formally, and after that there was a silence. For himself, Raoul didn't mind. He didn't mind anything as long as she stayed here, in this room. But he sensed a discomfort in her and wanted to ease it. He said, "A cigarette, perhaps," and pulled the pack from his pocket and looked down at it and remembered. *"Zut!* I am forgetting. With tobacco, I am uncivilized. For these one must have the brazen throat of a—of a *bouc."* His English was deserting him.

She opened her purse and took from it a pack of cigarettes. It was crumpled like his Caporals, but yellow. She said, "Mine are like that, too. English edition."

She held the pack up for him to see, smiling at him for the first time.

The smile took his breath away. He thought he smiled back, perhaps he was just staring. He didn't know. He felt gauche as a schoolboy, and hated himself Especially when her smile faded quickly and her eyes dropped from his. She was taking a cigarette from the yellow package, but this he knew was only an excuse. His lighter felt oddly heavy as he held it for her.

She said, "What the family asked me to do, M. St. Denis, was first of all to thank you . . . For—for what you tried to do—what you did

48

. . . They wanted you to know their gratitude—how much—how grateful we all are . . ."

She was in difficulty, and he said quickly, "I understand, madame —fully. It is bad fortune we were not found more soon."

Now the eyes were back on his. There was no trace of the smile in them. She said, "Mrs. Messenger—Adrian's mother—had something she wanted me to ask you . . . She spoke to me on the telephone— from New York. You see, she's ill and can't travel. She wanted very much to know—and I promised I'd ask you—she wanted to find out if Adrian was conscious at all. If he said anything she might like to know——"

Raoul heard the words with a third of his mind. The other two-thirds were concerned with the over-steady gaze and its meaning. Because he couldn't read it. He was a schoolboy again, and he couldn't read it.

"M. Messenger did speak," he said. "But you must please ponder that he was an injured man. Seriously injured, from a wound to his head. His words were no-sense, spoken in delirium."

She said, "I—we—we thought that would probably be the answer. Or that he hadn't spoken at all . . ."

Her voice trailed off into silence and she reached out to the ashtray beside her chair and dropped her cigarette into it, only half smoked. And she lifted the purse from her lap with one hand, putting the palm of the other on the arm of her chair.

Unmistakable signs of imminent departure. Which must somehow be stopped. By any means.

Raoul pretended he didn't see the signs. He said, thoughtfully, "There were names which he spoke. Different names, but over and again . . ."

She sat back, but she kept the purse in her hand. "Do you remember any of them, monsieur? Was one of them Mary?"

He wanted to lie, but couldn't bring himself to it. Not about this. He said, "No. This was not one of the names; not in my memory." He cursed himself silently for a sentimentalist. "This is the name of his mother, perhaps?"

"Yes," she said. "But if he didn't say it——" Her shoulders lifted, and again she sat forward, ready to rise.

49

His mind raced—and came up with an idea. He was doubtful about using it; but he had to do something. He said:

"There is one name which I remember with distinctness"—he pronounced it slowly, in syllables—"Jo-ce-lyn. This is your—your *nom-de-baptême*, madame?"

She said, "Yes," and at once he knew he'd been right to be doubtful about telling her. He wanted to hire large boys with big boots to kick him repeatedly.

She said, "I was probably the last member of the family, the last friend, he happened to see before the flight."

She was uncomfortable, and it was his fault. And now she would want to leave more than ever.

He jettisoned all scruple and began to lie. He said, "There were other names. But I have not thought of them." He put his left hand to his head with a rueful smile. "I too had suffered bangs on the cranium, if you understand. But now I shall make the effort, and I shall remember——"

It didn't work. Because this time she did get to her feet. "I wouldn't dream of bothering you any more," she said. "I've stayed far too long as it is."

He was on his feet too. The blue eyes were almost level with his eyes; and they were shockingly impersonal. He said quickly, "But I am not an ill man now, madame. There is nothing ailing with me. Three only ribs which are not yet entirely repaired——"

But the truth didn't work either. By some magic process, she was already nearer the door without seeming to have moved. She said, "Please, M. St. Denis—it's very kind of you, very kind indeed, but I'm not going to trouble you any longer."

The words were gracious enough, but behind them was a determined finality he knew he mustn't fight. He stepped past her and reached his left hand out to the door—and then checked with his fingers on the handle. He smiled suddenly, like a man who has just seen the answer to a problem.

"I see what will be best," he said. "I shall search in my mind for these names. And when I have found them—then I will communicate to you."

"Thank you," she said. "That's very good of you . . ." She looked at the door, waiting for him to open it.

"Then perhaps you will tell me to where I shall send a letter?" He hit just the right note. "Or telephone?"

It nearly worked. She started to open her purse—but then closed it with a snapping sound. She said, "Well—I—you see, I'm going away tomorrow, for several weeks——"

He didn't believe a word of it. But he said nothing, and she had to go on.

She said, "But I know some of the family will be writing to you. Mary Messenger certainly. Perhaps, if you reply, you could put anything you remember in your letters?"

There was nothing more he could do except say, "But of course!" He said it—and opened the door.

And she was gone.

There was a parking space almost immediately opposite the Nursing Home, and Anthony slid the Voisin neatly into it.

As he got out, he glanced at his watch and was surprised to see the hands at three o'clock. Reminded that he'd forgotten lunch in the rigors of the day, he felt suddenly hungry. But there was nothing he could do about it now. He'd spent too long with Flood, briefing him and deciding on the right approach to J. Slattery, and then wasted more time vainly visiting the first of the addresses Firth had given him on the telephone.

The establishment of Doctors Burton and Maxwell was the second, and as he went up the steps and reached for the bell-push marked VISITORS, the door was thrown open from the inside and he found himself, in considerable astonishment, face to face with the absent tenant of the first address.

She was even taller than he'd remembered from their one brief meeting, and on an even nobler scale. He thought again of what he'd said to Firth, "Cable address—Valhalla"—and then, as he saw her frowning introspection, felt that there must be trouble in Asgard. He raised his hat and was going to speak when he realized he'd been neither recognized nor noticed; she was already down the steps and striding off along the yellow chillness of Welbeck Street.

Place, time and mood were none of them right for a tiresome series of questions and answers, so he abandoned a momentary thought of pursuit and stepped through the door into a dull and decorous lobby.

There was a captive female in a cubicle, and he spoke to her through an inconvenient hole in the glass casing, asking for M. St. Denis. She looked at him with suspicious blankness, and he said, "Haven't they told you about me? Gethryn?"

"Oh yes, sir." The blankness dissolved. "Do you wish to go straight up? Or would you prefer to be announced?" She hesitated. "My instructions were to say nothing to M'sewer St. Denis before you arrived."

Anthony produced a card and wrote on it. "Send him this, will you?" he said. "I'll wait." He crossed to a chair and dropped into it and pondered the chances of Jocelyn Messenger having been to visit St. Denis and decided they must be odds-on, handsomely.

In the glass cubicle, the female pressed a bell-push on her counter and looked at Anthony's card and the handwriting under the engraved name. But it wasn't in English and she gave up trying to decipher it and waited for Nurse Bottsford . . .

Who, a few moments later, interrupted Raoul's search of the telephone directories on his writing-table, giving him the card and a look which verged upon the arch.

"Another visitor, m'soo," she said. "Not a lady this time."

Frowning, because none of the directories had yielded the information he was seeking, Raoul looked at the card. He saw the written message under the unpronounceable name and was astonished. It was four words only, but they were in his own language, and although at face value their sense was almost nil they brought memories. And great curiosity about the writer.

"Le cochon est mort." He stared at the silly phrase, and then at Nurse Bottsford. Ready to bridle under a lascivious Gallic smile, she was disappointed. The eye of M. St. Denis was the eye of a man who'd never realized she was a woman.

He looked at the card again. "Show the gentleman here, please," he said—and soon was facing a tallish man with grey temples and a lean dark face out of which green eyes looked at him with a smile in them.

Raoul smiled back. He said, with another glance at the name, "Tell me, M.——?"

"Gethryn," said Anthony.

A vague memory, not to do with the message, stirred in Raoul's mind. But he couldn't pin it down, and concentrated on the present mystery.

"Tell me, M. Geth-ryn"—he pronounced it in two careful syllables—— "What is all this about a dead pig?"

Anthony grinned. "There's a response—'À bas le cochon!'"

"Then seat yourself, monsieur." Raoul laughed. "And explain how it comes that you know this long-since code?" He still couldn't understand how this man with the odd name, this man he'd never set eyes on before, could have been connected with the operation which in '43 had destroyed the biggest Nazi ammunition dump in France.

Anthony said, "It was used on the Lazanne raid." He gave the date and the time. "Fifteen hours before the first explosion I talked to you from England. On short wave. For the occasion my name was Polidor Two. Yours, of course, was Ajax."

"Aha!" Raoul was delighted, holding out a hand which Anthony shook. "You will excuse this left, but the other could discompose my ribs." He sat himself on the edge of the bed. "It is a pleasure to tell you, monsieur, that you are the only officer of your État-Major of Intelligence that sends to us the precise help we wish at the precise time we wish it!"

He pulled out the pack of Caporals and offered them, with apology.

Anthony took one. "Once in a while I'm man enough," he said. And then, "You must be wondering how I found you. And what I want." He lit the cigarette. "I should explain I do odd jobs for the Government on occasion. Some diplomatic; some for the C.I.D.——"

"Ah, yes!" Raoul had pinned the elusive memory. "Gettrine! You know, there was once that my Editor was thinking that I should write about you. He names you the English Lecoq, and he is perhaps right." He grinned. "To deduce connection between Raoul St. Denis and Ajax, that is brilliance!"

"No deduction, I assure you." Anthony laughed. "Pure luck—and information passed on from the Special Branch . . . I only wrote on the card to make sure you'd see me. It occurred to me you might have had a bellyful of questions about the plane crash."

"And you are going to fill me more?" Raoul cocked an eyebrow at him. "Not to overflow, I hope."

"I don't think so. You see I'm not going to talk about the crash itself. Only about Adrian Messenger—the man you nearly saved."

"That is strange!" Raoul stared in surprise. "Only moments ago, there was another visitor to me about this poor guy. From his family." His glance flickered to the writing-table. "It is what which you wish to discover about him?"

"Anything," said Anthony. "And everything . . . Did you have any conversation with him before the crash? If you did, what did he say? If you didn't, did you happen to notice him and his general behavior? Lastly, did he speak at all while you were in the sea? And if he did, can you remember what he said?"

"And that is all?" Raoul asked. "Then okay . . . In the flight I did not notice him in particular. And I did not speak with him. That is simple." He paused, thoughtful. "When we are in the sea and I have grabbed him, he is first passed out but later talks. However, he is badly hurt to his head and the words are delirium only."

"Do you remember any of them?"

"In the most, they were names of persons. You wish to hear these? The rest was nothing—flapdoodle only."

Anthony repressed a smile. "What I really want is everything Messenger said. In the order he said it, and whether it seemed to make sense or not. In all probability it won't help. But I can't ignore the possibility that it might."

Raoul surveyed his visitor with curiosity. "There is a way with my mind I can sometimes use about remembering. You wish me to have a shot?"

"Please."

"So okay." Raoul put back his head and closed his eyes, and was silent.

The silence lasted for a full two minutes, and when he spoke his eyes stayed shut. He said:

"This is what I remember . . . After I have tied him safe, I am myself pooped. I too have a pass-out, and when I am back from it I hear him speaking. There is no—no variation to his words. They are level, a monotony . . . He said, 'Messenger—Messenger' many times . . . And then he says, 'Jocelyn—got—me—to—tell—Jocelyn—got

54

—me—to—tell—Jocelyn . . .' Then there comes nothing for a long time, I do not know how long, and when he speaks again he is shouting . . . I cannot remember this as the rest, but first there is something about a photograph and then there are two names, *George* and *Emma* . . . Aha, yes! First it is 'George' he shouts and then, a lot of times, 'Emma's book—Emma's book . . .' And then perhaps 'George' again . . ."

His words trailed off into silence, and this time the silence lasted so long that Anthony broke it.

"A photograph!" he said quietly. "And nothing else?"

"There was something——" Raoul still hadn't opened his eyes. ". . . Ah, yes! Some *baragouin* about brushes. About cleaning with brushes. Everything must be clean but there is one brush only . . . These precise words I do not remember, but they are like that . . ."

Now his eyes did open. "And that is all. No more words from him." He saw his visitor had been writing in a small, slim notebook. "After this, I see the ship. And before we are picked up, they tell me now, he is dead." He shifted position, stretching cautiously. "You have written all this?" he asked curiously.

"Yes." Anthony put away his pen. "Thanks very much."

"It has helped you?"

"I don't know yet." Anthony pocketed the notebook. "But I'm much obliged, anyway. Wonderful job."

"And we are finished?" Raoul was sceptical. "I did not see another question behind your eye?"

"On the observant side, aren't you?" Anthony laughed. "Since you press it, I was wondering about the stewardess, Rose Matson. She's too ill for interviews yet, but I could bear to know if she heard Messenger talking too."

Raoul shrugged. "It is possible, of course. But to me it seems she was all the time without consciousness." He lighted another Caporal, and watched Anthony's face. And said at last, "Now it can be my turn, hein?"

"To ask questions," Anthony contrived to be both bland and wary at the same time.

"Three small ones only. And then to request some assistance I need in a small matter." Once more Raoul's glance unconsciously flickered to the writing-table.

"Go ahead," said Anthony. "Anything I can do——"

"At first I wish to know, please, if Adrian Messenger was involved deeply in the *affaire* you now investigate?"

Anthony nodded. "Deeply is the *mot juste.*"

"But he was not on the wrong side for the law?"

"No." Now Anthony was curious. "Definitely not."

"That is okay then for my first question. The second is arising from your clear acquaintance with Mme. Jocelyn Messenger——"

"Clear?" Anthony looked at him and smiled. "I never said I knew her."

Raoul didn't smile. "You arrived so quick after Madame, you must have saw her as she leaves. But when I said to you there has been just now a visitor from the family Messenger, you show no surprise and do not ask what relative. So it is clear you have known she is who."

"Right!" Anthony's smile became a laugh. "And doosid lucid, as someone said once. *Whom* did your Editor christen 'the new Lecoq'?"

"Now tell me this, if you please"—Raoul still didn't smile—"You did not arrange with Mme. Messenger that she should make this visit to me?"

"Good lord, no!" Anthony was taken aback. "Oh, I see! You thought I might be double-checking? Finding out if you'd tell the same story to both of us? . . . My dear St. Denis, your only connection with this case is as a helper, not a suspect. Believe me!"

"Then all is okay." Again, with due caution, Raoul stretched. "And we come, please, to the small assistance you could perhaps give to me——"

"By all means." Anthony took out his pen again, and the little notebook, and began to write quickly.

"What is this?" Raoul was puzzled.

"The phone number you wanted." Anthony tore out the page, carefully. "And the address too, for good measure." He read out, "Paxman 04238. And 5 Whistlers Walk, Chelsea——"

Raoul interrupted, sharply. "But of what person is this the address?"

"My dear fellow, you underrate me." Anthony pointed to the writing-table. "I enter to find you searching the telephone directories.

I have just encountered your previous visitor—in whom, and in various ways, you subsequently express interest. The first time you mentioned this other visitor—*before* you exercised your deductive talents on me—you couldn't restrain a glance at said directories. A glance, I may add, you have subconsciously repeated several times. Particularly when you first introduced the question of getting help from me . . ." He shrugged, and smiled. "Need I go on?"

He watched the Frenchman's deepening frown with apprehensive amusement—and then was relieved. Because Raoul suddenly put back his head and laughed. And then winced as the ribs protested. And then replaced the laugh with a wide and delighted smile.

"*Riposte en tierce!*" he said. "The Maître represses the saucy student!" He took the paper from Anthony's outstretched hand. "And the joke is quite upon me!"

It was four o'clock when Anthony drove away from Welbeck Street.

And at that time, some fifteen miles away up the Thames, Jonathan Slattery was receiving a visitor in the small parlor behind his small shop on the corner of Pope Terrace in Twickenham, within sight of the river and Eel Pie Island.

Sitting back in his wheelchair, Mr. Slattery was studying a typewritten sheet just handed to him by his visitor. Mr. Slattery was small and fortyish, bright-eyed and one-legged. The visitor, a Mr. Flood whom Mr. Slattery had never seen before, was a spruce, quick-talking fellow of indeterminate age. He was also, so he said, the representative of a legal firm whose title had sounded to Mr. Slattery something like Wibberly, Wibberly, Sons and Wobberly, but probably wasn't that at all.

Mr. Slattery's bright eyes, a puzzled frown between them, looked up from the paper to Mr. Flood.

"Now what's all this to-do agyne?" said Mr. Slattery.

"I suppose it *is* unusual." Mr. Flood smiled cheerily. "But it's quite simple really. And it's twenty-five pounds in your pocket, of course. Not much in these days, I know but——"

"Twenty-five quid," said Mr. Slattery judicially, "'as always been a nice little lumpa lolly! . . . What I don't understand is 'ow I come to be gettin' it. *If*," he added, "get it I do."

Mr. Flood laughed; a genial sound. He took a wallet from his pocket and produced five new and crackling five-pound notes and laid them on the table at Mr. Slattery's elbow. "There you are," he said. "I think you'll find it adds up right." He sat back and produced cigarettes and offered them to Mr. Slattery, who shook his head. And then looked at the bank notes but didn't reach for them.

"And 'oo was the lolly supposed to be from?" he said.

"The estate of our late client, Harold Black," explained Mr. Flood in his rapid way. "Mr. Black was a wealthy man. Very wealthy. Our senior partner is his chief executor, and going through the deceased's papers a month or so after his death, found a list of eleven names—yours among them—each with a different sum of money noted against it . . . To cut a long story as short as I can, the executor, after discussion with Mrs. Black, decided that the estate would best be carrying out the testator's real if unexpressed wishes by seeking out the persons named on the list and disbursing the noted sums to them, although such sums were not included in the Will." Mr. Flood drew breath, smiled even more cheerily than before, and added an afterthought. "Of course, since these monies are unsolicited, unrecorded gifts of free-will, the taxes paid by the estate are all that is necessary, and any entry on your own income tax forms is *un*necessary."

Mr. Slattery looked at the money again. "*I* never knew no 'Arold Black," he said. "But on the other 'and, I never was one to take a dekko at the teeth of a gift 'orse, if y'know what I mean." He regarded Mr. Flood thoughtfully. "You want me moniker on anythin'? Receipt or some such?"

Mr. Flood shook his head. "Quite unnecessary," he said.

Mr. Slattery looked at the typewritten sheet again. "An' what's this 'ere?" he asked. "What do I 'ave to do with it?"

"Perhaps I didn't explain properly." Mr. Flood was patiently apologetic. "You don't *have* to do anything, Mr. Slattery. We—the firm—are just asking you to help us; but only if you want to. The ten names on that paper are the others against which our late client had noted the various sums. Many of them are difficult to trace—and we wondered if you could assist. You see, we still don't know if there was any connection between any of you. If there did happen to be—well, then you would recognize the name and possibly be able to give us a recent address."

"Come to think," said Mr. Slattery, slowly, "I don't see as 'ow I could land meself in any mess——"

"*Mess?*" Mr. Flood was shocked. "My dear sir——"

Mr. Slattery interrupted him. "Whichever way you look at it, cock, this is a bleedin' rum 'owjerdo!" He reached out a hand and took the money from the table and stowed it in a pocket.

"Unusual, yes." Mr. Flood was firm. "But nothing more."

"'Owsomever," said Mr. Slattery, ignoring this, "what the eye don't see, the 'eart don't grieve . . ." He lifted the typed list again and concentrated on it, reading the names over to himself in a mumbling monotone. "Bynebridge—Braddock—Dalkeith—Devitt—McGowan—Messenger—Moreton——" He hesitated, pondering, "Ormiston—Paxton—Pomfret . . ." He looked up at Mr. Flood. "Knew a Morton once," he said. "But 'e was Joe for Joseph. An' come to think of it, 'e spelt it without no E . . ." There was reminiscence in his voice.

"And none of the others are familiar?"

"Not a bloody one." Mr. Slattery shook his head. "Just a lot o' nymes to me. Sorry."

"Please don't apologize." Mr. Flood took the paper from Mr. Slattery's hand. "And thank you very much for trying to help." The paper disappeared into a pocket, and Mr. Flood gave signs of imminent departure.

But Mr. Slattery didn't notice them: a train of memory had been started. "Pore old Joe Morton!" He shook his head. "Bought 'is at Dunkirk, 'e did. The second day it was; in the mornin'. Come night an' I'd got my packet." He looked down at his pinned-up right trouser-leg, empty from the hip. "S'pose I was lucky, only losin' me barrel-an'-keg . . . If you can call it lucky, livin' in these sort o' times."

Mr. Flood, who had started to get to his feet, subsided onto his chair. "Dunkirk?" he said. "What were you in?" Subtly, he sounded and looked a different man . . .

When Flood finally left Twickenham, having used Mr. Slattery's telephone to call Anthony and arrange to be in Stukeley Gardens before six, it was a few minutes before five.

And at that time, at Scotland Yard, Superintendent Arnold Pike sent for Detective-Sergeant Thomas Gainsford Seymour, who was the officer he'd temporarily detached from other duties to do the first spade work on the case which the Assistant Commissioner insisted on referring to, sourly, as "this incredible Messenger business."

Sergeant Seymour arrived in a hurry—as is the way of Detective-Sergeants when summoned by the man they know among themselves as "Uncle Arnie." Sergeant Seymour had a folder of papers under his arm, and set it down on the desk as he obeyed Pike's gesture and pulled up a chair and sat. One of the new breed of C.I.D. career men—the old sweats call them the College Brigade—he was a well-built, casually well-dressed young man who looked younger than his thirty-one years and, until his nose had been put slightly but permanently out of straight in the light-heavy final of the previous year's Metropolitan Police Boxing Competitions, had suffered under the nickname Angel-Face.

Superintendent Pike looked at Sergeant Seymour through a cloud of pipe-smoke and said, "Well? Anything to report?"

Sergeant Seymour opened the folder. "I've sent memos to all the eight Chief Constables, sir, asking for full details of the accidents." He took a sheaf of eight flimsy carbon copies from the folder. "And I have personal notes to them asking for their private opinions, all ready for your signature." He took eight unfolded sheets, each clipped to its own envelope, from the folder. "And I've been over to the War Office, sir, and started Records checking on all the ten men on the list. They say it may take quite a while if we can't give 'em any more detail. And Major Hillyer gave me this note for you about it." He took a long, buff-colored envelope from the folder. "And I've been on the phone to Cardiff a couple of times, to Inspector Powell. I think they may have something for us on Bainbridge, sir. Powell said they'd phone us before six. Either he'll speak to me, or Chief-Inspector Evans may talk to you."

He closed the folder, now empty, and picked up the papers he had taken from it and set them neatly in front of Pike. Who grunted, and didn't look at them and said suddenly:

"What about the tenth man?"

"Slattery, sir?" Seymour felt he was being tested. "I understood he was being left to Colonel Gethryn."

"That's right." Pike grinned suddenly. "But you'd better watch your step with that 'Colonel,' my boy. He never did like it, and now it's wrong anyway. Before he left the Service this time they made him a General—and that he *won't* take. So it's plain Mister now, and don't you forget it!"

One of his telephones rang, and he picked it up and said, "Pike . . . Inspector Evans in Cardiff? . . . Yes—put him through." He waited, then in a moment said, "Hullo, how are you——" and thereafter was silent for several minutes, listening intently.

"Nice work, Taffy," he said at last. "Very nice. I'm much obliged to you . . . And you'll verify as soon as possible? . . . Thanks . . . Good-bye."

He hung up the phone and looked at Seymour. "Good man, Taffy Evans," he said. "He thinks they're on to Bainbridge. The man used to be a free-lance insurance agent, and Evans got the idea of checking on the big companies in Cardiff. Second shot he found a policy, wangled a description from the doctor, then had his men check back on all the D.U.* forms because I'd told him there was a strong possibility of death. Well, they turned one up from Bristol. Pulled out of the Severn six months ago. Advanced state of decomposition: body looked like it had been caught in weeds. Nobody anywhere had ever thought of Bainbridge; for the simple reason he'd never been reported missing. Seems he'd walked out on his wife a couple of times before, and she was sure he'd be back sooner or later . . . Well, the Bristol D.P.S.† said death had been by drowning, about another six months before. Which puts it around about the time Bainbridge left home. Cadaver's been disposed of, o' course, but the description's enough; there's a regular clincher. Malformation of the bone in both big toes that checks with the insurance doctor's notes."

Pike sat forward, knocking out his pipe in the ashtray on his desk. He shook his head, and looked at Seymour again, thoughtfully.

"You're a lucky young devil to be on this," he said. "It isn't only a Gethryn case, which in all my experience means it's a big one, but something tells me it's one o' those that may half-kill you with work but you'll never wish you were on something else." He sighed. "Mighty rare, they are—as you may have begun to find out . . ."

* Dead—unidentified.
† Divisional Police Surgeon.

He reached for a telephone. "Better let him know," he said, and dialed the private number of 19 Stukeley Gardens, and in a minute was saying:

"Pike here, sir . . . Well, it seems to be ninety percent now. To be exact, ninety point ninety-one——"

It was twenty-five minutes to six when Pike called Anthony from the Yard.

And that was almost exactly the time at which Mr. David Bronson from Vancouver was registering at the Gainsborough Hotel in Birmingham, a hundred odd miles away.

Mr. Bronson, perhaps because of a slightly stooping posture and somewhat shuffling walk, seemed ten years older than Mr. Hoag of Detroit, and even more than that senior to Mr. Lovett from Toronto.

Mr. Bronson, escorted to a room on the fourth floor, smiled pleasantly at the page who had carried up his two heavy suitcases, tipped the boy, locked the door after him, glanced around to make sure the windows of the room weren't overlooked by any others——

And then, for the first time since entering the hotel, took off his hat, revealing the same thick and neatly-trimmed and indeterminately reddish-brown hair as Mr. Lovett's and Mr. Hoag's.

Far too thorough in his methods to change walk or posture even in solitude, Mr. Bronson crossed the room and opened one of the suitcases, taking from it a leather dressing-case and two small, shop-wrapped packages. These he bore to the bathroom and set down; then, having stripped to the waist, took scissors from the dressing-case and stood in front of the mirror and proceeded to hack, in huge unrelated snips, at the thick hair on the top of his head.

When he had finished, the scalp was an odd sight. But he put the scissors back in the dressing-case and unwrapped the packages, revealing the content of one as a tube labeled "HAYR-ZOFF—The Magic Depilatory"; of the other a small flat jar bearing the words, "HELENE'S FOUNDATION MAKE-UP (Neutral Tone)."

He went to work again in front of the mirror, applying the cream to his poll with meticulous care. Finished, with the clay-like stuff spread smooth and thick, he spent the necessary ten minutes of waiting in turning on water to fill the bathtub and then clearing up every trace of his activities . . .

And very soon, bathed, robed and slippered, he was diminishing the startling over-whiteness of his scalp with judicious application of the product of Helene. With the result that when, half an hour later, he went down to dine in the grill-room, he was a quiet and pleasant and unmemorable gentleman. A gentleman who happened to be bald, of course, but with nothing in the least remarkable about his baldness.

He made a good and leisurely dinner, reading while he ate. The book was *Wintringham's Guide to Medeshire,* and seemed to interest him very much.

In London, at about the same time, Flood was dining with Anthony Gethryn. At Crockford's, and in that pleasant paneled chamber called "The Upstairs Room" which is reserved always for customers known and liked by old Mr. Crockford himself. They were three-quarters through the meal and, Anthony's lunchless appetite being sufficiently assuaged, were talking about Jonathan Slattery.

"You see," said Flood, "the minute I saw him in that wheelchair, with only one leg, I knew he couldn't be your heavy. So I used Story Number Four." He laughed. "Not that he swallowed it——"

Anthony interrupted. "Any danger of him talking? I can't see what harm he could do, but I wouldn't like it. On general principles, I wouldn't like it."

"He won't utter. Not after taking the twenty-five quid. Besides, he knows I don't want him to, and we were pals from the minute I found he got his packet at Dunkirk——"

"Dunkirk?" For a moment Anthony was puzzled. "Oh, yes—you and Dyson were in the flotilla, weren't you?"

Flood nodded. "We took Dyson's yawl. We were never anywhere near Slattery's mob, though. We got Sutherlands mostly, and he was 1st Wessex."

Then the waiter came, and it wasn't until they were drinking coffee that Anthony came back to the subject of this tenth man on the list; the one man who prevented Pike's ninety point ninety-one percent from being a full hundred.

63

"At the risk of being tedious," he said, "I'm going to ask you once more: Are you completely convinced Slattery's on the level?"

"Completely. If you met him, you'd say the same in two minutes."

"He showed absolutely no sign of recognizing any of the other names?"

"Absolutely none—apart from the Joe Morton business I told you about. And that was convincing in itself."

"All right. Then you realize what he's become? A liability—and an awkward one."

"How come?" Flood frowned. "Don't forget you know more about this whole flap than I do."

"Out of eleven men, counting Messenger, Jonathan Slattery is the only one who hasn't been murdered. Our unknown killer—my Mr. Smith Brown-Jones—has spent five years, a great deal of ingenuity and probably quite a lot of money in removing the others. So there's every ground for supposing he means to finish the job. We daren't suppose anything else."

"My God, that's right! Slattery's going to need protection. In fact he needs it now——"

"Exactly. I'll have to get hold of Pike within the next hour or so and see what we can fix. It's not going to be an easy job, because the protection mustn't show. Not to anyone. Particularly not to Slattery himself."

Again Flood frowned. "Don't see that last one. Seems to me he could help to look after himself if he was warned."

"Possibly. But as well as a liability, he's an asset. And if he knew, he wouldn't be."

Flood laughed. "That's vintage Gethryn if I ever heard any. I suppose it means something?"

"Sorry. In simple words for the novice, I mean Slattery's an asset because he's an innocent trap for Smith Brown-Jones, whom we *might* catch as he tries to finish off the last on his list. But we mustn't tell Slattery he's in danger, because then he'd very possibly start behaving differently. And if he did, and if Smith Brown-Jones has him under observation, which isn't improbable, then S. B.-J. might notice this and be on his guard. It's just as important not to tell Slattery as it is to make sure the watch on him isn't visible to anyone else . . . All clear?"

64

"Plate-glass." Flood was thoughtful. "This is really a hell of a do, isn't it? Ramifications two a penny."

Anthony lit a cigarette. "And I have an inescapable hunch we haven't even started."

"Meaning Smith Brown-Jones is such a genius he'll finish off poor old Jonathan without getting caught?"

"Meaning a lot of things. Meaning that for some reason or other it possibly isn't necessary for him to kill Slattery. Meaning that perhaps Messenger made a mistake and Slattery doesn't belong on the list and guarding him isn't a trap at all. Meaning we've got to bait the trap by guarding Slattery, and then behave as if there wasn't any trap or any Slattery either. Meaning we must go on chasing down every other lead we've got." He shook his head. "If you can call them leads." He looked at his watch and stood up. "I must go and ring Pike. Order brandy, will you? There's a good Curvoisier."

Flood ordered brandy, and had been sipping his for nearly ten minutes when his host came back, wearing an unaccustomed frown.

Flood grinned. "Trouble in Westminster?"

"Poor old Pike." Anthony picked up his glass. "It isn't his fault there are never enough men." He drank. "But they've got to look after Slattery and they know it." He slid a hand into his breast-pocket and brought out a long envelope and laid it on the table. "So let's forget that for a while. Let's talk about this."

"Why not?" said Flood. "What is it?"

"You'll see in a minute." He tasted his brandy again. "First let me tell you I spent a slice of this afternoon with Raoul St. Denis. I don't have to ask anyone from Fleet Street if they know who he is, so I'll just say that as well as being obviously a good type to have with you in a transatlantic air crash, he's also an ex-French Resistance leader of note, a charming fellow, and a quick-thinking, highly intelligent human being. The reason I went to see him was to find out if at any time, in the plane or out of it, he'd had any conversation with Messenger. He hadn't. But while they were bobbing around in the Atlantic, Messenger apparently did quite a bit of babbling. Stuff which St. Denis took for delirious nonsense. However, he's got one of those trick memories, thank God. Imagines himself back into the right circumstances and dredges everything up. Almost everything, anyway . . ."

65

He opened the envelope now, and took out two sheets. "While I was waiting for you to get back from Twickenham, I typed out what St. Denis quoted." He unfolded the sheets and handed one of them to Flood. "Before you read it, I'd better explain what he told me, particularly about the *way* Messenger spoke. Apparently the words came out as individual efforts, with no difference in stress and no vocal punctuation. You'll see I've typed them in groups, with notes after each group . . ."

—MESSENGER—MESSENGER—MESSENGER—

(Apparently repeated ad lib. Almost certainly an effort at self-identification.)

—JOCELYN—GOT—ME—TO—TELL—JOCELYN—GOT— ME—TO—TELL—JOCELYN—

(A wheel job: you can begin anywhere . . . Between this and the next words St. Denis remembers, there was an interval of indeterminate length, St. D. having been at least partially unconscious himself.)

—PHOTOGRAPH—

(St. D. remembers the word was used, but can't say how many times.)

—GEORGE—EMMA—

(As above.)

—EMMA'S—BOOK—EMMA'S BOOK—GEORGE—

(Apparently "Emma's book" was repeated ad lib before "George.")

BRUSHES. CLEANING. EVERYTHING MUST BE CLEAN BUT THERE IS ONE BRUSH ONLY.

(St. D. did *NOT* give these as Messenger's actual words. In this case, he could only remember the nonsensical sense they made.)

Flood read this through once, and then again, before he looked up. "Could be the way St. Denis thought it was, couldn't it?" he said. "Just delirium."

"It could be, of course. Or it could be a mixture. Or *all* of it could be sane, though I admit this looks improbable. What we mustn't forget is that Messenger had this business on his mind, whatever it is. And even if he was half-way round the bend when he talked, everything he said might still be connected with it."

"H'mm . . ." Flood picked up the typed sheet. "You recognize any of these names?"

"Yes." Most unusually, Anthony drained his brandy at a gulp. *"Jocelyn* must be Jocelyn Quist, the miniaturist. Who is also the widow of Adrian Messenger's brother Bernard. *Emma,* I've no knowledge of yet. *George* is probably George Firth, which at least supports the theory that the babble was an effort on Messenger's part to convey information on the obsessive subject."

Once more Flood studied the sheet. "I suppose so," he said slowly.

"Now take a look at this——" Anthony unfolded the second page from his envelope. "It's the results I got from working on the most promising entry, trying to see how many reasonable differentiations I could come up with. I was making allowances, of course, for Messenger's condition *and* the circumstances: he could have left out some words, and St. Denis could have missed hearing some words."

He handed the sheet across the table——

—JOCELYN—GOT—ME—TO—TELL—JOCELYN—GOT—
ME—TO—TELL—JOCELYN—

Possibility No. 1

JOCELYN GOT ME TO TELL (something to someone).

Possibility No. 2

(Someone) GOT ME TO TELL JOCELYN (something).

Possibility No. 3

(Someone) GOT ME TO (do something). TELL JOCELYN.

Possibility No. 4

JOCELYN: (Someone) GOT ME TO TELL (something).

Flood pored over the alternatives, nodding at each one. "Those're fine," he said. "If they get you anywhere. Do they?"

"Anyone can play!" Anthony said. "Try y'r luck, pretty gentleman

. . . Actually, I was wondering if you thought those four covered the reasonable possibilities."

"Depends what you call reasonable." Flood took out a pen and added, in neat quick script:

Possibility No. 5
JOCELYN GOT ME TWO (articles). TELL (someone).

He turned the paper around for Anthony to read. "How about that?"

"Well, well," said Anthony, reading. "At least we both saw the trap."

"Trap?" said Flood. "I don't get you. What sort of trap?"

"Phonetic." Anthony turned the paper over and pointed to a single line typed on the back. "Here's what I got eventually."

(Someone) GOT ME TOO. TELL JOCELYN.

"Oh, for God's sake!" Flood was self-contemptuous. "Why didn't I see that before?"

"I misled you." Anthony grinned. "Having gone through the same process myself. I gave it you the long way round to make sure there wasn't something I'd missed that might be even more apposite."

Flood stared down at the paper again, and pushed it away and began to trace patterns on the tablecloth with a spoon. "You *are* convinced this is all a one-man job, I suppose? Your Smith Brown-Jones as opposed to some—some organization?"

"'Who never doubted, never half believed'—especially in his own theories." Anthony looked at his companion curiously. "Let's say I think Smith Brown-Jones fits everything better. Much better. Why do you ask? Can't you swallow him?"

"He's a little sticky in my craw," said Flood, and looked up. "Take this plane business for instance: killing forty-odd people to get one! It's a question of conscience or guilt-complex or what-have-you. Organizations don't suffer from them. But one man!—he'd have to be a maniac——"

"So are we all, my boy, all monomaniac chaps—when you come to think of it. It's just a question of subject and degree. I think Smith Brown-Jones's subject is probably himself; and that's a self who's either frightened or ambitious or both. And I think the degree of his megalomania's a hundred-plus and sort of sharpens all the rest of him so he can keep it extremely well hidden."

"Could be, I suppose." Flood was still thoughtful. "And I also suppose you wouldn't buy the idea there *is* an organization, but that it's headed—*financed*—by Smith Brown-Jones?"

"I would not." Anthony shook his head. "I don't believe, and nor do you if you think, that a man who's spent the time, ingenuity and money that S. B.-J. has in arranging the deaths of ten men—I refuse to believe he'd be such a fool as to put himself in the power of even *one* other human being by letting that human being into any slightest detail of his extraordinarily dirty work."

"Okay—okay." Flood laughed. "I concede. I've just purchased one Smith Brown-Jones, latest model, all extras!" Again he shook his head. "But if you asked me to give odds you'll ever get him, they'll be on the prohibitive side . . . If he doesn't fall into the Slattery trap, you're sunk. Nowhere to start from; nothing to go on; no goal to aim at. Sisyphus Unlimited!"

"Well, well—The Derogator at the Dinner Table." Anthony surveyed him. "Let me quote the slogan of the Society of Sophisticated Super-Sleuths—'If at first you don't succeed, pry, pry, pry again.'" He looked at his watch. "Which reminds me, I've got to telephone again."

He pushed back his chair, and Flood said, "Jocelyn, I presume?"

"Obviously." Anthony was frowning. "I've been trying to get her all day—particularly since St. Denis gave me that stuff. I had a chance too—and let it go."

"Think she's ducking you?"

"Hardly." Anthony shrugged. "Though from the way she looked when I saw her, she's certainly got something on her mind." He stood up and walked across the room, making for the telephone-booth at the top of the stairs.

And a moment later was dialing Paxman 04238, hoping that this time it would be Jocelyn Messenger herself who answered.

But it wasn't. It was her housekeeper; the small, dour and obviously privileged Scotswoman with whom he had already spoken five times today, once in person at his abortive mid-day call. He repressed irritation, and identified himself, and with the utmost blandness asked if Mrs. Messenger had yet returned; and whether, if she had not, he could possibly be informed where he could get in touch with her.

But the blandness was in vain. The accents of Caledonia waxing ever thicker in his ear, he was told that the answer to both his questions was negative——

"And may I suggaist," said the telephone sternly, "that ye refrain from onny more calls this night."

The replaced receiver clicked violently in Anthony's ear, and he was still rubbing at it as he walked back to the corner table.

"No luck," he said to Flood. "I wonder where the damn woman's got to——"

The condemned woman was away on an outer edge of London, in Hampstead; a self-invited dinner guest in a charming house on one of those tree-shaded roads off the Heath which can still give the impression of being in the country.

The house was the temporary home, for their year in London, of her American friends, John Cameron the playwright and his wife Margaret. And now it was after dinner, and John was off in the study working, and she was restlessly roaming the drawing-room while Margaret, curled on a sofa by the fire, watched her with friendly curiosity. And said at last:

"Oh, come on, Joss! Sit down and unburden. That's what you're here for, isn't it?"

"Am I as transparent as all that?" Jocelyn dropped into a big chair. "Or are you just a witch?"

Margaret studied her. "If you were any other girl, I'd bet on man-trouble. But you, you *nun*——"

"P'raps man-trouble's like greatness," Jocelyn said. "Some achieve it——"

"Meaning yours has been thrust upon you." Margaret exhibited that rarity, a charming giggle. "Often the best way, don't you think?"

"You're impossible!" Jocelyn found a cigarette and lit it. Now she'd been brought to the point, she didn't want to unburden at all. But she had to make some show now. She said, "It's all poor Adrian's fault, bless him," and salved her conscience by telling herself it was partly true, anyway.

"Oh, I'm sorry, darling! I shouldn't try so hard to be funny . . . Wasn't that an awful thing!" Margaret shuddered. "Do you suppose it *was* a bomb?"

"I don't think I believe that story," Jocelyn said. And then remembered whose opinion had started it, and frowned at the fire.

"What did you mean, it was Adrian Messenger's fault you were upset?" Margaret was curious. "I know he was a great friend, but I don't think you meant his death. Or did you?"

"No. No, I didn't . . ." Jocelyn still stared at the fire.

"What's he done, then? Left you a couple of million?"

"Now I *know* you're a witch!" Jocelyn was taken aback. "No, it wasn't money. He wouldn't have dared—not after what I said to him once when he suggested it. But it's almost the same thing, damn it! It's a house. A lovely old Georgian house in Mayfair. In Whig Street. Adrian bought it when he left the Army. It was much too big for him, so he had it converted—beautifully—into three flats. He lived in the top one and let the others. He's left me the whole thing, including everything of his that was in it."

"Well, I think it was pretty darn nice of him." Margaret sat up suddenly, and pointed an accusing finger. "And this is all phoney! It isn't what's biting you, and you know it!"

"All right—all right!" Jocelyn got up restlessly. "And you're very clever!" She stood with an arm on the mantelpiece, looking down at her friend. "If you must know, it's something the family got me into. The Messengers, I mean. They sent me to see the man who tried to save Adrian—"

"Aha!" Margaret sat up again. "The Frenchman. Saint Something?"

"St. Denis. I found out he was in a Nursing Home in Welbeck Street—" Jocelyn stopped abruptly. "What am I *doing!* This is ridiculous. Confessions of a Sixth Form Girl, or I Was a Teen-age Iseult!"

Margaret stood up and crossed to a table against the wall and busied herself with glasses and a decanter and came back with two drinks. She gave one to Jocelyn and went back to the sofa with her own. She said:

"Now let's see, where were we? . . . Oh, yes, you're at this hospital, and you're going to be taken to the room of this Monsieur Beaucaire, or whatever his name is . . . I can see the whole thing. You stand by the bed, looking down at him. Propped on his pillows, he

71

gazes up at you. You're the most beautiful thing he's ever seen. He has smoldering dark eyes and a thin D'Artagnan moustache. His face is like Byron's, with a French accent. Both of you are spellbound, speechless. A faint flush stains the waxen pallor of his cheeks——"

"Oh Meg, you idiot!" Jocelyn took a stinging swallow of her drink and set it down. "He's only got some broken ribs, and he wasn't in bed. He wasn't pale. He's clean-shaven. His eyes don't smolder——"

"Okay—okay." Margaret's giggle came again. "But how's about the struck-speechless bit? That was right, huh?"

"Well—in a way, I suppose . . . I mean, there *was* one of those things——"

"You mean a click Nelson could hear in Trafalgar Square! So tell me for God's sake what's the trouble about meeting an attractive man!"

"Well—" Jocelyn picked up her glass again. "In the first place, I was vilely rude to him. This—this click as you call it, it upset me. I was—I was just *horrible!*"

"So what did *he* do? Slap your face or something?"

"I must say he didn't seem to notice anything. He asked me for my address—but I made some ridiculous excuse and didn't give it to him . . . And now I don't know what to do. I definitely think I'd better not see him again. But at the same time I hate him to think I'm as much of a bitch as I must have seemed . . ."

"Oh, nuts to that not seeing him again stuff!" Margaret was emphatic. "I know what I'd do. I'd get in touch with him—but quick. Call him up with some excuse. Did I drop my ration-book under the bed? Could he give me the phone number of the Eiffel Tower? Anything——"

"That would be fine—for you." Jocelyn surveyed her. "You're small, and dark, and awfully pretty. And somehow—God knows how!—you manage to look as if you needed protecting! . . . But you don't know how different things are when you're an outsize like me—a sort of natural-platinum moose!"

Margaret stared. "If you really want to know," she said, "I'd rather look like you than any woman I've ever seen."

"You're very sweet—and thank you." Jocelyn smiled a fleeting smile. "You don't understand, though. You have to *be* a moose to

72

know what it's like . . . You see, even the *idea* of a moose-girl in the throes of love is sort of funny . . ."

"What *is* all this?" Margaret was frowning now. "How much of a runt is this Beaucaire? Is he a midget or something?"

"*Midget?*" Jocelyn was indignant. "Why, he's *big!* He's bigger than I am, if you can believe it!"

"Then what in the name of Pete was the sob story all about?"

Jocelyn started to laugh. "I don't know," she said—and stopped laughing. "I suppose I'm just afraid . . . Afraid of—of being emotionally disturbed or something." She checked herself, horrified. "My God, did you hear that? Now I sound like a bloody schoolmistress!"

Margaret eyed her reflectively. "You're crazy," she said. "What you have to do is cut out all this self-analysis jazz. Shed these ugly neuroses, woman! Contact the guy if he doesn't contact you—and have a whirl, girl!" Suddenly, uncontrollably, she giggled again. "At least you don't have to be scared of him working too fast. Not with those ribs!"

"You—you monstrous creature!" said Jocelyn, and jumped as the door opened and John Cameron's face appeared around the jamb.

"Squaw Palaver?" he asked. "Or can an old brave horn in?"

"Oh please, John!" Jocelyn smiled at him. "I was on the point of yelling for help anyway."

"What's the trouble, Magnificence?" Cameron crossed the room and looked up at her. "Don't tell me you can't handle this little snippet." He looked down at his wife.

"She scares me," Jocelyn said. "She's a witch or something."

"Oh, sure. But give her the sign once in a while and you'll have no trouble." He sat beside his wife and pointed at her with extended first and little fingers.

"I thought you were supposed to be working," Margaret said. "What's the snag? Still that second act curtain?"

"Unh-unh." Cameron shook his head. "The old trouble—galloping lethargy." He looked at Jocelyn, still standing by the mantelpiece. "Talking about work; what are you doing, Joss?"

She shrugged. "Nothing exciting." She was staring into the fire again.

He looked at her curiously. "Didn't I see something in some column the other day? About you doing a miniature of some kid? It was a screwy sort of name—oh, yeah, Bruttenholm." He pronounced it phonetically, with all three syllables.

"John, you hick!" His wife was disdainful. *"Bruttenholm's* only the way they spell it! It's pronounced *Broom!"*

"Well, whaddya know," said her husband comfortably. "Another of these Cholmondeley-Chumly deals, huh? I can't keep up with 'em."

"That's because you're not a two-fisted snob like me! But you ought to know *Broom,* for heaven's sake! It's the family name of the Marquis of Gleneyre—and he's Jocelyn's uncle-in-law. And Marcia Bruttenholm's not just 'some kid,' let me tell you. She's the most beautiful debutante who's been presented at Court for years!"

"Okay—okay. I surrender." Cameron grinned happily. "I'll buy a copy of *Burke's Peerage* tomorrow . . . But what I really want to know's if Jocelyn *is* doing the work? Are you, Joss? And may I see it?"

But Jocelyn didn't seem to hear the question. She stared at him blankly for a moment—and then suddenly smiled. A wide and wholehearted and lovely smile.

"Your spouse may be a witch, John," she said. "But she gives first class advice!" She picked up her empty glass and held it out. "Somebody give me another drink."

"Well, *well!"* Margaret jumped up and took the glass in her left hand and held out her right.

"Put it there, Iseult!" she said.

CHAPTER FOUR

The next day was Saturday, and Anthony Gethryn, who had surprised himself by not sleeping well, surprised his skeleton household by appearing for breakfast at eight-thirty. And was barely through the meal before White announced a surprising arrival.

"Detective-Sergeant Seymour, sir," said White. "From Mr. Pike."

And two minutes later, in the study, Anthony was shaking hands with his visitor. Who said:

"The Superintendent told me to tell you, sir, that the A-C* had

* Assistant-Commissioner: in this case, of course, Sir Egbert Lucas.

okayed his recommendation that I should be detached from all other duty and report to you until further orders."

"My God!" Anthony was impressed. "What's happened? Did the Treasury up the Police Estimates?"

Seymour smiled. " 'Fraid not, sir. But Unc—but Mr. Pike did say he knew you'd be wanting a man and you'd better have the same one all the time." The smile became a grin. "He also said that if I was responsible to you, he couldn't be responsible for what you told me to do."

"I can hear him," Anthony said, and gave Sergeant Seymour a chair and a cigarette and lit one himself.

"Tell me," he said, "how much do you know about this affair?" Inclined already to approve of Sergeant Seymour, he was probing.

Clearly, and with admirable brevity, Seymour gave what was obviously the cut and polished edition of a briefing from Pike.

"That's fine," Anthony said—and then suddenly, "What d'you think of it? The whole thing?"

"I don't know, sir. Not yet." Seymour was cautious. "It's—well, it's definitely out of the ordinary. I will say that."

"Hardly an over-statement!" Anthony laughed—and shot another question. "What would you choose as the most important piece of the puzzle so far?"

"Slattery, sir." Seymour had no doubts about this. "In fact, if there's no attempt on him, I don't see how we'll ever get the guilty party."

"If you must know, nor do I." Anthony's approval was waxing. "But that doesn't mean we're not going to try . . . What's been done about the watch on Slattery, by the way? Know any details?"

"Yes, sir. There are two men in an unrented shop across the street. They're working as painters, and can cover the front. Behind Slattery's place—he and his wife live on the premises, you know—there's another man. He's taken a room in the next street, and his window overlooks Slattery's back door. Those are the daytime arrangements. I'll find out later what they're doing for nights."

"H'mm." Anthony pondered. "Sounds all right as far as it goes." He caught a fleeting expression in Seymour's face. "You got something more?"

"Well, I had been thinking Slattery would be safer at night anyway. Being in a wheelchair and not going out much after dark, I

75

should think. I mean, he'll be safer *unless* the killer changes his pattern altogether." Seymour smiled, a trifle uncertainly. "I could easily be off the beam on this, though."

"I don't think so." Anthony wondered whether the youngster had come to the same conclusion he himself had reached the night before. "What's your idea of this pattern? You don't mean just making the deaths look accidental? Or do you?"

"No. It's a bit more than that, sir. I'm thinking about the *kind* of accident he uses." Seymour leaned forward, more at ease every moment. "All but one of 'em are definitely connected with going from one place to another; with *traveling*. The one exception might be Bainbridge, but he was fished out of a river and was probably en route somewhere when he got it."

"If it's any satisfaction," Anthony said, "I reached exactly the same conclusion. Only I took a lot longer to reach it." He smiled. "I can see it's going to be a pleasure to work with you."

Seymour colored to the roots of his tight-cropped blond curls. He mumbled, "Thank you, sir," and hurried back to business. "Of course, it doesn't get us anywhere——"

"There I disagree," said Anthony. "Profoundly. It tells us something about the man we're after—the man I've christened Smith Brown-Jones. And that's all to the good, however nebulous it is. Because he's a subject on which we're far too ignorant." He began to pace the room. "And a damned unpleasant subject, too! Fascinating as a problem, of course. But not pleasing, Seymour, very far from pleasing . . ."

He stood at the window and stared out at his oblong of garden, in summer one of the brightest in London, but bleak and bare now under the dun-yellow winter sky . . . He shivered, and went on staring out as he spoke.

"You know, Seymour," he said, "even in this sort of work, it's rarely one runs into true, unadulterated evil . . . If I were to count the murderers I know for whom I've had no faintest shred of sympathy, for instance, I wouldn't use all the fingers on one hand." His shoulders moved again. "But this one! This one's straight out of the *Ancient Mariner!* . . . I wonder how many of those ten men felt him behind them . . ."

He swung around in a sudden movement, and laughed. "Sorry about the melodramatics," he said, and crossed to his desk.

"*Ancient Mariner?*" Seymour said. "Coleridge? . . . Oh, yes! 'Like one that on a lonesome road——'"

Anthony nodded. "'Frightful fiend,' when you come to think of it, is hardly an exaggeration . . ." He reached for pen and paper and grew businesslike. "Let's get to work. The first thing I want you to do is visit Updyke and Wallace, the press-cutting people." He scribbled a note and handed it over. "Give 'em this, and you'll see Martin Updyke himself. Tell him I want urgent, comprehensive coverage on Adrian Messenger, past and present."

"Right," said Seymour.

"Then get started on your own big job for the weekend. Which is to get in touch, *un*officially, with as many as possible of the widows or closest relatives of the men on Messenger's list. Objective three-fold. First and most important, get the men's military histories, if any. Second, discover from the relative you talk to if the other names on the list, plus the name of Messenger, were ever mentioned by the man, and if so in what connection. Third, find out whether there is or has been any faintest suspicion that the 'accidents' weren't what they seemed . . ."

Anthony was watching Seymour's intent face. "That's a tall order," he went on. "But I'm going to make it taller. I want this done, but I'd rather not have it done at all than give anyone any inkling there's anything wrong. We mustn't—and I mean *must not!*—run any risk of publicizing in any degree that there's any sort of investigation going. I can't make that too strong."

"I understand, sir. With an unknown quantity like your Smith Brown-Jones, we can't run the risk of him picking up anything from anywhere." Seymour paused; added hesitantly, "There's one thing, though—you're not forgetting Mr. Pike's written personally to all the local Chief Constables concerned? Mainly about the 'accidents,' of course—but the answers might cover the other things too. Especially military service."

"No," said Anthony. "I haven't forgotten. But double-checking can't hurt and might help. Especially when it takes in the personal viewpoint. And it may be quicker, too." There was curiosity as well as approval in his look. "You seem to agree military service is important. Mind telling me why?"

Seymour flushed again, but managed a grin at the same time. "Because finding the link between all these characters has to be, sir; in order to get any clue to the motive. And I remember Mr. Pike saying you thought the War might be the answer." He got to his feet. "If there's nothing else, I'd better get going. When d'you want me to report?"

Anthony pondered. "Oh, let me know how you're doing sometime tomorrow. Or Monday morning, if you like." He smiled. "I don't expect miracles, you know."

He was watching Seymour, after an instant of hesitation, start for the door when another thought came. "Wait," he said. "While you're with Updyke, tell him to dig up anything he can on all the 'accidents.' From anywhere." He considered a moment. "And that *is* all," he said, and again saw a momentary hesitation. "Unless you have something?"

"Well, not really, sir," Seymour said. "But I *was* wondering what line you were going to follow yourself——"

"My dear chap!" Anthony was contrite. "I should have told you. My target for today—the *private* life of Adrian Messenger . . ."

In Chelsea, near the river and not far from Battersea Bridge, Whistlers Walk is an address about which even the oldest of London's taxi drivers have to think twice.

There are only five houses in Whistlers Walk, two on each side and one sealing the end of the little street, turning it into a cul-de-sac. The four houses which face each other are massive "villas" dating from the middle days of Victoria; but the fifth, which at this time was Jocelyn Messenger's, is from a more gracious age. Smaller, low and half-timbered, it looks out at the Thames from the windows of its one upper storey; and to each side and behind it, surrounded by its own wall of once rose-red brick, is far more ground than can be boasted by any other dwelling place in this part of London. There are trees inside the wall, too; not only several of the city's ubiquitous planes, but a pair of oaks and a big beech which rears over the door of the smaller building at the back; the studio that once was a stable.

It was ten-thirty when Anthony parked the Voisin in front of

Number Five and got out and looked around him. At some time during the past half hour, the sun had struggled through the yellow blanket and now shone pale on the grey stone of the Embankment, striking gleams from the river. Yesterday was the first time he had ever been in Whistlers Walk, and he studied the front of the house with renewed pleasure as he went up its three low steps and rang the bell. And waited, girding himself for final battle with the small and Scottish Cerberus.

But battle wasn't waged. This morning, Caledonia's representative was subdued rather than stern, wary instead of wild. She hardly let him speak before she said, "Ye're to come in, if ye please—" and took his hat and coat, and led him to a charming, book-walled room at the back of the house, and muttered something he couldn't catch, and left him. He heard her voice again just outside the room, apparently speaking over a telephone; then almost at once, looking out of the french windows at the surprising garden, saw Jocelyn Messenger walking quickly toward him from her studio.

The blue linen of her overall matched her eyes, and the sun glinted in her hair. She was smiling and vivid and long-striding, and it was clear to Anthony that for this morning at least the clouds had lifted from Asgard. He found himself simultaneously disliking the task ahead and realizing how right George Firth had been to imply one-sidedness to Adrian Messenger's devotion.

He opened the window for her, and she stepped into the room and shook hands with him. A cool, firm handshake which matched the rest of her.

"I'm sorry about being so unavailable yesterday," she said. "And I have a sneaking feeling Sheila was rude to you, though she won't admit it. She's a tactless little dragon sometimes."

"Useful thing round a house, a dragon," Anthony said. "And any treatment I got, I probably asked for." He followed her to the fire, and sat in the chair she suggested, and waited for an opening.

It wasn't long coming, because she sat herself to face him, and looked at him and said, "I'm delighted to see you, Mr. Gethryn. But I'm also a little curious . . ." She laughed. "What do I mean, a *little?* I'm dying!"

"This isn't the sort of call I wish it was," he said. "You see, there

79

are times when I do an odd job or so for the C.I.D. and I'm afraid this is one of them."

She was grave now, studying him. "Now I'm more curious than ever——"

"It's about Adrian Messenger," said Anthony. "And I want your help."

"Poor Adrian!" Her face clouded. "But what in the world could he have to do with the Police?"

Here it was, and he might as well get it over quickly. "I'm afraid his death wasn't accidental," he said. "In my opinion—which is the official opinion too—he was killed. Murdered."

She stared at him, the blue eyes wide in shocked amazement. "Then—then there *was* a bomb!"

"Yes." Anthony was grim. "Most definitely there was a bomb."

"How *horrible!*" She shuddered—and then suddenly stiffened, looking at him with frowning intentness. "What did you mean, *Adrian* was murdered? The bomb means all those poor people were —in a way. But it sounded so—so personal when you said it."

"Yes," said Anthony again. And then slowly, "Messenger's life seems to have been the sole objective of whoever wrecked that plane."

Pure reflex brought Jocelyn to her feet. "But it's *impossible!* . . . Who could conceivably do such a thing!" She heard her voice rising and controlled it. "This just doesn't make any sense! Adrian didn't have any enemies. He—he was a *quiet* person . . . Oh, I can't believe it!"

"I know it sounds like a badly plotted nightmare." Anthony was sympathetic. "But that's often the way with truth."

"You sound so *sure!*" Jocelyn sank back onto her chair. "But how can you be?"

"He told us himself," said Anthony. "And if that sounds cryptic, it won't when I've given you the story from the beginning——"

He gave it to her; and was surprised to find how little time the known facts took to tell. She listened in silence, and intently. And when he'd finished, she said slowly:

"It still sounds like a nightmare; but a different kind. The kind you *have* to believe!"

And then she said, "What can I do? I don't see how I can help, but I'll try. I'd like to."

"Then I'm going to bombard you with questions." Anthony produced a paper which he unfolded and gave to her. "That's a copy of the list given to George Firth by Messenger. Do you remember having heard him mention any of these names?"

Jocelyn studied the list carefully, weighing each entry. "No." She shook her head. "I'm sure he never did."

"Can you suggest anyone else, some other close friend, I could put the same question to?"

"No, I don't think I can . . . Adrian was an odd sort of person, in a lot of ways. He was awfully—what's the word?—reticent. It sounds silly, but except for me and possibly General Firth, I don't think he had any friends. Hundreds of acquaintances, but no *friends*."

"Are you counting family? I know his father's dead, and his mother's in America. But isn't there anyone else he was close to?"

"Oh, how silly of me! He adored Aunt Mildred—and Uncle Roderick too, if it comes to that——"

"The Gleneyres!"

"Yes. Of course they're his *great* aunt and uncle really. But somehow he treated them more like parents."

"And he might have confided something to either of them? Something he wouldn't have told you?"

She hesitated. "I—I suppose so," she said. "Particularly to Aunt Mildred."

"Thanks, I'll remember that." Anthony was thoughtful. "Now another tack: were you seeing Messenger fairly frequently during the last six months?"

"Oh, yes. Two or three times a week at least."

"Did you notice anything unusual about him at any time? I mean, was there any difference in his manner? Did he seem worried about anything, for instance?"

"I—I'm not sure . . . That sounds silly, but you've got to remember he was a moody sort of person anyway, so one didn't notice his ups and downs so much . . ." She was silent, frowning as she wrestled with memory.

"Don't worry," Anthony said. "We'll skip that one——"

She looked up. "No—wait. I don't want to give you any wrong

ideas, so I'm being careful. But I think I did vaguely notice something—the last two or three times he was here."

"What sort of something?"

"Like one of his worried moods, but a little different. As if he was sort of excited as well as worried . . . I'm afraid I'm not making much sense——"

"Oh, but you are." Anthony smiled at her. "Try and make some more, though. Did you say anything to him? Ask him what was the matter or anything?"

"I may have . . . Yes, I believe I did. But I really wasn't paying any more attention to it than I would have to any of the moods, you see. That's the trouble . . . Oh, wait a minute! I remember telling him he seemed awfully jumpy, and I hoped the Atlantic crossing would cure it. Something silly like that——"

"Ha!" Anthony was alert. "And what did *he* say?"

"I'm sorry—I don't think I—— Oh yes, I *do* remember. He said, 'If it doesn't, nothing will.' I believe those were his exact words."

"Now that," said Anthony, "is very interesting. Very interesting indeed!" He lapsed into silence, rubbing reflectively at his chin.

Watching him, Jocelyn stood up and pressed a bell-push by the mantelpiece. And went back to her chair as he said:

"Did he say anything about his reason for going?"

She shrugged. "I believe he mumbled something about 'business.' And I'm afraid that's a word which makes my ears close up automatically."

"Could that have meant literary business?" Anthony was persistent. "Something to do with his work?"

She shook her head. "When Adrian said 'business,' he always seemed to mean 'money-business,' and nothing to do with his writing . . . He was always very *solemn* about money," she said. "Like most very rich people."

"I know exactly what you mean." Anthony gave her a quick smile. "But let's get back to the American visit. He told George Firth he'd be home in a fortnight. Is that what he said to you?"

"Just about. What he actually said, I think, was that he'd be gone for 'two or three weeks.'"

"Did he mention any particular place he was going to in the States?"

"I'm not sure . . ." She sighed, looking at Anthony with an apologetic little smile. "I must be sounding perfectly moronic, but I'm afraid I don't remember things if they don't particularly interest me——"

She stopped abruptly, shocked by her own words and their implication. A faint flush crept up from her throat to her temples. She said, "I don't know about real policemen, Mr. Gethryn, but I hope I can treat you like a confessor. About—about personal things, I mean . . . What I'm trying to say is that I'm afraid I—I wasn't so interested in Adrian as he was in me——"

She stopped again, and Anthony jumped to the rescue. "Don't give it another thought," he said. "All I want are some facts. As pants the hart, I pant for detail. Any crumb!" He looked at her with an eyebrow raised. "Just *something* about this trip. A place-name, a plane-time, a remark about the weather—anything!"

She pondered—and was surprised by a new flash of memory. "Oh, yes! He mentioned California—something about it being hot there and having to take two sets of clothes because it was going to be cold in Canada——" She stopped as she saw Anthony's expression. "Didn't you know he was going to Canada as well?" She was surprised.

"He didn't say so to Firth. Go on—please." Anthony made no attempt to conceal eagerness.

"He was going to be in America—California, I suppose—only for a day or two. Then he was going on to Canada. But I'm certain he didn't say exactly where."

She relapsed into another brow-furrowed silence—and the door opened and the little Scotswoman entered and departed; wordless, but leaving behind her wine glasses and a decanter of sherry which to Anthony's pleased surprise turned out to be wholly admirable.

Jocelyn said absently, "Poor Adrian sent it to me last year, from Portugal—" and then, suddenly, "I've just thought of something else about California. I'm sure he mentioned someone's name." She hesitated. "Now what *was* it?"

"The name of the person he was going to visit?"

"Yes . . . Oh, damn—*why* didn't I pay more attention? . . . It was in the studio, the day before he left . . . I was working on sketches of Marcia, and Adrian was sort of wandering round . . . He said something about flying, and how amazing it was to think it was only going to take him a few hours to get to America——" She covered her eyes with a hand, concentrating. "And then only a few more to get to Canada after he left the—the—*Someone's* in California . . . The name's just round the corner in my head . . . Oh, I've got it— no, no, that wasn't it. Oh, damn and blast!" She sat straight and looked at Anthony with a rueful twist of her mouth.

He thought, fleetingly, how lovely she was, and to hell with scale. He said:

"Don't press, and it may come back. Tell me something else." He paused, picking the words for his most vital question yet. "Thinking back, are you sure Messenger never said or wrote anything to you which might have been construed to mean he was in danger of his life?"

"Of course I am!" She sat very straight and her eyes were indignant. "If he had, don't you think I'd have said something about it by this time?"

Anthony grinned, raising his hands. *"Peccavi!"* he said. "Also *Kamerad!* . . . Let me try again: Can you recollect any word or action of Messenger's which at the time seemed unremarkable but which now, in the light of what I've told you, could possibly be interpreted as meaning he thought he might be in danger?"

"No!" she said. "Absolutely and positively no!" Indignation gave way to curiosity. "What makes you think there was?"

Openly, Anthony studied her. There was no doubting her; not about this, nor about anything else. He said, slowly:

"I found out what he said before he died. The person who heard it thought, not without reason, that it was delirious nonsense. But I don't agree."

He paused—and Jocelyn sat straighter than ever. "You must have been talking to Raoul St. Denis," she said, with an oddly flat delivery he decided it would be best to ignore. He said:

"Yes. We found we were old war-time associates, and he obliged me by performing a remarkable feat of memory. He gave me what was probably an almost perfect verbatim report." Anthony considered showing her his typed interpretations, but decided against it. "I won't bother you with all the ins-and-outs, but I ended up with a near-certainty that Messenger was trying to say that someone had *'got him too,'* and was asking St. Denis to *'tell Jocelyn.'* "

She was moved. "Poor Adrian," she said softly. And then, "But I don't understand it. I think M. St. Denis must be right about delirium."

"It's possible, of course." Anthony shrugged. "But somehow I don't think so. I think I've misinterpreted; because whichever way you arrange the words, they're too near making sense not to have any meaning . . ." He paused again. "There were two other names he kept saying, by the way. *George,* and *Emma.* Would you know who they are?"

"I imagine *George* is General Firth," she said at once. "But I don't think I ever heard of any *Emma . . .*"

"Another author, possibly? 'Emma's book' seems to have been repeated several times."

She shook her head. "No. I don't think so. There's Emma Jane Winston, of course." She smiled. "But Adrian couldn't stand her work, and I feel certain he'd never even seen her personally." She picked up her glass—then set it down and jumped to her feet.

"Holton!" she said triumphantly.

"Emma?" said Anthony. "Or California?"

"California." The triumph had faded, and she was shaking her head dejectedly. "But it isn't right. As soon as I said it aloud, I knew it was wrong. Oh, *hell!"*

"I still say forget it," said Anthony. "Then it'll come, in one glorious burst of light and music. At the most improbable moment." He looked at his watch. "I'm sorry to keep you so long, but there's just one more point: George Firth tells me Messenger's lawyers are Abercrombie and Smythe. I was wondering if by any chance you happen to know either of them personally?"

She looked surprised and, he thought curiously, a little uncomfortable. She said, "Yes I do—Gilbert Abercrombie. Why?"

"Because I'm trying to devise a way of getting myself an hour with Messenger's private papers. Without exciting too much curiosity——"

"Oh I see . . . Yes, of course——" He saw the faint flush again, and then a sudden determination.

"You don't have to talk to Gilbert at all. Or anyone except me," she said. And explained, concisely but with a certain stiffness, the bequest of the Whig Street house and its contents.

"They've taken all the business and financial stuff," she said. "But everything else is still there. In his desk in the study."

She stood up and crossed to a writing-table near the french windows and took something from the drawer and brought it back and held it out to him. "Here are the keys," she said, and sat down again. "All you have to do is bring them back when you've finished. It's the top flat: you can go up the front stairs, or there's an outside flight at the back."

Anthony weighed the keys in his hand, and smiled. "I wonder," he said, "what I'd do without you? A thousand and one heartfelt thanks!" He got to his feet. "I'll reward you by taking myself off——"

Again she was surprised. "No more questions?"

"Not just now. Only a request." There was something in his tone which made her look at him sharply. "I have to ask you, with all the pomp and red-taped circumstance I can command, not to reveal to anyone what we've been discussing."

She smiled. "If that's a request," she said, "I can't imagine what an order would be like." The smile vanished. "But of course I won't."

She stood up to face him. She was closer to him than at any time before, and he was momentarily surprised by the novel sensation of having to look up, from his own six-feet, at a woman's eyes.

"I only wish I could have helped more," she began; then suddenly checked at a new thought.

"Oh, but p'raps I can!" she said. "I mean, really *do* something." She was eager now. "Please fill that glass and sit down again, and I'll tell you——"

It had been, you will remember, half past ten when Anthony arrived in Whistlers Walk——

And at that time, in the lobby of the Gainsborough in Birmingham, the bald-headed Mr. David Bronson of Vancouver was availing himself of one of those up-to-the-minute services on which the hotel prided itself, the Travel-Advice Bureau.

Mr. Bronson sat in the little glass-walled office and explained his needs to the current Advisor, whose name was Smathers, and who was already thinking how pleasant and easy a client had fallen to his lot this morning. Because all Mr. Bronson wanted was, first, to discover whether he could go by train from Birmingham to Deyming in Medeshire without returning to London; and, second, to ask advice as to the best place to stay for a week or so in Deyming itself.

Having ascertained that Mr. Bronson wished to travel the next day, Mr. Smathers selected a train; informed his client there would be one change only, at Dorminster; arranged for the actual purchase of Mr. Bronson's first-class ticket; stated emphatically that the Gleneyre Arms Hotel in Deyming was the *only* place to stay, and concluded this triumphal session of service by telephoning then and there to the hostelry in question and reserving a room for Mr. Bronson as of the following evening.

Mr. Bronson expressed himself as not only gratified but surprised by Mr. Smathers' promptness and efficiency, which he said was something he hadn't succeeded in finding in any London hotel. Mr. Smathers beamed under the treatment, liking Mr. Bronson more with every moment; so much in fact that when an hour or so later he found Mr. Bronson in the lobby and presented him with his railway ticket, he took advantage of the final flourish allowed him by the Gainsborough management and invited Mr. Bronson to a pre-luncheon *apéritif* in the hotel's new and resplendent American bar.

Mr. Bronson accepted with every evidence of pleasure, and over their drinks confided to Mr. Smathers that this was his first visit to "the old country"; and that being about to complete this afternoon the single piece of business which had brought him to Birmingham, was planning to spend the last weeks of his trip in a search for truly rural England.

This led to the truly cosy discovery that Mr. Smathers was himself a native of Medeshire and could give assurance that this County contained some of the most beautiful and unspoiled country in the British Isles. A fact which Mr. Smathers put down to Medeshire's luck in numbering among its landowners two or three old families who still had the wealth and ability to keep up their estates—

"Notably, of course, Lord Gleneyre," said Mr. Smathers. "A wonderful man, Mr. Bronson. A true aristocrat, in the finest sense of the word."

"Yes, I'm sure," said Mr. Bronson, and turned the subject with deft unobtrusiveness. He had momentarily taken off his glasses, and was rubbing gently at the corner of his right eye, where a little muscle had started to twitch.

It had been a quarter to twelve when Mr. Bronson and Mr. Smathers had entered the Gainsborough Bar——

And at that time, in London, Anthony Gethryn was leaving Whistlers Walk. He stood at the front door with his hostess and gave her final congratulation on her idea for being of active help. Like most good ideas, it was simple: she was in any event going down to Deyming Abbey the following day, and now would volunteer to discover from the Gleneyres, without arousing in them any suspicion of anything out of the way, whether Adrian had confided anything to either of them within the past months which had struck them as in any way unusual.

"I'll be back on Monday afternoon," Jocelyn said. "If I don't find out something sensational, I'd better wait till then to phone you, hadn't I?"

Anthony smiled. "Unless," he said, "that mental fanfare comes and you remember the California name——"

As he spoke, he stepped out through the front door she was holding open, and saw a taxi pulling up beside the Voisin. He turned to say good-bye—and realized that, for this instant at least, Mrs. Jocelyn Messenger had ceased to be aware of his existence.

Looking past him, her eyes had widened in astonishment, and once more he saw the flush creep up from her throat, darker this time. He turned his head to look at the taxi again, and saw that its passenger was getting out—stiffly and cautiously. A giant of a man in a grey suit and topcoat; a man whose shoulders looked somehow familiar and then, as their owner turned his head, were recognizable as the shoulders he had first and last seen covered by a white silk robe with a red dragon embroidered on its back. Ajax, it was apparent, didn't believe in telephony; at least not as opposed to personal appearance.

Anthony raised his hat. He said, "Good-bye, Mrs. Messenger," and went down the steps.

Raoul St. Denis was paying the taxi driver. He saw Anthony, and was plainly surprised. He hadn't yet looked up at the door of Number Five. He said:

"Good morning, Lecoq. May I gather you are hot and heavy upon the trail?" He smiled, but the smile didn't reach his eyes.

It occurred to Anthony to be glad that this man couldn't be on any opposing team, and he made haste to say what instinct told him was that rarity of rarities, the right thing which is also the truth. He said:

"The trail's so cold, my friend, and so tenuous, that I've been enlisting help. Charming and most efficient help." He made a gesture which drew Raoul's eye to the front door of the house and found himself forgotten for the second time in as many minutes.

A salutary experience, he thought, and watched as Raoul removed his hat—awkwardly, with his left hand—and Jocelyn Messenger moved out of the doorway and down to the second step to greet him.

She was smiling a smile which made Anthony envious, academically at least, of her new visitor, and he turned to his car and opened the door and was about to slide into the driver's seat when a new thought came and he looked back.

"Mrs. Messenger!" he called—and both of them turned. He was relieved to see that now St. Denis's smile at him was wholehearted. He said to Jocelyn, "That ukase against discussion——" and waited.

She said, "Don't worry. I won't forget."

"Good," he said. "But it's withdrawn as regards your present company. Provided you pass the order on."

He didn't wait for a reply, but tipped his hat again and turned back to the Voisin. As he started the engine and backed around, he saw that the front door of Mrs. Messenger's house had closed, leaving the steps bare . . .

Having for the past three or four years boasted one of the few remaining London landlords with the money to keep up his property in the style to which it ought to have been accustomed, Number Twenty-one Whig Street was credit to the shade of John Nash; and a pleasure to the eye both inside and out.

But to Anthony Gethryn it was proving just one more bead of frustration to add to his steadily lengthening chain. Almost an hour spent in Adrian Messenger's flat, mostly at the big desk in Adrian Messenger's study, had left him with nothing more than the conviction that Adrian Messenger's was the most private of all the posthumous private lives he had been forced at one time and another to investigate. Obviously, the man had had taste, money and imagination. But he had also, it seemed, been the possessor of one of those ultra-orderly minds which, especially in regard to all forms of document, believe in a place for everything with very little of anything in it.

Finished with the last drawer in the desk, which contained two completely disinteresting files marked CORRESPONDENCE, Anthony sat back and glanced at his watch, and realized he was hungry. He stood up and looked at the top of the desk again, its beautiful softly gleaming surface unlittered by anything save the big bronze-bound blotter, a telephone and an engagement pad bound in dark green leather. Just to check—because he had done it once before—he lifted the cover of the pad and verified that the virginal top sheet was dated the preceding Sunday. Which had been the day after its owner had left for the foreign parts he was never going to reach . . .

Anthony sighed, and picked up his hat, and was almost out of the room when thought of an omission in his search suddenly struck him.

He went back to the desk and rectified the omission by lifting the copper-bound blotter and looking underneath it——

And there, glaring up at him, lay last *Saturday's* sheet of the engagement pad; the sheet for the actual day of Messenger's departure. At the top, in ink and neatly aligned in the division marked "A.M.," was the entry "9:30—Airport," but below this, in pencil, a note was scrawled diagonally across the rest of the paper:

"*Mrs. A. (Sara) Kouroudjian—Windicotes—Purling—Surrey.*"

Anthony stared at it, and sat in the desk chair again and pushed his hat to the back of his head and went on staring. There was an old, familiar tingling somewhere in him: he hoped it wasn't playing him false. Both entries seemed to be in Messenger's handwriting, but the second looked as if it had been written in haste. Which meant—which had to mean when taken in conjunction with the date of the sheet and its position under the blotter—that this had been written by Messenger immediately before he left.

And it meant more, thought Anthony, as he studied the related positions of the phone and the engagement pad, balancing them against the angle of the scrawl. It meant, again almost certainly, that the scrawl was the result of a last-minute telephone call, probably incoming.

He reached for the telephone himself, and as he dialed wondered again about the validity of the tingle.

His call was answered. By a Scottish voice which, after he had identified himself, was civil enough though still faintly draconian. It supplied the information that the lady it called Mrs. Maissenger had gone out to luncheon, with someone it called the Frainch gaintleman. But it regraitted that it did not know where the meal was to be eaten, nor at what time the lady would return.

"Never mind then," said Anthony. "Thanks very much. Tell her I called, will you?"

He hung up, and folded the paper and stowed it in his wallet, and within a couple of minutes was in his car again, heading for St. James's Street and lunch.

Had he been five seconds earlier crossing Piccadilly, he would have seen the taxi bearing Jocelyn Messenger and her host a little further eastward, toward the restaurant of Aristide Mazarin . . .

In which establishment, an hour later and in the middle of a meal which cheerfully flaunted its excellence in the grim but fading visage of Austerity, Raoul St. Denis chanced in conversation to use the word, "California"——

With results which caused among the other guests even more interest than before in him and his lovely companion. For she clapped a hand to her forehead and said "*Dalton!*" in a voice obviously much louder than she'd intended. And then colored, and laughed a small embarrassed laugh, and leaned across the table and said something to the big Frenchman.

What she said was, "I'm awfully sorry. It was just that I remembered something. It's all part of what Anthony Gethryn wanted me to tell you . . ."

And then she said, "I think I ought to phone him," and made a gesture to keep Raoul in his chair, and herself stood up . . .

91

But she failed to reach Anthony Gethryn, both at Whig Street and his own house.

For Anthony Gethryn, having decided over a quick and solitary meal to follow his hunch concerning the importance of Mrs. A. (Sara) Kouroudjian, was already driving out of London toward the country town of Purling, forty miles away.

He knew, of course, that he might be wasting his time; but reflected gloomily that in this affair time was the only thing of which he seemed to have any supply at all. He remembered Flood's remark, "Ramifications two a penny," and felt like adding, "frustrations free."

He might have been cheered had he been able, at this moment, to watch Thomas Gainsford Seymour at work. Hatless, with a briefcase under his arm and looking as little like a policeman as any human well could, Seymour was standing on the doorstep of Number Eighteen Wellington Square in North London. He was talking with a haggardly handsome, fortyish female whom he addressed as "Mrs. McGowan," asking if she could spare him a few moments of her time.

"We-ell, provided you're not going to sell me anything . . ." There was a note of doubt in Mrs. McGowan's voice, but a definite gleam of approval in the eyes which took in her visitor from shoes to golden head.

Seymour winced at the mere and vulgar thought of salesmanship. He protested, with a virile boyishness nicely calculated in its appeal, that all he wanted from Mrs. McGowan was help. He was, it seemed, assisting in the collection of material for the appendices of a new military work entitled *Troops of the Town* and dealing with the magnificent work and war-record of the London Regiments—

Here he zipped open his briefcase and glanced at a convincing sheaf of notes. And said, "I understand your late husband was with a London regiment, Mrs. McGowan—" and then broke off as the lady interrupted him.

"What are we standing out here for?" she said. "Come in. Might as well be comfortable—"

Whereupon Mr. Seymour stepped over the threshold, already certain that the information he needed was as good as received . . .

As has been stated, this glimpse of his new assistant thus efficiently at work might well have cheered Anthony. But it is doubtful if a scene being enacted at about the same time, beyond another side of London, would have had the same effect.

The exact location was Mr. Slattery's small shop at the corner of Pope Terrace in Twickenham. Outside it, at front and back, the arrangement of the invisible trap for Mr. Smith Brown-Jones would have pleased his christener. The two pseudo-workmen continued their admirable performance of painters at work in the vacant premises opposite the Slattery front door; and their colleague the pseudo-writer continued to watch over the rear of the premises from his window in the next street.

But inside, it was a different story. Had Anthony been able to hear the conversation in the parlor behind the shop, he would most certainly have been disturbed. Seriously disturbed.

Huddled in his wheelchair, as close to the small fireplace as he could get, Jonathan Slattery stared at nothing and didn't so much as turn his head when his wife came in and set down a tray which clattered genially.

He said, dully, " 'Tain't teatime yet," and his wife said, cheerfully, "I know. But I thought a cuppa might cheer you up like." She laid a hand on his shoulder. "With a drop o' the old and bold in, eh?"

Her husband made an effort. He sat straight and grinned at her. "Now you're talkin', girl," he said, and shot the chair in one rapid thrust of its wheels across the room to a corner-cupboard from which he took a squat bottle that he bore back to the fireside with care. He waited while Connie Slattery filled two cups with dark, dark tea from the pot and then into each cup himself poured from the bottle a generous tot.

His wife dropped into the old rocking-chair on the other side of the hearth. They lifted their cups, and sipped cautiously, and almost achieved harmonics with their simultaneous "A-aahs!" of appreciation.

They drained the cups in a silence which persisted as Connie refilled them, and then refused the lacing her husband offered.

"Not for me, ducks," she said. "But you 'ave another. Do you good, it will."

Jonathan Slattery obeyed her, and smiled at her again, and raised the cup to her. " 'Ere's lookin' at you, Con!" he said.

But after that he fell silent, staring at the fire once more. Until Mrs. Slattery said, with a sort of gentle suddenness:

"It's no good, ducks—*I* know you're bothered. *And* I know what's botherin' you." She stood up and brought him a cigarette and held a light for it. "You can't put no blinkers on *me!*"

Her husband turned up to her a face of injured and bewildered innocence. "'Oo's bothered?" he demanded. "Jest because a bloke feels sorter down-like, does 'e 'ave to be *botherin'?*"

Mrs. Slattery took his empty cup and set it on her tray. She said placidly, "It's that Mr. Flood an' the twenty-five pound, ain't it? . . . 'E left you 'is number. Why don't you get 'im on the telephone and explyne?"

"You know what?" Her husband spoke with something more than asperity. "You're goin' loopy—that's what!" He snorted angrily, but without looking at her. "Why in the 'ell should I be worryin' about *that* 'owjerdo? Now I'm askin' you—*why?*"

"'Cause you are, that's why." Connie Slattery was unperturbed. "Because you didn't play fair with Mr. Flood, if you want it in plyne English."

"Whadjer mean, didn't play fair!" Mr. Slattery's indignation mounted. "I didn't do no 'arm to this 'ere Flood, did I? Nor no 'arm to 'is firm! Nor to this 'ere Mister Whotsitnow 'oo left all the lolly! . . . You're rockin' wrong at last, Con—that's what you're doin'!"

"All right, ducks." Mrs. Slattery was still calm. She picked up the tray—and then set it down again. Mr. Slattery was staring at the fire once more. She crossed to his wheelchair and stood behind it and reached over its back and put one hand on each side of Mr. Slattery's head and dropped a kiss on his pate, in the exact center of the bald spot.

"Never mind, Johnny-o," she said. "You do what *you* think, boy."

It was a quarter to four when Anthony drove into the little town of Purling and over the bridge and up the hill toward where, so the A.A. man at the crossroads had told him, stood the house called Windicotes . . .

It was large and well-kept in well-kept grounds. It was also empty

—and a farm laborer walking by the gates gave information that its "people" were away.

Anthony let him go, and turned the car and drove slowly back down the hill. He considered, briefly, a visit to the Purling Police Station, where by identifying himself he could get such information as the town contained as to the present whereabouts of Mrs. Kouroudjian. And then, deciding against it as being likely to arouse too much local curiosity, he remembered that the Superintendent of the Surrey Constabulary was an old friend of Pike's, and stopped at the Post Office and shut himself in a phone-booth and called Scotland Yard . . .

It was a darkening and bitter half past four when, back in London's outskirts again, he crossed the river at Putney and headed for Chelsea; fifteen minutes later when he rang the bell of Number Five Whistlers Walk, and two minutes later still when the little Scotswoman, after a short conversation over an inter-house phone, led him across to the studio.

Charming outside, this was even more so within. It was long and high and the whole northern section of the roof was glass. At one end fir logs crackled in a fireplace of dark red brick and at the other a big stove glowed. Around the stove and under the glass roof was all the pleasing litter of a painter's workplace, but about the hearth were order and comfort; deep chairs and a sofa and a low round table upon which stood a tea service on a silver tray.

As he entered, Jocelyn rose from one of the big chairs and from the other side of the hearth, on the sofa, Raoul St. Denis raised a hand in greeting. Permeating the comfortable glow of the place, lending an invisible nimbus to the man and woman already in it, there was an atmosphere of felicitous and personal excitement which for want of a better word Anthony was forced to describe to himself as "romantic." He answered Raoul's gesture in kind, and smiled at Jocelyn as she came to meet him. And looking at her was suddenly smitten, albeit with a pleasantly wistful benevolence, by consciousness of his years.

"I hope you don't mind my dropping in like this," he said, and was interrupted.

"I've been hoping you would," she said. "I've been trying to get in touch with you all afternoon." She took his hat and coat and led him to a chair near the fire. "I've remembered that name Adrian said. The California one." She was triumphant. "It was *Dalton!* . . . Does it mean anything? Does it help?"

"Dalton?" said Anthony, and thought about it. And shook his head and smiled. "It rings no bell now. But that's not to say it won't be important later. So it's good news—and I needed some, God knows!" He stretched his hands out to the fire, and was asked whether he wanted tea or a drink and chose the tea. Which was admirable, and accompanied by a scone which could only have been baked by a Scot and was richly saturate with butter. He devoured it and accepted another and murmured, "Austerity, where is thy sting?"

"Everything's from Aunt Mildred at Deyming." Jocelyn laughed. "Moral: Marry into a farming family." She was sitting on the floor by the low table, and the firelight glinted on her hair.

Anthony drained his cup. He sat back and pulled out the Whig Street keys and laid them on the table, and Jocelyn said quickly, "Did you find anything that helped?" She caught his glance at Raoul. "It's all right. I've just finished telling him all about it. Everything you told me."

Raoul nodded. "Past doubt, an extraordinary affair!" He smiled. "It is for the Police a lucky job they have a late-style Maître Lecoq at work."

Anthony shook his head. "I never felt further from masterdom, my dear fellow. Gaboriau wouldn't have owned me." He looked at Jocelyn. "On your other question," he said, "I did find this." He produced the sheet from Messenger's engagement pad. "Under the blotter on his desk. Plainly the result of a phone call just before he left." He handed her the paper. "Name mean anything to you?"

She read it out slowly, frowning. "'Mrs. A. (Sara) Kouroudjian,'" and shook her head. "I've certainly never heard it. Or seen it."

"There's no doubt, I suppose, that it's Messenger's writing?"

"It couldn't be anyone else's." She was decisive. "But he obviously wrote it in a hurry." She reached out to the sofa and handed the sheet to Raoul, but went on looking at Anthony. "I wonder who she is? Do you think she might be important?"

"I seem incapable of thinking these days." Anthony was gloomy. "So I'll say I *feel* she is." He gave a rapid account of his fruitless trip to Purling, ending with his call to Pike. "He may possibly dig something up," he said. "Even if it's only an address where the woman could be reached."

Raoul was still studying the sheet. He said, "Is there nothing to be learned from the servants of M. Messenger? A valet, perhaps, or a—a maid-of-all-kinds?"

Jocelyn shook her head. She said, "Adrian didn't have any *regular* servants. I mean, none of his own. He used these Retainers Unlimited people——"

She hesitated at Raoul's expression, and Anthony cut in, "Messenger's housework was done by a company, a business firm. It's an ex-soldier's project—expensive, but I believe very good. A team-work thing, with a different *équipe* for each kind of work—cleaning, cooking, and so on. You may never get the same people twice running."

Jocelyn said, "That's right." She was surprised. "But how did you know?"

"George Firth told me. Because I asked about servants at the beginning." Anthony looked over at Raoul. "Add this arrangement to Messenger's over-developed sense of privacy, and you'll see domestics won't help."

"So!" said Raoul. "Then I think of it is *who* that gives to M. Messenger the name and address of this lady." He looked at Anthony now. "Or perhaps you prefer that I close my big mouth?"

"Far from it." Anthony shook his head. "Go ahead, my dear Rouletabille."

"Okay. At first then I will say it does not seem it is the lady herself who talks with M. Messenger across the telephone. This is because what has been written is in the highest degree unnatural for her to be saying. So then the person who tells this is a person M. Messenger has requested for the information; perhaps in friendliship, perhaps to be imbursed. *Alors*—every effort should be put out to discover this person, who in probability knows a great deal of M. Messenger's doings in this affair."

He stopped abruptly—and Jocelyn, who had been watching him intently, turned to Anthony. "He's absolutely right, isn't he?" She was enthusiastic about the rightness. "But how on earth could you find out who it was? There's no way of tracing phone calls nowadays, is there? Not when they're dialed? . . . Oh, wait a minute! Just suppose it was Adrian who made the call, and to somewhere outside London! Then it *would* be on record, wouldn't it? Might that be worth trying?"

Raoul said, "Would not a notice, a—an advertisement in the newspapers be more in the point?" He shifted on the sofa; and grimaced and put his right hand to his side. "But it is sure M. Geth-ryn has thought before of all this——"

"No." Once more Anthony shook his head. "I was with you up to a point, Rouletabille, but I'm not any longer. You see, I'm sure Messenger didn't institute that phone call. And I'm doubly sure the person who gave him this name and address knows nothing which would be any use to us."

Jocelyn stared at him. "That's very sweeping!" she said; and he repressed a smile at the unconsciously proprietary indignation.

"It all hinges on Messenger's character," he said. "You didn't know him, St. Denis, so you're absolved." He switched his gaze to Jocelyn. "But I'm surprised at *you!* In the first place, the phone call must have been incoming, or a man of Messenger's aggressively tidy habits wouldn't have noted the information it provided in a slapdash scrawl. He'd have been ready with a nice neat piece of paper, not the engagement pad . . . Secondly, as to the importance of the caller, I can't believe that Messenger—this intensely private, even secretive, man who hasn't told his closest friends anything at all about this intricate and dangerous business—I *can't* believe he'd divulge anything about it to some outsider, whether they were getting information for him as a favor *or* being paid."

"Of course not." Jocelyn wasn't indignant any more. "I should have known that all the time!" She looked at Raoul.

And Raoul looked at Anthony. "Then it is only Mme. Arménie with whom you are left? But when you find her, it will be difficult to know the—the approach, I think." He stood up cautiously, and again unobtrusively pressed his right hand to his side.

In one smooth movement, Jocelyn got to her feet. She said, "I think you're in pain, and I'm sure you ought to be back in Welbeck Street. In bed." She was severe.

The object of the severity seemed to enjoy it. "But I assure you, madame," he said, "I have no pain to talk of. It is merely the tape which itches me like a devil. From here to here I am encased like a dead Pharaoh." He turned to Anthony. "All the time, monsieur, it

98

becomes more clear to me why you appear down the mouth with your investigations. So many trails, but all so cold!"

"And old," said Anthony. "Like me. I seem to be suffering from a mixture of *Melancholia Frustratio* and *Anno Domini*."

Jocelyn said, "But I thought you told me this morning you *did* have one chance of catching the murderer? Or am I all wrong? It was something about a trap he might walk into. I'm certain you used the word trap——"

"I did. But any verbs I used were conditional. In their iffest mood, I assure you. However, if you'd like details——"

He rapidly outlined the Slattery situation, and when he'd finished Jocelyn stared at him and said, "I just don't see why you're depressed. It looks as if all you had to do was wait." She turned to Raoul. "Don't you think so?"

"I am not sure." The Frenchman's eyes were fixed on Anthony. "If in his experience M. Lecoq is not happy, there will be reason."

"Nothing so dignified as Reason." Anthony's smile was wry. "As I said before, I seem to have given up thinking. All I can say is the whole Slattery thing *feels* too easy . . . What I ought to do is hire a crone to read my tea-leaves for me!"

Raoul sat on an arm of the chair nearest the fire. He still watched Anthony's face. He said, "Are you not expecting too much of your efforts in a too-short time, monsieur?"

"*Efforts!* My dear fellow, you mustn't dignify my vague flutterings in this case by using a big strong word like that!" He laughed; a bitter sound. "The Compleat Detective in Six Lessons. From Mr. Micawber!"

"Lecoq, *mon vieux*," said Raoul. "I think that you beat out your brain without necessity. Against the stonewall of a single thought." His tone hadn't changed. "The thought that this criminal is possessed with an aim of great proportion which you feel inable to prevent him reaching because you do not yet know it."

"That's very good——" Anthony stared at him.

"But you forget that the criminal in the question has been having five years in which to work, while you have been having less days." Raoul suddenly smiled. "But there is, of course, always the possibility that I speak through a hat."

"No indeed!" Anthony was emphatic. "You're very good. In fact, you're brilliant." He stood up and crossed to the hearth and threw a half-smoked cigarette among the glowing logs.

From the sofa, Jocelyn broke the silence. "*Criminal* doesn't seem the right word somehow." She shuddered. "I keep wondering if he's one of those psychopathics who just kill for the sake of killing——"

"No, no!" Again Anthony was emphatic. "However secretive Messenger was, he at least left us the knowledge there was a reasoned pattern here."

"But what sort of a human being could possibly——" Jocelyn broke off, her shoulders twitching to another shiver.

"I can't tell you what sort of a man he is in fact." Anthony was pacing now. "But I'll draw you a nice unrecognizable portrait of what he must appear to be . . . A man who doesn't appear at all. The face in any crowd. The man in any street. The ineluctable bystander. The invisible, unmitigated norm. A sort of Abominable No-Man!" He ceased the pacing and stood with his back to the fire and surveyed his listeners.

"I've christened him Smith Brown-Jones," he said, and looked at Raoul. "As you might say, Jean Blanc-Dubois." He looked at Jocelyn. "And you were very near the mark, worse luck, with your psychopathic, motiveless killer. Because until and unless we discover at least a hint of his motive, he's working with all the advantages of the true psychopath and none of the drawbacks."

"Not if the Slattery trap works," Jocelyn said. "Then it doesn't matter."

"But M. Lecoq," said Raoul, "is without faith in the trap. A distressing jam for him, I think. Because with no facts to lean upon he must still struggle to discover the objective of Jean Blanc-Dubois."

On its table near the door, the telephone began to ring. It sounded very loud, and very insistent.

"Now who on earth——" said Jocelyn, and stood up and went to the instrument and lifted it.

"Hullo?" she said. "Yes, he's here." She sounded surprised. "Hold on a minute." She turned and held out the receiver to Anthony. "It's for you. Scotland Yard."

He crossed to her. "I took the liberty," he said, "of telling them I might be here if they couldn't get me at home."

He said to the telephone, "Gethryn here. Who's this? . . . Oh yes,

Horlick—" and then listened for long moments and said at last, "Yes . . . Yes . . . Thanks very much."

He hung up, and came back to the hearth and stood with his back to the fire again. "A small rift in the cloudbank," he said. "That was one of Pike's men. Telling me about Mrs. Kouroudjian."

He smiled suddenly. "Mrs. Kouroudjian, my children, *has* got something to do with the thing, tra-la! Tra-la several times! Mrs. Kouroudjian has only recently acquired her exotic surname; is in fact still away on her honeymoon. Aboard the yacht which the male Kouroudjian maintains even in these 'ard times. They have no wireless phone aboard—but they're expected back, at Spithead I believe, within the next few days . . ."

He broke off. "Forgive the ebullience," he said. "This may not lead to anything at all; but at least it's not another frustration."

"You can't stop there!" Jocelyn was indignant. "What is she? Who is she? *How* do you know she's connected with the case?"

Anthony wasn't smiling now. He said, "Mrs. Anton Kouroudjian, until a few days ago, was Lady Pomfret. Widow of Sir Francis Pomfret . . . And Sir Francis Pomfret drowned in a sailing 'accident' five years ago. He was the first on Messenger's list to die . . ."

CHAPTER FIVE

The next day was the eighth since Adrian Messenger's death, and the third since Anthony Gethryn, at dinner with Lucas and Firth, had at one stroke both inaugurated and entered the case.

It was also a Sunday, but far from sabbatical in tone for anyone connected with the investigation. To the C.I.D., of course, the seventh day was always as filled with labor as its predecessors, but in their several ways Anthony and most of his non-official team were exceptionally active.

After Flood, perhaps Raoul St. Denis was the least affected. But he also was busy—talking to his Doctor, paying his bill, arranging to move back to the borrowed flat and re-hire the old Norman maid who went with it. And all this business, after all, was direct result of his brief association with Adrian Messenger, Anthony Gethryn and Adrian Messenger's sister-in-law.

Who was possibly the earliest starter, taking her car out of its garage next her studio at the dread hour of seven A.M. and setting out on the sixty-mile drive to Deyming Abbey. A drive through an iron-grey, sleet-flooded, slippery-highwayed winter's day. A drive which should have been both tedious and nerve-wracking but somehow wasn't either, because of the new and wonderful sense of being alive which filled her.

A close second to her in the matter of early starting was Seymour. Also driving—and disliking every mile more heartily—he was on his way from Hampshire, on the edge of which county he had spent the night, to Mostyn-Underhill in Suffolk, trying to skirt the sprawl of London in the process . . .

At eleven A.M., the firm of Updyke and Wallace, Press Cutting Agents, came into the picture. In the person of Miss Madeleine Bixby, one of the best and most trusted of Martin Updyke's personal staff. Miss Bixby arrived at the firm's dingy but efficient offices in Shaftesbury Avenue to the sound of church bells. She entered by Martin Updyke's private door, and pulled off her hat and coat and gloves and dropped them in a listless heap and found herself two aspirin tablets and a long, long drink of water and sat heavily in Martin Updyke's chair.

Miss Bixby, whose name doesn't matter to this story but whose then state of health most definitely does, was suffering from an advanced hangover and far too little sleep. Not having reached her own bed until after dawn, she was here only by reason of loyalty to the firm, desire for the considerable overtime money this task would net for her, and an ever-present realization of which side her bread was buttered.

She got wearily to her feet, and swallowed more water to down more aspirin, and found the two new box-files marked "A. R. GETHRYN—*Urgent*," and set to work——

At almost exactly the same time that Anthony Ruthven Gethryn himself, the innocent cause of her travail, finished dutiful letters to his wife and son and began to pace his study from door to garden-windows, losing himself in thought and clouds of pipe-smoke.

Half an hour later he rang for White, and, after asking that excellent person to provide what would have been unprovidable by anyone else in London on a Sabbath morning, settled down to his typewriter.

It was nearly one when White returned—whence, only he or his Maker could have told—bearing with him a large baize-covered bulletin board and a handsome supply of drawing pins . . .

And in Birmingham it was two-thirty exactly when Mr. David Bronson of Vancouver boarded the train which was to carry him on the first leg of his journey to Deyming in Medeshire. A Sunday "slow," it wasn't scheduled to reach Dorminster, where Mr. Bronson would have to change for Deyming, until three-forty. And after that the rest of the journey would take another hour and a half; a prospect of inevitable tedium which had led Mr. Bronson to purchase an armful of the latest magazines.

Alone in his first-class carriage, a trifle chilly but otherwise comfortable enough, Mr. Bronson was leafing through his purchases when he struck by chance upon a slim and aggressively unsensational periodical called *The World of Books.*

He was about to discard it in favor of *Country Life* when his eye was caught by the first paragraphs on a page headed, "The Publisher's Parlor," apparently the work of some person or persons lurking coyly behind the nom de guerre, *Henrietta Street.*

> Chatting the other day with Leslie Orcott (of Orcott and Haskins) I brought up the sad topic of Adrian Messenger's tragic end, wondering whether he had left behind any unpublished material . . .
>
> It seems that at the time of his death, the brilliant young novelist was engaged upon a work of non-fiction, dealing with his varied experiences in World War Two. Tentatively titled *The Single View,* the book, Leslie assured me, had promised to be Messenger's major contribution to the art of letters . . . "An opinion," Leslie said, "which I give unhesitatingly; in spite of the fact that it is only half-finished!"
>
> According to Leslie, *The Single View,* even in its present state, is infinitely superior to any of the spate of Personal Reminiscence War Books. "Even the half-finished ms," he averred, "constitutes for the reader an emotional and intellectual experience. So much so indeed, that we are seriously thinking of publishing it, incomplete though it is."

The effect upon Mr. Bronson of this pedestrian piece of literary gossip was in inverse ratio to its placidity. For a brief instant, which he wouldn't have permitted himself had there been any other occupant of the carriage, his whole appearance altered. Subtly, but all the more remarkably for that.

By its sudden tension, the man's whole body seemed to lose its middle-aged slackness and become taut and hard and ten years younger. Behind the horn-rimmed glasses, the eyes lost their benign and slightly foolish calmness, sharpening to a fierce and driving intensity. The kindly mouth tightened to a thin-lipped slash, and the lower jaw thrust out, lending the whole face a look of wary ruthlessness. The one remaining likeness to the Mr. David Bronson who had boarded the train was the little twitching muscle beside the right eye, a minor affliction which only struck him (or Mr. Lovett of Toronto, or Mr. Hoag of Detroit) at certain moments of psychological stress . . .

But at the train's first stop, which was the small rural station of Barton Cross, Mr. Bronson was Mr. Bronson again. And the little tic was now pulsing so gently as to be virtually unnoticeable. Looking from the carriage window, Mr. Bronson saw the Guard of the train (whom he carefully called Conductor) and in his pleasant way appealed to this official for help concerning his ticket, explaining that he had been en route for Deyming, but had now reconsidered and wished to go straight on to London . . .

At five o'clock, some fifteen minutes after Mr. Bronson had reached his new destination, Seymour arrived at Stukeley Gardens. He looked tired, and his face had new and un-cherubic lines in it and even the close-cropped blond curls seemed limp. He stretched his legs out to the study fire and took a long and grateful swallow of the drink which, after one first glance, Anthony had prescribed. And he saw with curiosity the big bulletin board hanging on the wall by the desk. Pinned to it were paper strips of varying size, some with only a word or two typed on them, others with many.

Anthony saw the scrutiny and grinned. "Been giving myself the illusion of working," he said. "Tell me what you've got and I'll have some more *facts* to stick up there. God knows we can use 'em!"

"Did fairly well on Military service, sir," said Seymour. "Not so good on the other heads. Nothing, to tell the truth. No suspicion of any 'accident.' Only one relative who even remembered a couple of the other names, and then not in any particular connection."

"As expected." Anthony was unperturbed. "Now tell me how many service records you've got."

Seymour sat straight and pulled out a notebook. "Well, there are seven here, sir." His tone was deliberately flat.

"Seven!" Anthony was delighted. "Congratulations!"

Seymour beamed. "Not all my doing. Three I got at the Yard. Out of replies to Mr. Pike's letters to the Chief Constables. They came in this morning. I took the service records out, and Mr. Pike's going to talk to you on the other stuff tomorrow. But he wanted me to tell you he doesn't think there's anything that's going to help."

"Again as expected." Anthony shrugged. "When did you have time to go to the Yard, by the way?"

"Just a few minutes ago, sir. Stopped on my way back from Suffolk."

"Suffolk?" said Anthony quickly. "Pomfret?"

"That's right." Seymour caught the tone. "Why? Anything new developed?"

Anthony pointed to the last strip on the right of the board, and Seymour stood up to look. The slip contained only the heading, "SARA KOUROUDJIAN."

"Pomfret's widow remarried," said Anthony, and told the tale of the engagement pad. "What did you get about him?"

"I was lucky," Seymour said. "His place, the Manor House, has been sold. But the landlord at the Boar's Head in Mostyn-Underhill used to be butler there." He glanced at a page of the notebook. "Pomfret left no children; no close relatives. Widow went abroad right after the funeral; never came back. Pomfret served in the Suffolk Light Infantry, 8th Battalion. Ended up with the rank of Major. Foreign service, India-Burma. Invalided out six months after cessation. Age forty at time of death, which was by drowning. Sailing 'accident.' Boat was found overturned, presumably by squall. Pomfret's body washed ashore later. No witnesses. No suspicion in locality."

"Nice going!" said Anthony. He unpinned the biggest sheet from the board and rolled it into his typewriter. "Now: this is a list of the ten men, with Messenger added. There are three headings—*Unit and Rank, War Theater,* and *Relative.* I've filled in Messenger and Slattery. You dictate your seven to me, alphabetically."

"Right," said Seymour. "We start with Bainbridge then——"

He began to dictate; and ten minutes later Anthony rolled the list out of the machine and studied it:

Name	Unit & Rank	War Theater	Relative
Bainbridge, P.	2nd. Batt. Caermarthen Regt. (Cpl.)	India-Burma	Widow
Braddock, J.	4th Batt. Queen's Y'kshire Regt. (Pte.)	India-Burma	Mother
Dalkeith, I. J.	3rd. Forfars (Capt.)	Greece; India-Burma	None living
Devitt, J. M.	5th. Batt. London Rifles (Sgt.)	India-Burma	Widow
McGowan, C.	21st. Middlesex (L. Cpl.)	Egypt; India-Burma	Widow
Moreton, R. F.	Hampshire Fus'lrs (1st. Lt.)	India-Burma	Widow
Ormiston, C.			
Paxton, A. T.			
Pomfret, F.	Suffolk Light Infantry (Major)	Egypt; India-Burma	Widow (Now Kouroudjian)
Slattery, J.	2nd. Batt. 1st. Wessex (Sgt.)	France	Wife
A. Messenger	10th. Hussars (Major)	France, Libya; India-Burma	Gleneyres

In silence, Anthony stood up and pinned the sheet back on the board. And in silence frowned at it. Beside him, Seymour shifted uneasily, and waited. And finally couldn't stand the silence any more.

"Sort of jumps out at you, doesn't it?" he said. He reached out and pointed to the entry for Slattery. "Except this one . . . Any chance his record's incomplete, sir? Easy enough to be in France first, then India-Burma later. Like Messenger himself."

"Not this one," said Anthony. "Lost a leg at Dunkirk." He was still frowning.

"I'd have sworn we'd got something." Seymour was unhappy. "When I collected four India-Burma's on my own, and then got three more from the Yard, I was ready to bet we had it."

Anthony shook his head. "The link's got to be constant, damn it!"

"Even if Ormiston and Paxton turn out India-Burma too?" Seymour wasn't giving up yet. "What would you say then, sir?"

Anthony turned to look at him. "I don't know," he said. "To hell with J. Slattery, anyway. I'm not even going to think about him till we've got the rest."

Which, for all its veracity of intent, was a statement as far from the truth as its utterer had made in many years . . .

It was six o'clock when Seymour left Stukeley Gardens——

And at that time, in the parlor behind his Twickenham shop, Jonathan Slattery was trying to explain to a visitor why he had telephoned to request the visit.

The visitor was Flood, who was silently thanking his stars that something—possibly some sentimental association with Dunkirk—had made him give the little man his phone number.

"I was tryin' to get you all yestiddy afternoon," Slattery was saying. "*And* last night. I would of tried y'r office, but I couldn't remember the name o' the firm——"

"Oh, that's all right," said Flood, who couldn't either. "What's the trouble, if any?" He had studiously kept his eyes from the little pile of neatly folded five-pound notes on the table by the wheelchair.

But now Slattery picked them up. "It's about this 'ere money," he said. "I been thinkin', an' so's the wife, as 'ow I didn't oughter keep it." The small bright eyes, earnest in the small lined face, were fixed on Flood's. "So 'ere it is back." He held out the notes.

Flood made no move to take them. "Why?" he asked.

"'Cause I ain't got no right to the bleedin' stuff. That's why!" Slattery had flushed; a man angry with himself and therefore with the world. "If you want it in black an' white, cock, I think this 'ere lolly was meant for me cousin Joe. Joe useter be the owner o' these 'ere premises—until a couple o' years ago, when 'is wife kicked off. Then 'e wanted to sell, so me an' the missus, 'avin' a little put by, we decides we'll take a bash at it, see? . . . Now, *I* didn't never know no 'Arold Black 'oo wanted me to 'ave twenty-five quid. I toldjer that. But I never toldjer 'as 'ow there was another J. Slattery, the J. indicatin' Joseph. So now I *am* tellin'! I'm sayin' this 'ere money was prob'ly meant for Joe, see? So tyke it, fer Crysake!" He leaned further forward in the wheelchair, brandishing the notes at Flood.

Who still ignored them. And said, "You say this money was *probably* meant for your cousin? Have you asked him if *he* knew Harold Black?"

"No, cock!" said Slattery with increasing violence. "No, I 'aven't! I 'aven't arst 'im because I don't 'ave no super'uman powers, see? *I* can't 'old no spiritual communication with no one 'oos pushin' up the muckin' dysies, see?"

"Keep your shirt on, chum," said Flood mildly, slipping a little in characterization but masterfully concealing excitement. "Tell me: when did your cousin Joseph die?"

"Bit over a year ago," said Slattery, and proceeded to save Flood a lot of trouble. "Bit o' bleedin' bad luck, it was! 'Im 'avin' served on three muckin' fronts and then to go fer a muckin' Burton over a muckin' motor-bike accident! . . ."

It was after seven-thirty, at Stukeley Gardens, and Flood and Anthony were sitting in the bright little bar into which Lucia Gethryn had converted a far-from-bright butler's pantry.

"And so," said Flood, nearing the end of his first drink and a succinct report, "you're still out twenty-five pounds. I persuaded him to keep it. He's Cousin Joseph's next-of-kin anyway." He drained his glass. "Honest little bloke. Felt he was taking money under false pretenses. I wished I could tell him that's what it was given under."

But Anthony was disinterested in money. "Thank God you left him your phone number!" he said—and then, "I don't suppose, by any remote chance, that you found out what front or fronts *Joseph* Slattery served on? If he served at all?"

"As it happens, I did. When our Jonathan gets talking, you don't have to use a spade." Flood was curious. "Why?"

"Let's have the answer." Anthony was intent. "Questions later."

Flood shrugged. "Cousin Joe was with the Eighth in Libya," he said. "Tank Corps. Later, he went to Burma and India, on a transfer." He picked up his empty cocktail glass and examined it with meaning.

Anthony replaced the empty glass with one twice its size, and filled this. "The Cup of Ghent!" He presented it with a flourish. "For Aix-type newsbearers!" He came out from behind the bar. "Bring it with you," he said, and opened the door and led the way along the hall to the study and switched on lights and beckoned Flood over to the desk and the bulletin board.

"Look at this!" He pointed to the sheet he and Seymour had been working on. He picked up a pencil. "*And* this!" Opposite the name *Slattery, J.* he drew a heavy line through the word *France*, writing *Libya; India-Burma* in its place.

He stood back and watched Flood scan the list. He said, "To quote the seraphic Sergeant Seymour, 'Sort of jumps out at you, doesn't it?' In fact, my fluvial friend, I'll give you fifty to one the histories of the remaining pair show *India-Burma* too."*

Flood said, "No takers," and ran his finger down the column headed *Unit and Rank*. "I think Joe Slattery was a Sergeant," he said. "But I don't know what regiment he was transferred to in India—"

"Doesn't matter," said Anthony. "There isn't a man on there who belonged to the same outfit as any other."

Flood still stared at the board. "You mean the link's purely geographic?" He sounded dubious.

"In part, certainly. As for purity, I shouldn't think so . . . What're you trying to do? Subdue my senile enthusiasm?"

Flood laughed. "It only struck me India-Burma's quite a bit of territory to look for links in."

"Give me time, give me time! What I may find, after some heavy

* Anthony would have won his bet. Although by the time he received the information it was no longer necessary to the progress of the case, the War records of Ormiston and Paxton did, of course, show them to have served in the India-Burma War Theater.

digging, is that all the ten, *and* Messenger, were on some special operation together."

But Flood only grunted. His eye had been caught by the next slip on the board. A narrower slip, with words he recognized typed one below the other, except at the bottom, where a couple of lines ran straight across the paper. The words were in groups, with an extra space dividing one group from the other. He ran his eye down them: "*Messenger . . . Jocelyn-got-me-to-tell-Jocelyn . . . Photograph . . . George-Emma—Emma's-book-George . . . (Brushes—Cleaning—Everything must be clean—But there is one brush only.)*"

Flood tapped the slip with a forefinger. "So your '*Someone got me too. Tell Jocelyn*' wasn't right after all. You wouldn't have this up here if it had been."

Anthony shrugged. "I hope it wasn't. Because Jocelyn knows nothing, so it doesn't make sense for Messenger to ask for her to be told, unless he was completely delirious. Which I don't want to believe."

He dropped into a chair. "If I look at those bloody words often enough, I *may* see something else."

Flood took a pull at his drink and looked at the other slips on the board; slips, otherwise blank, which were headed "ACCIDENTS," and "SARA (POMFRET) KOUROUDJIAN," and then "??DALTON??" . . .

He started, nearly dropping his glass. "What's this Dalton?" he said.

Anthony looked at him sharply. "Name of someone Messenger was going to visit in California. Why?"

"Doesn't it mean anything to you? Not even in connection with this?" Flood pointed to the *War Theater* column of the first list.

"Not a thing. Nor to anyone else who's seen it. Not even to George Firth; because I phoned him and asked. What are you trying to say?"

"That your missing link isn't missing any more." Flood drained the Cup of Ghent and set it down. "Five hundred to one your Dalton in America is some relation of the late Brigadier-General Sir Hugo Dalton, killed in action in '43. And a thousand to one the ten blokes on the list, *and* Messenger, served under Hugo Dalton on a special force he trained in India and took into Burma in '42. 'Operation Dacoit' it was called. Sort of junior preview of 'Operation Chindits,' which was Wingate's better and later and more publicized effort."

Anthony was out of his chair. "My God!" he said. And again, "My God!"

And reached for the telephone . . .

The man he was trying to get was Guy Dennison. Guy Dennison was at the War Office, and Guy Dennison not only owed a good turn to Anthony Ruthven Gethryn but was aware of it. He was also in a position to obtain replies to the pair of questions Anthony Ruthven Gethryn urgently needed to ask.

When Guy Dennison was finally run to earth, not in person but at the other end of perhaps the fiftieth telephone line Anthony had tried, it was almost ten o'clock. Once found, however, he took up little time. In answer to Anthony's first question he said, "Can do. Phone you before lunch tomorrow," and to the second replied, "That might take longer. Buzz me Tuesday."

Which left a phone-sick Anthony at liberty to disrupt the brief Sunday-evening peace of Superintendent Arnold Pike. Which he did, driving himself out to the terra-cotta wilds of Fulham and inter- rupting a chess game between the Superintendent himself and a friend who might have stepped straight from the pages of Mr. Pooter's immortal diary.

Alone with Pike for ten minutes in a chill and little-used dining- room, Anthony apologized, refused a drink, briefed his host on the Dalton link, and went on to the matter of the three replies Pike had already received to his Chief Constable letters. As Seymour had suggested, he was told these had contained nothing of use except the military histories. Under the "Accident" head, results had been completely negative: never at any time, it appeared, had there been any suspicion at all that anything connected with the deaths had been other than it seemed.

"And frankly, sir," said Pike, "I don't think we'll get anything from the other seven either."

Anthony agreed. "But we couldn't afford not to try," he said, and went on to talk about the real reason for this visit. Which was, of course, l'affaire Slattery and the discovery that the "J" had indicated a defunct Joseph instead of the extant Jonathan.

"So now," he said, "you can gladden the heart of our Sir Egbert by taking those six men off the job . . . A job," he added bitterly, "which they should never have been on."

And that was all for Sunday . . .

Monday morning, when Anthony rose to it at eight, was bright but cold, with the sun balled yellow in a slate-grey sky and a wind with a razor-edge. There was nothing of note in the morning post, but as he finished breakfast, a messenger arrived and White brought him a large, thick envelope from Updyke and Wallace.

He took it to his study and sat at his desk and ripped it open. It contained two separate folders of press-cuttings, one labeled "ACCIDENTS," the other "MESSENGER."

He opened the second folder first, and ran his eye quickly over thirty or forty cuttings which the most cursory examination showed as valueless. A condition which, although there was no way he could have known this, was due to the classic hangover of Miss Madeleine Bixby.

The contents of the "ACCIDENT" folder seemed, as he began to read them, to be as useless as the others. Until he reached the penultimate paragraph of the last cutting of all, which was from a rural Highland weekly, dated two years before, and dealt, taking a whole page in the process, with what it called the "GLEN QUHILAIR RAILWAY DIS-ASTER." Which, as the list of fatalities revealed, had been the cause of the death of the third man on Messenger's list, Captain I. J. Dalkeith.

His attention caught, Anthony read the whole thing again. Slowly and thoughtfully. And was still staring at it when Seymour arrived fifteen minutes later.

Anthony gave him a chair near the fire and looked down at him and said, "You're early. For which many thanks."

"Something turned up, sir?" Seymour's blue eyes took in the litter on the desk and the big cutting still in Anthony's hand.

"Yes. Two somethings, in fact." Anthony tapped out his pipe and gave a terse account of the Slattery situation and began to fill the pipe again. "You know Scotland?" he said. "The Highlands?"

"A little." Once more Seymour's eyes went to the cutting, now on the mantelpiece.

"Good. Because that's where you're going. As soon as we can arrange it. Or sooner."

"This couldn't be about Dalkeith and that railway smash, could it?" Seymour was puzzled.

"It could indeed. In fact it is. Why shouldn't it be?"

"Well, sir"—Seymour was uncomfortable but tenacious—"it's just that I've always thought this was probably the one accident in the ten that was the real thing. The train had three carriages on it, and thirty-two people, if I remember. It somehow came off the rails on a hillside curve in this lonely country. All the people were injured, most of 'em seriously, but only fifteen were killed. Now a chap as bright as Smith Brown-Jones surely wouldn't run all the risk and do all the work entailed in wrecking the train on a long-odds chance like that!"

"Hold those horses, my lad!" Anthony picked up the cutting. "You haven't had the advantage of seeing this little gem from the Scottish fourth estate. Until I'd read it, I was following almost exactly the same line of thought as yours. But now——" He let a shrug finish the sentence, and handed over the yellowed page. "See for yourself."

He refilled the empty pipe, watching as Seymour quickly scanned the triple columns and finally looked up, shaking his head.

"Sorry, sir," said Seymour. "Afraid I don't see what you're driving at."

Anthony lighted the pipe. "P'raps you don't understand Mr. Smith Brown-Jones as well as I do," he said between puffs. "Think of our references to Coleridge the other day, and then consider the end of that account again." He pointed to the cutting. "The part about the heroic and self-effacing motorist who labored so magnificently in the rescue work——"

Seymour frowned, and re-read the paragraphs under the sub-head *Nameless Samaritan* and looked up in wordless and puzzled enquiry.

"Don't you see?" said Anthony. "It removes your long-odds objection. Stalking his quarry, Smith Brown-Jones finds Dalkeith is going to be on this branch-line train in the Highlands on a certain night, let's say a week ahead. So he goes up there beforehand, an innocent tourist. And scouts the terrain. And finds a suitable, lonely locale. And makes his arrangements for 'accidental' derailment. Then all he has to do is *happen* to be driving by, probably the only car on

113

a deserted road, at the time the train comes off the rails and rolls down the hillside——"

"Jesus *Christ!*" said Séymour, comprehension dawning.

"You see what I mean?" Anthony's tone was deliberately flat. "All Brown-Jones has to do is be early on the scene of the shambles, and *locate* Dalkeith. If Dalkeith's dead, fine. If he isn't—well, render him so, if you follow me. Very simple really, under cover of apparently herculean efforts at rescue work."

Seymour said, "*Christ!*" again, and became conscious that his robe of correct C.I.D. impassivity had slipped. "Yes," he said, with elaborate casualness. "I suppose you're right, sir. Unpleasant type, Mr. Smith Brown-Jones."

"Hardly a type, Seymour; let's hope he's *sui generis.* Brilliant, though. Except that, just conceivably, he may have overplayed his hand in Scotland." Anthony pointed to the cutting still in Seymour's hand. "Re-read the panegyric about the nameless and selfless Samaritan, and you'll find there must be several people who'll remember him. From Dr. Dougald downward . . ."

Seymour stood up. "A description!" he said, the robe slipping again.

Anthony shrugged. "We mustn't expect too much. On the other hand, we have to try . . ."

It was eleven o'clock when Seymour, arrangements for his journey completed, left the house . . .

It was eleven-thirty when Dennison called from the War Office. As promised, he had the answer to Anthony's first question. He said:

"Reference Dalton, Major-General Sir Hugo, killed in action 1943." He was laconic as ever. "Next-of-kin is widow. *Née* Fothergill, Marjorie Constance. She's living in La Jolla, California. Address: 110 Seabird Avenue . . . Got that? Right. Buzz me tomorrow on question two."

It was noon when Anthony came to the end of a protracted telephonic session with a helpful overseas operator, and hung up secure in the knowledge that he would probably be talking with Lady Dalton at about six-thirty that evening.

It was just after he'd finished lunch—at two o'clock, to be exact—that Jocelyn Messenger telephoned. Back in Chelsea after her overnight stay at Deyming Abbey, she had nothing, she said, to report.

"At the risk of sounding too pleased with myself, though, I know I did a good job." Her soft deep voice was clear and alive in Anthony's ear. "I mean, the way I handled it, if Adrian *had* done anything really unusual lately, either Aunt Mildred or Uncle Rory would have been bound to tell me——"

"*'Really unusual'?*" said Anthony sharply. "Forgive the pounce, but don't forget we're looking for any deviation from the norm in Messenger's recent behavior. Anything! Even parting his hair on the other side——"

"I know." There was a momentary smile in her voice. "But there wasn't a thing, apparently. From what they told me, it seems Adrian must have been more himself than usual. Except for hunting a few times, he just lost himself in the library, even after dinner . . . I'm sorry I couldn't be more useful . . ."

"Oh, but you have been," Anthony said. "Your 'Dalton' was a big step." He told her quickly of the India-Burma-Dalton's-Dacoits link. "I take it he never mentioned this particular operation to you?"

"No . . . The War was one of the many things Adrian would never talk about . . ."

It was only a few minutes past six when Anthony found himself speaking across five thousand miles to the widow of Major-General Sir Hugo Dalton.

As is usual with transatlantic conversations, the reception on both sides was slightly better than that of a call to his club. Also, and mercifully, Lady Dalton, born Marjorie Constance Fothergill, proved a woman of few but clearly related words. Accepting without hesitation his mendacious groundwork, she answered his main questions readily . . .

Yes, she knew the late Major Adrian Messenger slightly . . . Yes, she had invited the late Major Messenger to stay a couple of days in California on his way to Canada . . . Yes, the invitation had been the result of a letter from Major Messenger stating that he wished to see her on a matter apparently connected with his service on the staff of General Dalton . . . No, she had no idea what this "matter" could have been . . . No, she recognized none of the other names recited to her . . . She was sorry not to be more helpful to Major Messenger's executor . . . She was at the service of Major Messenger's executor if any more questions arose . . .

And that was all for Monday.

On Tuesday, at eleven in the morning, Anthony phoned Dennison at the War Office——

And was told Colonel Dennison was in conference——

And paced, and tried to possess himself in patience——

And at five minutes past noon answered the telephone to Dennison himself. Who said:

"Your second question: I've located two Londoners who survived Hugo Dalton's Burma jaunt. Got a pencil? . . ."

Which led to the institution of several more telephone calls by Anthony, and two interviews which, together with the time consumed in phoning, plus driving, took him through the day until four-thirty in the afternoon.

But fruitlessly. Although both men—*quondam* captain and sergeant-major—responded readily enough to Anthony's gambits, they had nothing of any apparent value to offer. Dalton's three-hundred man force, it seemed, had been divided into three prongs of a hundred men, each prong having a different objective. And neither the captain nor the sergeant-major had been in that prong which Adrian Messenger had commanded. The captain remembered Messenger, but had not known him well. Neither he nor the sergeant-major remembered, except with the utmost vagueness, any of the ten men on Messenger's list. And, finally, both corroborated what Dennison had gloomily hinted; namely that in great contrast to Wingate's later Raiders the casualties among Dalton's entire force had been devastatingly heavy . . .

On which depressing note, Anthony took himself home, the hope that he might somehow get the whole missing story from an ex-Dacoit fading rapidly.

He was still depressed, and wondering whether to go out or dine at home by himself, when White came to the study to announce a visitor.

"A Miss Bixby, sir," said White. "From Updyke and Wallace. She'd like to see you personally if possible—"

"Show her in," said Anthony—and, mildly curious, found himself greeting a well-dressed and attractive and extremely nervous brunette.

She explained the nervousness at once and with admirable clarity, producing from her bag an Updyke and Wallace envelope containing a single cutting.

"It's my fault absolutely, General Gethryn," she said. "You should have had this in Monday's batch. But somehow I missed it. I *do* hope it isn't important."

She was so frank, and so worried, that Anthony forgave her the "General." He smiled at her and said, "I don't suppose so. It's only a matter of twenty-four hours anyway."

He took the envelope and opened it, and was faced with those paragraphs from *The World of Books* which had so abruptly changed the plans of Mr. Bronson from Vancouver; the paragraphs concerning Adrian Messenger's half-finished work, *The Single View.*

As he read his lips formed a soundless whistle—and he frowned—and muttered a savage "Bloody idiot!" under his breath.

"Oh, it *was* important!" Miss Bixby's pallor increased. "I'm *terribly* sorry—"

"No, no! All exhibitions of annoyance were to my own address, I assure you." Anthony gave her another smile—and after five minutes of small talk and a glass of the best sherry she'd ever tasted, sent her happily off.

She was hardly out of the house before he'd found the publishing firm of Orcott and Haskins in the phone book. Uselessly, it turned out, because by this time it was nearly seven o'clock and the only person left to answer the phone was a late-working accounts clerk who suffered from a cleft palate and complete ignorance as to the possible present whereabouts of either of the firm's partners . . .

Regretfully leaving enquiries for the manuscript for tomorrow, Anthony punished himself, over a lonely meal, with reflections on his own inadequacy.

There's no doubt about it, he thought, *I must be slipping . . .*

*Great Detective, investigating private life of dead writer, fails even
to ask what sort of book said writer was writing at time of demise!
. . . Walk up, ladies and gentlemen—see the Magic Metamorphosis!
Lecoq-to-Lestrade under your very eyes! . . .*

He was still in the same mood an hour after dinner. Until, prowling
the study, his eye fell on the *World of Books* cutting, and he absently picked it up, absently running his eye for perhaps the twen-
tieth time over its archly pedestrian periods—

And two words in the last paragraph leapt out at him as if they
were on fire.

"My *God!*" he said . . .

CHAPTER SIX

Flanked by jagged, achingly empty bomb sites, the Hotel Alsace lay
between the Thames and the center of that historic but meretricious
London thoroughfare, the Strand. Its main buildings and theatered
forecourt unharmed, the Alsace was then, as it had been before, is
now and probably always will be, one of the best hotels for those
peoples who still refer to themselves as English-speaking; a combination mecca and home-from-home for visiting Americans, a *sine
qua non* for domestic and imported practitioners in the dramatic
and other lively arts.

At ten o'clock on this Tuesday night—the same Tuesday night that
Miss Bixby had called at Stukeley Gardens with the news-cutting
which had so belatedly changed Anthony's frame of mind—the
famous grill-room of the Alsace was in that state of flux where the
early diners have left, the middle-period diners are finishing, and
the first comers among the supper clientele are beginning to drift in.

Among the middle-period finishers, at one of the most coveted
corner tables on what Americans call the mezzanine, was a handsome but strangely assorted party of four which had drawn through-
out the evening more than an ordinary share of looks and comment.
Mr. and Mrs. John Cameron were entertaining their friend Mrs.
Jocelyn Messenger and her friend M. St. Denis, and the aforesaid
strangeness of the assortment lay in the marked disparity of size be-

tween hosts and guests. As John had remarked in an early aside to his wife, when the urbane and ubiquitous Mario had led the party to its table, "I feel like Whosis, King of the Trolls. Thor and Brünnhilde to dinner, and nothing in the cave but dwarf-seed!"

The looks and comment, however, had not been concerned with the party as a party. While several people knew the Camerons (*he's that American playwright, you know*—Neap Tide, *and that other thing Rex Harrison did last year*), opinions were varied as to his guests, the very big man and the big but lovely blonde. Particularly the lovely blonde. Theories as to her identity flew thick and fast, running a gamut which made her everything from the Crown Prince of Sweden's fiancée to a newly-discovered and sensational film star from Reykjavik. Or, as was insisted upon at the far end of the room by a General's wife from Sevenoaks, a sister of Laurence Olivier . . .

Serenely unaware of these fancies, but fully conscious that she was looking and feeling her best, Jocelyn Messenger was enjoying herself. As much as she had ever enjoyed herself in her nearly-to-be-completed three decades of life. Perhaps more. That feeling of aliveness, of excitement in and through the mere fact of existence, still pervaded her delightfully. It had been increasing with every hour of every one of the days since she had met Raoul. In the good canoe *No Self-Analysis* she was riding the rapids—and to hell with where they took her!

She forced herself back to present surroundings and found that Raoul was telling the Camerons about the miniature of Yvonne d'Ete she had done three years ago; the miniature of which, it now appeared, Raoul's paper or magazine or whatever it was had published an enlargement——

"Did you ever see the original?" Margaret was asking.

"But yes indeed!" Raoul said with enthusiasm. "This, it is work most exquisite. Top tip-notch, absolutely!"

As Margaret was seized with a fit of coughing, having perhaps inhaled too deeply on her cigarette, a page appeared at the table and looked from John Cameron to Raoul and said, "Mr. St. Denis? . . . You are wanted on the telephone, sir."

"Hein?" Raoul was surprised, but made his excuses and pushed back his chair and in a moment was walking away in the page's wake.

Margaret looked after him. "He's not only charming, he's terribly

119

attractive!" She studied Jocelyn facing her. "And you, Miss Moose—you're shining! You're perfectly *beautiful!*" Her face crinkled into its impish grin. "Maybe I was wrong about broken ribs, huh?"

"How would I know yet, you horrible woman!" Jocelyn saw with relief that John Cameron was paying no attention, being deep in a discussion of brandy with the sommelier. "Remember it's only four days and six restaurants since I met the man!"

"Oh days—schmays!" Margaret was enjoying herself. "What's time got to do with it? And who said love laughs at clocksmiths? Or was it me?"

The sommelier's keys clinked as he walked away, and John was with them again. To Jocelyn's relief he was suddenly interested in a stir at the far end of the room, near the forecourt entrance, where Someone and Someone's entourage were being shown to a very large and much beflowered table.

"Enter right," John said, "V.I.P. Incognito. With muted hautboys——"

"Who is it?" Margaret turned to look but there was a pillar in her way.

Jocelyn looked too, but could see nothing save people, mostly men, surrounding some central figure.

"Who is it?" said Margaret again—and John, still looking, began to laugh.

"*Viva La Roma!*" he said. "*Ecco La Busta!* . . . And here I was thinking it was Royalty!"

"What on earth are you talking about?" Jocelyn peered again and saw a dark and striking young woman, expensively underclad, being seated at the head of the big table.

"It's just that new Italian job, honey." Margaret was no longer interested. "Another of these 50-20-39's! Calls itself Lisa da Vinci. Didn't you catch *Invincible City?* Or *Nero?*"

"Oh yes," said Jocelyn, who had seen neither film. She was wondering what was keeping Raoul so long, and who could have known he'd be here.

And then he arrived. He took his chair to face her and looked apologetically at the Camerons and said, "If you will permit——" and Margaret, with one of her most brilliant smiles, started a politely animated discussion with her husband.

Raoul leaned stiffly across the table. "This was our friend Geth-ryn who is at the telephone," he said. "Something of much importance has popped up for him. Something with which it appears I can assist. He wishes that I go to his house, if possible at once." He shrugged. "I have told him the decision is not mine——"

Jocelyn interrupted. "Of course you must go," she said, thinking what fun it was to give him orders. "John and Margaret will understand—and we've finished dinner anyway." With a sudden breathless excitement she saw the hand of Providence in all this. The rapids were going faster and so was her heart.

"But you must promise me one thing," she said. "I'm terribly curious; I've *got* to know what it's all about! So come and have a drink when you've finished——"

And she said, "Never mind how late it is . . . It's Sheila's night off, so come straight round to the studio. I'll be waiting for you."

She turned to the Camerons. "Raoul's worried because he's got to leave," she began. "He's afraid you'll think he's being rude——"

And two minutes later, having shaken hands with John Cameron and raised Margaret's fingers to his lips, Raoul was walking off toward the forecourt entrance.

It must have been the other hand of Providence which made Jocelyn raise her head to look after him, for the second time, at exactly the moment when he passed—obviously without noticing it in particular—the table of the young woman who had been born Bianca Poggioli but in these days was known to the world as Lisa da Vinci.

She caught sight of Raoul's back just as he'd gone by—and jumped to her feet with a throbbing contralto cry of his name, followed by an even deeper *"Carissimo!"* Knocking over her chair, a glass of champagne and a flower vase, she surged at him as he turned; surged with both hands outstretched and every curve in undulance . . .

Though brief, the meeting was filled with drama for the many hungry-eyed watchers. Signorina Poggioli was not only bored with England and Englishmen, she was also (at least since she had become Lisa da Vinci and a law unto herself) an ardent exhibitionist. Neatly avoiding Raoul's move to take only one of the outstretched hands, she threw both arms around his neck, and stood on tiptoe, and planted her lips squarely upon his as the pliant outlines of the rest of her conformed meltingly to the rest of him . . .

After that, it was all over in a matter of seconds, with Raoul's deft extrication of himself, the exchange of a few words, his formal bow and departure. And Miss da Vinci returned slowly to her table, smiling to herself; half-wistfully as she remembered a certain two-year old episode in Capri, half-triumphantly as she considered the havoc her performance had inevitably aroused in the breasts of at least three males among her entourage . . .

Undoubtedly she would have been more gratified still had she been aware of the damage wrought in another, but feminine, breast at the far end of the room . . .

The clock on the mantelpiece in Anthony's study showed the time at five minutes past eleven. Below it, glass in hand and comfortable in a big chair near the glowing fire, Raoul St. Denis looked up at his host with curiosity. And smiled, not without a touch of bitterness.

"*Eh bien*," he said. "Having passed through a sonofbitch experience, I am arrived. So now, first tell me how you have found me on the telephone. And then in what way is it I am to help."

"The first is easy." Anthony stood with his back to the fire. "When I got no answer from either your phone or Jocelyn Messenger's, I thought it probable you were dining out, very possibly together. So I made a list of the most likely restaurants and started ringing them. The Alsace was fourth." He had been smiling, but the smile vanished. "What I want," he said, "is to pick your brains again. Or p'raps I should say that trick memory of yours."

"Which means, I conceive, that I am to go back into the cruel sea, hein?" Raoul sketched a shudder, and drank, and set down his glass. "Okay—shoot ahead!"

"You don't take the plunge just yet." Anthony was unusually somber. "Before you do, I want to know what *sort* of voice came out of Adrian Messenger when he babbled at you. What was its pitch, its timbre? Was he gasping? Did he stammer? In short, my friend, what did he *sound* like?"

"So?" Raoul's gaze was more curious than ever, but he wasted no time. "It was not a voice of great deepness. It was less deep, as example, than yours or my voices." His eyes took on an absent look. "It was perhaps like this——"

There was a long pause and then from his mouth a labored, breathless sound; a sort of high-pitched mutter which said, "*Messenger—Messenger—Messenger——*"

The absent look went away, and he spoke in his own voice. "Something as that," he said. "I am myself not hot as the *imitateur*, but this was pretty like."

"Good." Anthony moved away from the hearth, and behind Raoul's chair. "Now *I'm* going to try it. Don't look at me; just listen." He paused; then gave as close an imitation as he could. "*Messenger—Messenger—Messenger* . . . How's that?"

"Too deep—a little." Raoul was judicial. "And perhaps too precise in pronouncement."

Anthony tried again. "*Messenger—Messenger—Messenger——*"

"Excellent! Completely A-1!" said Raoul, and watched in observant silence as Anthony crossed to the board hanging by the desk and took a long slip of paper from it and came back to the hearth.

He sat on the leather-padded fender-seat and looked across at the Frenchman. "I'll explain all this flummery later," he said. "Just bear with me for a few minutes. What I'm going to do is ask you to go back into that cold, cold sea while I do my best to imitate Messenger's voice and go through everything you told me he said. All *you* have to do is stop me if you hear anything wrong. In my voice; in any word; in *anything*. I hope that's clear."

"To the farthest degree."

"All right, then." Anthony stood up. "Here goes——" He reached over and switched off the light near Raoul's chair, leaving it in a soft half-light, and went back to the fender-seat and studied the slip of paper.

After a moment Raoul said, "Okay." He didn't open his eyes.

Anthony let another half minute go by. He hoped fervently he could again produce the voice that had been called completely A-1. He said:

"*Messenger—Messenger—Messenger*"—and aroused no word or movement of objection in his listener. Emboldened, he repeated the name three times more. And then let the voice trail into silence.

And then started on the wheel of ". . . *Jocelyn—got—me—to—tell—Jocelyn*," and went around it three times.

And waited again, longer than before. And then tried, much

123

louder. *"Photograph—photograph"*—and still got no protesting reaction, and drew a deep silent breath . . .

And said, *"George—George,"* and then *"MS book—MS book—MS book——"*

And finally dared an even greater departure with, *"Photograph—George—MS book—photograph—George—MS book——"*

He let the Messenger voice fade into silence for the last time. And stood up and crossed to the lamp by Raoul's chair and turned it on again.

"That's all," he said. "I gather you heard nothing wrong?"

Raoul opened his eyes and sat straight, wincing slightly at a reminder from his ribs. "This was a *tour de force!* The voice and words to the life. Or perhaps one would say death." He studied Anthony's face. "I see in your eyes a triumphous look of discovery, I think. Or do I kid myself?"

"You do not." Anthony picked up his glass from the mantelpiece and drained it. "Adrian Messenger was an author. He was at work on his third book when he died. He didn't say the name *Emma* to you, or the words *Emma's book.* He said what I said just now, and you accepted, '*MS book.*' MS being an English abbreviation for *manuscript,* and nowadays broadened in sense to include *typescript.* That much seems certain. But to go a bit further, I am also inclined to believe he was saying what I said to you last. To which also you didn't object. I said, '*Photograph—George—MS book——*' Which can be interpreted, '*There is a photograph of George in the typescript of my book.*'"

"O-ho!" said Raoul and pursed his lips in a soundless whistle. "Is it possible that this Georges may be known to you?"

"Not at present. One of the worst of my many mistakes has been to assume it was his friend General Firth. Now I've found it can't be—and I'm faced with the distressing fact that something like every ninth child in the Commonwealth answers to 'George'! . . . Another mistake I made, and a worse one, was to ignore Messenger's current work completely. Because his first two books were novels, I acted on the idiot assumption that the third was going to be another. Whereas, as I discovered only this afternoon, it's actually a volume of *personal* War reminiscence——"

"For this I am in fault." Raoul shook his head sadly. "When you say it now, in your own voice, '*MS*' sounds in my ear most unsimilar with '*Emma's*.' But in the sea I have not distinguished this——"

"My dear fellow, you're not to blame at all. In the circumstances, a phonetics professor might've heard it just as you did."

As he spoke, Anthony moved away from the fire, crossing to the desk. He was reaching for the telephone when his eye fell on the *World of Books* cutting, and he picked it up and crossed back to Raoul and gave it to him.

"Read this," he said. "While I go another ten rounds with this bloody telephone . . ."

It was nearly two in the morning when Jocelyn realized the sleeping pill wasn't going to work.

She sat up in the strange bed and swung her feet to the floor. Outside, an east wind had broken up the dark clouds, and moonlight poured in through the window she'd left uncurtained, so that she didn't have to switch on a light to see around the unfamiliar room. The room which was the spare bedroom of the flat which had been Adrian's but now was hers.

For the first time, she wondered if she'd been a fool to come here. Mightn't it have been better, more satisfactory all round, to have stayed in Whistlers Walk and waited till he'd arrived? Then she could have let him know, in any one of a hundred ways, just how she felt . . .

But did she want to? Was it or wasn't it better this way? With him just wondering, and guessing, and probably worrying about her and what she was doing?

Yes it was, she decided. Definitely! Because, on top of everything else, she was still so angry she probably wouldn't be able to retain any dignity. And that would be fatal: it would make him think he mattered——

Yes, she'd been right. The momentary doubt must have been caused by the sedative trying to work, momentarily lessening the churning, stabbing ache inside her. But now the ache was back at full strength. As strong or stronger than it had been at the Alsace when she'd taken leave of John and Margaret, refusing to let them drive her, and had found a taxi to take her home and kept it waiting while she changed out of her new dinner dress and threw a few things into a suitcase and then had herself driven to Whig Street, not even leaving a note for Sheila to find in the morning . . .

And so here she was, sitting on the edge of the bed in a cold strange place, shivering and churning and aching. And wondering with part of her mind *exactly* what the churning and the ache were about. Trying to live up to her father's patiently and insistently reiterated precept that the only person in this world she must never in any circumstances try to fool was herself . . .

She had reached the point of telling herself that, under the protective anger, the emotions involved were jealousy, wounded pride and something else she defined vaguely as fear, when she became aware of how bitterly cold she was.

And no wonder, she thought, sitting in nothing but sheer silk pyjamas in this ice-box of a room with a knife-like draught stabbing in from the window she had opened! She realized now that being unfamiliar with the transatlantic luxury of the heating system Adrian had installed, she must have pushed the wrong buttons on the control-panel before going to bed . . .

The panel was in the passage, half-way between this room and the living-room and study at the far end. She got to her feet and started for the door, shivering uncontrollably . . .

Her fingers were almost on the door handle when she heard a sound from the passage. A sound which, in spite or because of its brevity and the dead silence which followed it, was immediately and terrifyingly recognizable . . .

Someone—someone outside—had somehow unlocked the back door of the flat! The door at the head of the exterior staircase which led up from the walled garden; the door which, between this room and the kitchen, was only a few feet away from her . . .

The silence was broken again. This time by a faint groaning of hinges as the back door was opened. Opened cautiously. Stealthily . . .

Another silence—and then a faint *click-clock* as the door was closed . . . And then, after another breath-stopping period of no-sound, a faint faint creaking, more felt than heard, as something—someone—moved along the passage. Toward this room. Toward her . . .

A moment ago she had been vaguely defining fear as the least of the three emotions which governed her. But now, although of an entirely different kind and terribly far from vague, fear was the only thing she could feel. In the age-long instant between one barely perceptible footstep-creak and the next, her mind showed her the whole horror. Showed her with luminous, inescapable clarity . . .

Realization of the idiot folly she had shown in coming here was an added sickness . . . So Adrian had in some way half discovered some sort of incomprehensible plot at the core of which was his own in-human killer; the killer Anthony Gethryn had called by the half-funny, half-frightening name of *Smith Brown-Jones.* In the back of her head, behind all the other thoughts she could hear Anthony's voice—*"The face in any crowd . . . The invisible, unmitigated norm . . . With all the advantages of the psychopath . . . A sort of Abominable No-Man . . ."*

What could be more likely than that this No-Man might somehow want something from the place where Adrian had lived? What could be more certain than that, if he found someone in his way, he would kill them as unhesitatingly as he had killed Adrian and God knows how many others? . . .

Now the ghost-creaking footsteps had passed; they were nearer the study and the living-room . . .

So it must be only terror which was making her feel there was someone just outside this door, only inches from her. Someone so near she thought she could hear breathing . . .

An idea came. The telephone! There was one on the table by the head of the bed . . .

She held her breath, and inched away from the door and then in two silent strides was reaching out for the thing . . .

In some faraway corner of her mind she was wondering how, even at this hour of the night, the heart of London's west end could be so absolutely and horribly silent . . . And then, even as her hand touched the smoothness of the telephone, a car-engine sprang to life somewhere in the street below . . .

If her fingers hadn't been numb with cold, the violent involuntary start she gave might not have mattered. But as it was, the receiver slipped out of her hand—and struck against the table-leg with a crash which thundered in her ears . . .

And not only in hers. For the door was flung violently open and the fierce gold-white beam of an electric torch stabbed at her eyes, dissolving the moonlight and outlining her against the paneled wall . . .

A scream swelled up in her throat—and then turned to a choking gasp as the light was cut off and she heard the astonished voice of Raoul—

It said something astonished in astonished French—and a surge of relief left her sick and shaking. She swayed, and sat heavily on the edge of the bed . . .

And a switch clicked, and the light in the ceiling came on, and she could see Raoul in the doorway.

Suddenly she didn't feel faint any more. She felt strong, and very, very angry. Twice as angry as she had before.

She said, "What the hell are *you* doing here?"

He stammered something in a mixture of French and English. The first word she really heard was the name "Geth-ryn," but after that gathered that it was Anthony Gethryn who had broken into the flat, because immediate entry was imperative and neither of them had so much as considered the possibility of her being here—

Suddenly and acutely conscious of herself, she cut the recital short. Her face expressionless, her eyes on Raoul's, she got to her feet and stood very straight and pulled the gaping pyjama jacket together and buttoned it up to her throat.

"Could you remove yourself while I get something on?" she said. "Or is that asking too much?"

It was fifteen minutes later, and in the living-room of the flat Anthony was in mid-explanation.

". . . So having suddenly discovered the MS might be vitally important," he was saying, "I had to try and find it as quickly as possible, or even quicker. I managed to get hold of Leslie Orcott's phone number, and got him out of bed—only to find out the script wasn't with the publishers at all, Messenger having refused to leave even part of it with them after they'd read it. So it was almost certainly here. So St. Denis and I went to your house, to borrow the key. But there was no one there, and I decided that in the circumstances you wouldn't mind if I took liberties with the lock of this back door. Which, by the way, you ought to get changed at once; it's far too easy to spring." He paused, with a rueful half-smile. "I can only offer apologies, and hope our performance didn't upset you too much. I feel—and I know St. Denis does too—that we ought to be kicked for not even considering you might be here——"

Jocelyn interrupted him. "Why should you? It was just a sudden idea I had." She didn't look at Raoul. "And of course we've got to find the manuscript!"

She stood up. "We'd better try the study first," she said, and crossed to the door, passing Raoul as if he weren't there and leading the way across the passage to the study.

She switched on lights and stood in the middle of the room with Anthony, looking around, while Raoul hovered by the door watching her. With the shining hair pulled severely back, with the white scarf at her throat and the dark tailored robe covering the silken pyjamas, she was so beautiful it made his heart ache.

She said suddenly, "I wonder——" and crossed to a cupboard let into the big bookcase which took up the whole of the wall facing the windows.

"I don't think so," said Anthony. "I looked there on Saturday——"

She said, "But I remember coming here one afternoon when Adrian had just finished working. The typist was putting something away in here." She opened the cupboard door, revealing neatly ordered shelves of stationery. She considered these for a moment; then stooped and pulled out two boxes marked "CLAIRMONT BOND— THE ARISTOCRAT OF TYPING PAPER—1 REAM."

She took them to the desk and set them down. "I'm not sure," she said. "But let's see——"

Under the title-page "THE SINGLE VIEW—by—*Adrian Messenger*," the first box contained one hundred and seventy-nine pages of beautifully typed script. The second box contained one carbon copy of the same work.

"I thought I remembered," Jocelyn said—and Anthony beamed at her.

"And you didn't even cry 'Heureka!'" he said. "You're wonderful!" His eyes glinted, their green oddly deepening as he lifted out the contents of both boxes and searched through them for something he didn't seem to find and then concentrated on the latter pages of the top script, reading intently as he bent over the desk.

Jocelyn pointed to the desk-chair. "Why don't you sit down?" she said. "Or mustn't detectives work in comfort?"

"Thanks," said Anthony absently, and absently stripped off his overcoat and dropped into the chair, never taking his eyes from the typescript.

"And I'll get us a drink," said Jocelyn. And turned and went out of the room, again not seeing Raoul as she passed him.

He followed her. Along the passage and into a small but delightful dining-room. On the chiffonier were decanters and glasses, and busying herself with these, Jocelyn was elaborately surprised when he spoke behind her.

"I could perhaps assist!" he said.

Turning, she gave him a bright and elaborate smile, aimed impersonally over his left shoulder. "Oh, thank you *so* much!" she said. "There's a beautiful American refrigerator in the kitchen. If you wouldn't mind getting some beautiful American ice-cubes out of it, we could be really luxurious——"

But when he returned with the mission fulfilled the dining-room was dark. She was back in the study, a tray set on a side-table near her chair. She was watching Gethryn as he pored over the typescript; watching so intently that she seemed hardly to notice Raoul as he set the bowl of ice-cubes carefully down beside the twin decanters marked SCOTCH and BOURBON. He had rehearsed a speech, but before he could use it Anthony sat back and said suddenly:

"Mrs. Messenger: when you arrived here tonight, did you go all round the flat?"

"We-ell, sort of," Jocelyn said. "Why?" She smiled at him and added, "And couldn't the name be Jocelyn?"

"I'm flattered, and it shall be." Anthony's answering smile was brief. "Did you get any impression—any feeling—that someone else had been here lately?"

"No. No, I don't think I did." She was thoughtful. "Of course, I knew you'd been here on Saturday. And then the Retainers Unlimited people are still coming in twice a week." Her eyes widened. "Are you thinking someone's broken in?"

"I'm afraid I know it."

"Who?" Raoul's voice was edged, incisive. "Your—your—I forget the English—your Jean Blanc-Dubois?"

"Smith Brown-Jones. Yes. Probably yesterday."

"But how can you possibly know?" Memory of the panic she'd felt half an hour ago brought Jocelyn to her feet.

"Come here and I'll show you." Anthony separated three sheets from the pile of typing and set the rest aside, handing two of the three to Jocelyn as she came to the desk. "Run your eye over these," he said. "Pages 38 and 101. Selected at random."

He waited till she had scanned them; then gave her the third. "Now look at this—page 174." He watched her study it. "See any difference?"

She looked at it again; then set it down by the other two and made comparison. She said, "I don't see anything——" and found Raoul beside her and moved away, and excused the movement by crossing back to the table by her chair and beginning to pour drinks.

Anthony picked up the first two sheets and gave them to the Frenchman, starting the same routine with him.

There was silence—until Raoul said suddenly, "O-ho! . . . Here, on *this* page, there is the difference that some of the *lettres majuscules* —ah, yes! the *capital* letters—are not in position. They are more high a little than the other letters, I think."

"Right." Anthony nodded. "But it isn't just *some,* it's all of 'em. Which means, even by itself, that the hands which typed page 174 didn't belong to the person who typed all the others. The typeface is the same, obviously from this typewriter here"—he pointed to the machine on its own table near the desk—"but not the touch."

Jocelyn came back, carrying two drinks in which ice tinkled. She set one down at Anthony's elbow. She said, "Scotch; I hope it's right . . . What did you mean, *'even by itself'?* Is there something else besides the capitals?" She handed the second glass to Raoul without looking at him.

"Two more things," said Anthony. "First, all the other pages in the script have twenty-seven lines. But this one"—he held up the suspect sheet—"has twenty-six. Secondly, on all other pages every semi-colon is followed professionally by two spaces. On *this,* all three semi-colons have just *one* space after them——"

Raoul said, "M. Messenger himself was typing it, perhaps?"

Jocelyn said, "Adrian *hated* typewriters!" She looked at Anthony, not Raoul. "You mean Smith Brown-Jones broke in here, and found the manuscript, and calmly took out a page and *retyped* it. With alterations!" She couldn't repress a shiver.

Anthony said, "Exactly." He held up the spurious page 174 again. "You both saw this, so you know that in a paragraph round the middle of the page are the names of several men, none of which we've seen before in this case." He read them off. "I maintain that the original page had another name in here; the real name of Smith Brown-Jones himself." He waited a moment, looking from Jocelyn to Raoul, and then went on when they didn't speak. He said:

"I've told you about the India-Burma-Dalton's-Dacoits link already. So when I say that this page, number 174, is right at the beginning of what was obviously going to be the India-Burma section of Messenger's book, you'll realize there's a pretty sound basis for what I'm saying, even without the physical evidence——"

Jocelyn said, "Wait. Don't scare me any more, just tell me something else. Why did you say it was probably *yesterday* that Smith Brown-Jones was here?" She shivered again.

Anthony said, "That was a slip. I should have said it was *certainly* yesterday . . . When I talked to Orcott on the phone tonight, he mentioned I was the *second* person in two days who'd asked about Messenger's manuscript." He was talking to Jocelyn only now. "St. Denis knows, because he heard me talking; but I'd forgotten you didn't. The first enquirer was a man who telephoned his office on Monday. His name was something like Swanson, Orcott said, and he was an American. He explained he was a war-time friend of Messenger's and had met him again in Paris last year. Messenger had talked about his book and asked whether Mr. Something-like-Swanson would check over the proofs on the part he knew about. Now, Mr. Something-like-Swanson had not only seen the news of Messenger's death in the airplane crash—and been greatly saddened thereby—but he had also happened to read an item in a dim periodical called *The World of Books* which prophesied that Orcott and Haskins might publish Messenger's book, unfinished though it was. And he wondered, did Mr. Something-like-Swanson, whether it wouldn't be a nice gesture on his part, and a sort of memorial to his defunct friend, if he checked over the MS anyway? For free, of course! So when, he asked, could Mr. Orcott let him look at the manuscript? Whereupon Mr. Orcott told Mr. Something-like-Swanson that the publishers didn't have the manuscript in their possession yet. Whereupon Mr. Something-like-Swanson stated that he was in Britain on business and would be traveling constantly during the next week or so but would, upon his return to England's great metropolis, contact Mr. Orcott again . . . Whereupon, of course, Mr. Something-like-Swanson rang off, drew a deep breath and became again Smith Brown-Jones. But now a Smith Brown-Jones possessed of the almost-certain knowledge that the manuscript he *must* examine was on the premises legally occupied by Adrian Messenger at the time of Adrian Messenger's death. The address of which premises—even if he didn't know it already, which of course he did!—he could readily ascertain from any phone directory."

Anthony stopped abruptly. He tilted back the desk-chair and said, "*Phew!*" And mopped at his forehead, and suddenly grinned at Jocelyn. "Forgive the tirade," he said. "But I was a lot quicker than Leslie Orcott, I assure you."

Raoul said, "Oh yes. Very much!" And he smiled at Jocelyn too.

But she didn't seem to know he'd spoken. She went on staring at Anthony. Who was leafing through the script again and suddenly said:

"Jocelyn: you mentioned a typist of Messenger's. Did he always have the same one?"

Jocelyn said, "Yes. She did all his work. Both the other books."

Anthony said, "I suppose it's too much to hope you know her? Her name? Or where she lives? Anything!"

Surprisingly, Jocelyn began to laugh. "Don't think I'm hysterical," she said. "You'll understand when I tell you. She's a sweet little roly-poly of a spinster. About fifty. With that blue-grey hair. She's terribly respectable, and breeds canaries. I don't know her address— but I couldn't possibly forget her name!" She began to laugh again. "It's unbelievable! Gwendolynne LaDoll!" She spelt it out.

Anthony looked at her in awe. "*Wonderful!*" he said. "On the whole surface of this sorry planet there can't conceivably be more than one of 'em! . . . Where's a phone book?"

He may or may not have been wholly right, but certainly there was only one LaDoll, Gwendolynne, in London. She lived, it appeared, at Number Fourteen Glendon Mansions in the Fulham Road —and in something less than three minutes from the moment of having heard her name, Anthony was talking to her on the telephone.

He was grave and mellifluous and completely reassuring in his slightly pompous courtesy. And he was again chief executor for the late Adrian Messenger. He regretted infinitely having to disturb Miss LaDoll at such an hour; only a matter of the gravest expedience which this most certainly was, could excuse it . . .

Miss LaDoll, sleepy at first but always and touchingly eager to help, was quickly lost in the mendacious, multi-syllabled maze of explanation the telephone gave her of the circumstances which had created the expediency. Lost, but willing and able and ready to answer the questions which were asked her . . .

Oh, yes, said Miss LaDoll, she had typed the whole of poor Major Messenger's wonderful book *The Single View*—as far as it had gone . . . Oh, yes, the last page she had typed was number one hundred and seventy-nine. Definitely. She remembered very well, because she had a wonderful memory for numbers . . . No, she had no extra carbon copy of the work: Major Messenger never had more than one carbon made and always insisted on keeping that . . . Yes, she had always done Major Messenger's work at Major Messenger's flat, always on Major Messenger's own typewriter, which had a special elite typeface . . . Yes, she did work for other people, of course, but Major Messenger had for several years been her best and favorite client . . .

It was at this point that the self-styled executor of Major Messenger drew a deep and silent breath, and gripped the telephone more tightly, and broached the most important matter of all.

"Now just one more question, Miss LaDoll," he said, in tones even more measured and mellifluous than before, "and then, if I may, I will say good night and make an appointment for you to visit me tomorrow. A visit for which, I hope, you will permit me to remunerate you . . . This final question—and it is *most* important—concerns some photographs, possibly mere snapshots, which my fellow executors and I believe Major Messenger was intending to have reproduced in this new work. Do you know of any such projected illustrations?"

"Well now——" The light precise voice was hesitant in Anthony's ear. "All I could say is there *was* a big buff envelope marked 'Photographs' which Major Messenger kept with the manuscript. It was always in the first-copy box. We kept the manuscript in boxes, you see—Clairmont Bond boxes—and Major Messenger kept this envelope in the top one . . . No, I never saw the photographs. The envelope was sealed, you see—not that I would have looked if it hadn't been . . ."

And that, really, was all. Having elicited the information that the envelope marked "PHOTOGRAPHS" had been in the box the last time Miss LaDoll had been in the flat (which had been, it seemed, only a few days before Messenger's death), Anthony contented himself, still reassuringly mellifluous, with engaging Miss LaDoll to come to Stukeley Gardens at eleven this morning, apologizing again for having so rudely interrupted her slumbers, wishing her a temporary good-bye, and gently replacing the receiver.

He surveyed his audience—Jocelyn in a chair at his right, Raoul still standing at his left. He said, "You got that, I suppose? The photographs *were* in this box." He tapped it with a forefinger. "But now they aren't." A deep frown furrowed his forehead. "You won't know what I mean, and it's too complicated to explain just now, but forgive me while I mutter maledictions on a winsome young woman called Bixby!" Suddenly, disturbingly, he crashed a fist down on the desk. "If it hadn't been for that little bitch," he said, "I might've had the pleasure yesterday of meeting Mr. Smith Brown-Jones. Here, in this room!"

He stopped, abruptly. "Sorry. I seem to be getting temperamental in my old age." He picked up his neglected drink and took a long pull at it.

And no one said anything for what seemed like a long time. Until Jocelyn broke the silence.

She spoke to Anthony; she still wasn't looking at Raoul. She said, none too steadily, "He—he's sort of unique, isn't he? Your Abominable No-Man, I mean . . ."

"I hope so," said Anthony. "Fervently!"

Raoul said, "Because this man has done here what he wished and then thrown his hook does not mean that he might not in possibility return? Perhaps for some other reason he has only found later?" He was looking at Anthony as he spoke, his face set, the eyes narrowed.

It occurred to Anthony, for the second time in three days, to be glad this man wasn't an opponent. He shrugged as he answered, "It's possible he might come back, I suppose. Unlikely, but still possible."

Raoul spoke to Jocelyn now. He said, "There is one thing clear: you must not stay in this place."

She did look at him now. With a sort of impersonal coolness. And she gave him another of the impersonal, over-his-shoulder smiles. She said, "To borrow a phrase from Margaret Cameron—you're telling *me!*" She looked at Anthony. "Give me three minutes and I'll be ready."

Raoul said, "M. Geth-ryn will wish to go quickly to his home, with this MS." He pronounced the letters carefully. "To study over it. I will engage a taxi——"

On her way to the door Jocelyn stopped. She looked around at him with another of the smiles. She said, "Oh, I'm sure Anthony won't mind driving us. We can drop you on the way to my place . . ."

And so Raoul was "dropped," outside his flat, at exactly five minutes past three. And Jocelyn was in Whistlers Walk three minutes later . . .

Anthony, hurtling back through empty streets to Knightsbridge, was home and in bed by three forty-five. The east wind was still blowing, and except around its edges the sky was cloud-free, with the stars still bright in a firmament which seemed to promise a clear day.

But then, half an hour later, the wind dropped completely. And the clouds closed in again, low and smooth and heavy, and the river-mist began to pile up under them, mixing with all the smoke from the sprawling city until the atmosphere became a blackish yellow, thickening and darkening in the still cold air . . .

So there was no dawn that Wednesday——

A simple phrase which smacks of science-fiction and the horror of such erstwhile imponderables as Martian invasion or deflection of the sun—except to the Londoner. For him, it means simply the arrival of a new and true pea-souper of a fog.

And this was indeed a pea-souper. In all her fifty-odd years Miss Gwendolynne LaDoll (Dolly to her friends) couldn't remember a worse one.

She had set her alarm clock half an hour later than usual to compensate for her disturbed sleep; but when, on its faithful blare, her eyes opened to darkness and her ears to oddly muffled semi-silence, she knew what was happening. Just to check, she padded to the window and peeped out. She murmured, "Oh, dear!" to herself in the approved tone of disgust, but secretly was excited and uplifted by this departure from the norm: as, indeed, were far more Londoners than might be imagined.

Miss LaDoll, switching on lights all over the flat, bathed and dressed, and then attended to the needs of the twenty canaries she kept in the little spare-room she had converted to an aviary. Over her breakfast, she listened to news on the wireless, learning that while most of London's usual traffic was inoperative, the tube trains were running, as also (though not according to schedule, of course) were the wonderful, wonderful L.P.T.B. buses, which even now Miss LaDoll had to think twice about before calling them L.G.O.C.'s.

She determined to keep her appointment with poor Major Messenger's executor. In the first place she was curious; in the second, the executor had sounded such a *nice* man. And then there was the money, of course, to say nothing of the adventurous feeling of a journey in the fog. A very simple journey it was, too, she reflected. All she had to do was go out, grope her way along to the next corner, wait for the right bus, and eventually get put off in Knightsbridge. Right at the end of Stukeley Gardens . . .

And it might be nice and triumphant, she thought, if she could manage to be punctual in spite of the fog. She looked at her watch. It said nine-twenty, which meant she had an hour and forty minutes for a journey which in ordinary weather would take little more than a quarter of an hour. Humming to herself, she put on her new warm coat over her trim grey suit, chose the neatest and plainest of her hats, said good-bye to the canaries—and sallied from Glendon Mansions.

That dreary but usually busy thoroughfare, the Fulham Road, was today a half-seen river of yellow-black darkness; a hushed river along which the occasional lights of occasional vehicles moved slowly and gropingly.

The fog stung Miss LaDoll's throat, and she paused for a moment to pull her scarf up over her mouth. Her eyes smarted too, but there was nothing she could do about this, and she started bravely off, her eyes straining to see the pavement ahead, not yet having to resort to wall-feeling. After all, she thought, it's only a few yards to the bus stop. She couldn't miss it, because it was right by the bomb site where the library used to be. She didn't know—she had no way of knowing—that, as she had left the shelter of the Glendon Mansions doorway, another pedestrian had come out of the darkness at the corner of the building and was following her.

He was an ordinary enough figure in the murk. A man of middle-size—or over, or under—with overcoat collar turned up and hat-brim turned down. The only things about him which might have set him apart from the majority of his fellows were that he wore soles of thick sponge-rubber which deadened the sound of his footfalls, and that—if one had been close enough to see his face—there might have been noticeable the involuntary twitching of a little muscle at the corner of his right eye . . .

Like Miss LaDoll, Anthony waked at eight. And like Miss LaDoll, he quickly became conscious that once again London was in the throes of a true pea-souper. Unlike Miss LaDoll, he groaned and rolled over in bed and went to sleep again . . .

He got up at nine-fifteen, and decided to miss breakfast and asked White to bring him coffee in the study. He drank the coffee, and put more logs on the fire, and smoked a couple of cigarettes. And found himself pacing restlessly, wondering whether it was only the fog which was making him uneasy.

To stop the pacing he sat at his desk, and was faced with the two "Clairmont Bond" boxes of typescript which Jocelyn had let him bring away from Messenger's flat. They brought to mind a necessary chore, and he picked up the telephone and called Scotland Yard.

He couldn't get Pike, but was satisfied with Horlick. He told Horlick briefly of the obvious visitation by Smith Brown-Jones to Adrian Messenger's flat, and arranged for a C.I.D. unit to visit the place as early as possible (keys to be obtained from Mrs. Messenger) to see whether the intruder had left any traceable clues to his identity.

"He won't have, of course," said Anthony wearily. "But we've got to try." He thought of something else. "And while you're at it," he said, "get somebody to check with Retainers Unlimited, the company that looks after the housework in the flat. Again, you won't get anything, but again we have to try."

When he hung up, it was ten o'clock. Looking through the windows at the dirty and swirling and unnatural darkness, he suddenly wondered whether Miss LaDoll would have the temerity to face it, and decided to call her and say that he would visit her instead. What he wanted—her fervently-to-be-hoped-for memory of the missing name on the spurious page 174—was far too important a matter to be delayed. He wished now he hadn't decided against putting the question when he'd spoken to her from Whig Street.

He remembered her number, and dialed it. And waited while the phone at the other end rang vainly a dozen times.

He hung up. She must have started, he thought. But when she'd arrive, God only knew . . .

There was nothing he could do except wait. But the unease in him persisted, even increased. It now seemed somehow connected with Miss LaDoll. He tried to shrug it off—and thought he'd look over Messenger's manuscript once again, and pulled the top-copy box toward him and opened it——

And stared appalled at something he hadn't noticed before. Something he felt he should be shot for not having noticed.

A small rectangular patch, darker than the surrounding whiteness, at the upper left-hand corner of the title-page. Darker, and faintly shining. And faintly—very faintly—sticky to the finger-tips.

A patch which shouted of its origin, which must certainly have been a small gummed label that had been stuck onto the paper, not too firmly, and then removed——

Removed because it bore the printed name and address of the professional typist who had done the work. A label like the labels always stuck to copy-work of his own, typed by his faithful Miss Bracknell. A label whose purpose was two-fold; advertisement, and ready reference for employers as to the typist's address and telephone number.

And the knowledge possibly contained in the memory of Gwendolynne LaDoll (*Expert Typing—Lowest Rates—Literary MSS a*

Specialty) must certainly be, though from the reverse point of view, as important to Smith Brown-Jones as it was to Anthony Gethryn . . .

It all went through Anthony's mind in a fraction of the time it takes to write, so that it was only a second or so after he had first opened the box of typescript that he was calling Scotland Yard again.

This time he was luckier, catching Superintendent Arnold Pike himself. He said, "Pike? Gethryn. This is urgent! Gwendolynne LaDoll, of 14 Glendon Mansions, Fulham Road. Small, middle-aged, grey-haired. She may or may not be on her way to see me. She certainly needs protection. I don't know what they can do in this murk, but for God's sake get onto Kensington and tell 'em to send a man to Glendon Mansions. And a couple more to try and pick her up if she's really left. I repeat, this is *urgent!*"

"Right, sir," said Pike, and the phone clicked off . . .

He rang back some fifty minutes later; fifty minutes during which Anthony three times started out to the garage for his car and three times sternly checked himself. Incredibly, the fog was growing darker and thicker and less penetrable, so that it seemed unlikely he could even find Glendon Mansions, let alone be of any help . . .

When the phone rang, he was in the hall, coming back into the house from the last excursion. He picked up the extension and heard Pike's voice, and didn't like its tone.

He said, "Gethryn here——" and waited.

Pike said, slowly, "About Miss LaDoll, sir: I'm sorry to have to tell you the lady met with an accident. In the Fulham Road, only fifty yards from Glendon Mansions. About an hour and a half ago——"

Anthony said, "My God!" And then, "Is she still alive?"

"No, sir. Death must have been instantaneous." Pike's voice came slower still. "She seems to have slipped off the kerb in front of a bus. Driver knew nothing till he felt a front wheel go over something——"

"All right," said Anthony heavily. "That's enough."

And then he said, "Have you ever felt like a murderer? . . . Not a pleasant feeling Pike. Not at all pleasant . . ."

He hung up.

CHAPTER SEVEN

Whenever Anthony looked back at the case afterwards, it always seemed to him that the murder of Gwendolynne LaDoll, for which he never ceased to blame himself, really marked the first turning-point.

Because from that morning the whole tempo of the affair seemed to change. Instead of being a procession of slow-moving days, each producing some small crumb of new knowledge, it became a confused and sporadic succession of sterile pauses and far from sterile events, all such events (though connected within the vague framework of the mystery) seeming entirely disassociated one from the other—

Until the last one, which unexpectedly proved to be the missing catalyst. And, as Anthony said later, "shed a mystifying half-light over the whole business."

This period—it covered a fortnight—always appears in his otherwise orderly memory as a series of isolated scenes; the series including scenes in which he himself took part, and also scenes which, without him as a participant, came to his knowledge or imagination later.

In his mind he always calls them the "Time-Whens" . . .

The time when, during an argumentative hour at Scotland Yard, Anthony Ruthven Gethryn was interrupted by Egbert Lucas, who said:

"Wait a minute, Gethryn, please let's take things as they come. I sympathize with your feelings, but we must still deal with matters in due order——"

"Oh, by all means!" It was Anthony's turn to cut in. "The bloodier the business, the redder the tape. I was only trying to save a little of that valuable ingredient, time. Can't I take it for granted that you people have done everything you ought to have done, and get on to things I really want to know? Like the results of your investigation of Messenger's flat?"

"Negative, sir." Pike spoke quickly, before Lucas could open his mouth. "No unidentified fingerprints. No trace of illegal entry"—he smiled—"except what you made yourself. And as for Retainers Unlimited, we'll have to give them a clean bill of health."

"As expected." Anthony shrugged. "But not as hoped." He got to his feet. "So I'll take myself off and let you get on with your other work: there must be a lot of empty stable doors left in London that need shutting."

Lucas groaned, putting a hand to his head. But Pike said, "Just a minute, sir, there's one other thing. About Miss LaDoll——"

"Witnesses?" Anthony turned quickly from the door.

Pike shook his head. "No chance of that, I'm afraid . . . But there's a report from Kensington that her flat was entered the same morning she was killed. Someone really went through the place, but there's nothing to show what was taken. If anything."

Anthony digested this. "Very thorough, Mr. Smith Brown-Jones!" he said. "Doesn't miss a trick, does he? *We* knew there wasn't another carbon of Messenger's manuscript—but S. B.-J. had to make sure . . ."

The time when a new guest arrived at the Gleneyre Arms Hotel in Deyming, and signed the register with a dashing scrawl which read, "D. Bronson—Vancouver, B.C."

Having completed this duty, Mr. Bronson took off his hat, revealing his bald pate, and looked around the paneled hall with beaming approval.

"Very nice!" said Mr. Bronson. "Truly old-world!"

Mr. Robert Twombley, who was the inn's host and lessee, smiled at his latest visitor. "So glad you could come to us after all, Mr. Bronson."

"So am I—so am I!" Mr. Bronson was quietly genial. "Hope I didn't inconvenience you, by the way. Putting off my reservation the way I had to."

"Not at all, sir." Mr. Twombley shook his head. "And now you're here, I hope you'll be with us for a nice stay."

"It'll certainly be a week," said Mr. Bronson. "Longer, I hope." Again he looked around him with approving interest.

And again Mr. Twombley smiled, approving of Mr. Bronson as much as Mr. Bronson obviously approved of his surroundings. "I wonder, sir," said Mr. Twombley, "whether you would like to go straight to your room? Or whether you would care to join me in a glass of sherry?"

"That second proposition sounds mighty good!" Mr. Bronson rubbed his hands. "I'll take you up on it. With pleasure."

"Splendid," said Mr. Twombley, and led the way across to an open doorway at the far side of the hall.

Over the doorway a picture hung; the portrait of a young and striking man in hunting pink. It caught Mr. Bronson's eye, and he stopped to study it.

"Who's this?" he asked. "Fine-looking youngster."

"That, sir," said Mr. Twombley, plainly delighted by the question, "is an early portrait of the present Marquis of Gleneyre . . . A great gentleman, Mr. Bronson! And a fine landlord! I only wish we had more of his kind left."

"Oh, so that's Lord Gleneyre, is it?" Mr. Bronson was interested. "I've heard of him. Great sportsman, I believe——"

As he followed Mr. Twombley into the bar, Mr. Bronson took off his glasses and rubbed at the corner of his right eye, where a little muscle was twitching . . .

The time when Raoul St. Denis called at Number Five Whistler's Walk.

His ring was answered by Sheila, from whose Caledonian features all traces of the dragon were wiped by a large smile as she saw who the caller was.

She said, "Good morning, m'sure," and Raoul gave her an answering smile as he raised his hat.

"And to you, mademoiselle. I see that as usual you are in a pink . . . Tell me: you have heard perhaps from Mme. Messenger? When she will return?"

"No, sir." Sheila shook her head. "No, I have not. As you're knowing, she was gone Waidnesday, and the truth is I've had no word from her since."

Raoul pondered. "I will be most grateful, then," he said at last, "if you might in possibility tell me to where I may write a letter?"

It appeared that Sheila might. And Sheila did; so that three minutes later Raoul was walking away, studying a slip of paper upon which was printed, in neat block capitals:

"MRS. JOCELYN MESSENGER,
c/o THE RIGHT-HONOURABLE
THE MARQUIS OF GLENEYRE, K.G.
DEYMING ABBEY,
MEDESHIRE."

The time when Seymour returned from Scotland and came straight to Stukeley Gardens.

Again Seymour was tired and looked it. He bore no resemblance to that Seymour whose nickname had once been Angel-face. He showed, in fact, such signs of dejection that Anthony wouldn't hear a word from him until he had been given an outsize drink, and the most comfortable chair in the study, and after that several minutes in which to enjoy both in silence.

"You look far from gruntled, my lad," said Anthony at last. "What's the trouble? No description of the Samaritan?"

"I wouldn't say *no* description." Seymour was glum. "Far from it." He pulled out a notebook. "Want to hear the whole story, sir? From the beginning?"

"By all means." Anthony sat on the fender-seat. "Fire away."

Seymour dropped the notebook on his knees, and drew a breath. He said, "First I tried in Edinburgh for relations of Dalkeith's. But he doesn't seem to have had any—except some cousins in England . . . So I made my way up to the Highlands, near Glen Quhilair. As you know, I was a couple of days longer than I'd meant to be; but it was a tough job rounding everyone up . . ."

He picked up the notebook again. "However," he said, "I eventually talked to nine of the people who'd helped in the railway 'accident.' Only five of 'em had come in contact with Samaritan Brown-Jones, but they all remembered him perfectly well. They were the Doctor, the local Constable, the Parson, a ghillie, and a Parish Nurse. They all thought S. B.-J. was a sort of ultimate in selfless heroism. And they were all only too glad to describe him for me!"

He drained his glass, and turned over a page of the notebook. He said, "Dr. Alistair Dougald, who's six foot three and blue-eyed and a

144

greying blond, said the man was *'under middle height; darkish and strongly built'* . . . The Constable, who's five foot nine and on the plump side and a black-haired Celt, said the man was *'a tall, brawny chiel; fair, with blue eyes in his face'* . . . The ghillie, who's about my size, said the man was about my size, *'with nothing special to him a man would note'* . . . The Nurse, who's a little bit of a thing, said the man was *'a Haircules of a fellow, and had red hair on the head of him'* . . . They all four agreed he was an American."

Again Seymour stopped, and this time Anthony put in a word. "What about the Parson?" he said. "Why keep him up your sleeve?"

Seymour said, "Because he's the only one that gave me anything at all, sir. Not much, but something." Again he turned a page. "The Parson said, *'the man was of medium height, possibly a little over. None of us could see him very well. You must remember it was the middle of the night and the only lights we had were car-lamps and the flames from the burning wreckage. But I would say the fellow was about thirty-five. He was clean-shaven, with nothing remarkable about his face. I don't agree he was an American. Something of a student in accents, I detected in his speech the typically Canadian OU. I don't know whether you've ever noticed it, Mr. Seymour, but the Canadian OU is unique. Where all other English-speaking people pronounce OU as a diphthong, the Canadian (unless, of course, he comes from any French-Canadian district) makes a separate sound for each letter. The word about, for instance, he pronounces as ab-oh-oot'* . . ."

Seymour looked up, obviously through with this witness. And Anthony said, thoughtfully, "Canadian, eh? And Messenger was going on to Canada from California . . . Well, three cheers for the Parson."

"The Reverend Hamish MacFarlane," Seymour said. "A wonderful old man, sir." He glanced at his notes. "He had something else, too—for what it's worth . . . I think I've got his exact words here. He said, *'the only peculiarity I noticed about the man, Mr. Seymour—and I put it down to nervous exhaustion following his truly great efforts in succouring the injured—the only peculiarity I noticed was a little tic or twitching muscle, by the corner of his right eye.'*"

Seymour closed the notebook and put it back in his pocket. "And that's all, sir," he said. "Precious little, too, for the time I put in." He was downcast.

In sympathetic silence, Anthony stood up. He took Seymour's empty glass, and refilled it, and gave it back to him. He said, "Get outside that, and don't be so glum. I say three more cheers for the clan MacFarlane . . . I don't know about the tic; but Canada might turn out to be very useful." He was still thoughtful. "Very useful indeed . . ."

The time when, at Deyming Abbey, all three of the resident Bruttenholms chanced to take breakfast at the same time as their guest.

The log fire crackled cheerfully, and an unexpected sun shone through the leaded windows of the room that once had been an Abbot's private parlor.

For the three adults at the table, the meal was over. Only Derek Bruttenholm, Viscount Saltmarche, was still eating, satisfying a twelve-year-old appetite sharpened by convalescence from the recent mild attack of measles which had taken him out of school one whole delightful month before the Christmas holidays. He finished his third piece of toast and marmalade and reached for more, winking across the table at his friend Jocelyn, whom he privately considered to be one of the very few females in the world worth talking to.

Jocelyn answered the wink with another one, topping it off with a benign smile. She thought fleetingly that Derek was probably the only orphan she would ever know for whom she would never feel sorry. She hadn't known his father and mother, both of whom had died six months before she met and married Bernard Messenger. But she did know that with grandparents like Uncle Rory and Aunt Mildred, the next Marquis of Gleneyre was a lucky boy.

She studied Uncle Rory and Aunt Mildred in turn. The Marquis, looking so hale a sixty that it seemed impossible he could be past that by more than twenty years, was indulging his lifelong passion for sensational journalism by reading *The Daily Picture*. The Marchioness, a lovely little figure who, from her neat and shining white hair to her tiny slippers, would have delighted the heart of a Boucher or a Fragonard, was going through her morning's post-bag.

Jocelyn smiled at the unconscious pair as benignly as she had at the boy. She felt benign today, for upstairs in her room were not only

146

the letter she had received yesterday from Raoul, but also her almost completed reply. Which had been very difficult to write, but which at last had reflected, subtly and only between its lines, exactly what she now felt. Which in turn was that she had been behaving like an illogical schoolgirl. When she came to think, it had been plain from the beginning that the Signorina Da Vinci was a shape from the past and not the present. And who was Jocelyn Messenger to imagine that any man she happened to fall for must *ipso facto* have been some sort of virgin Bayard until he met her!

She smiled again, this time wryly and at herself. She didn't even like Bayards; not of any kind. And she didn't mind shapes, however startling, so long as they weren't contemporary and made her just another shape (an outsize one) in a collection . . .

She felt a sudden, almost irresistible urge to rush upstairs, now, and pack, and leave for London at once. But she knew she mustn't: they expected her to stay at least another week . . .

So—so why shouldn't she get Aunt Mildred to ask Raoul down?

Why not, indeed! They'd all been wanting to meet Raoul anyway, hadn't they?

She sat back, and lit a cigarette, and watched Aunt Mildred, waiting for an opening.

The Marchioness had just unfolded an air-mail letter from New York. She said, "Oh, here's one from Mary!" She scanned the sheet eagerly. "She seems to be feeling *much* better . . . Oh, and she's had what she calls a *most* charming letter from that very gallant Frenchman!" She looked at Jocelyn, "By the way, my dear, did you ever see any more of him?"

"Yes," said Jocelyn. "Yes, I did." She felt herself colouring, but couldn't do anything about it.

"And will again, do I gather?" The young eyes of the Marchioness were brightly enquiring.

"Yes. I think I very likely will." Jocelyn had mastered the blush now. "As a matter of fact, Aunt Mildred, I was going to ask you——"

"*Hah!*" said the Marquis suddenly. "'Straordinary coincidence!" His tanned face and white moustaches appeared from behind *The Daily Picture*. "Here you're talkin' about this fellah St. Denis—and I'm starin' at a picture of him!" He stretched out a long arm and handed the paper to his wife. "Good-lookin' chap. Doosid pretty gel he's with, too!"

"H'mm——" Lady Gleneyre looked from Jocelyn to the picture; then at Jocelyn again. She handed on the paper without a word.

Jocelyn looked at the picture, and then at the print below it. Which read, "Sharing a joke at the *Société de Paris* luncheon—M. Raoul St. Denis and the latest toast of theatrical London, lovely French ballerina La Nicole . . ."

Another shape! Not from the past this time, but obviously contemporary.

In her mind, Jocelyn was already tearing the unfinished letter into a thousand shreds.

And then, at last, *the time when* they telephoned to Stukeley Gardens from Scotland Yard with the news that Anton Kouroudjian's yacht had put in at Southampton . . .

Determined, though expecting little, Anthony got himself up in the small hours of the next morning and drove to Southampton. With comparative ease he traced his quarry to the Hotel Majestic, and by noon was in the Kouroudjians' suite, from which the male Kouroudjian was handily absent, and beginning his talk with the former Lady Pomfret.

She looked, sounded and behaved far more like someone called Pomfret than like someone called Kouroudjian. Typical of that vanishing breed of whom it used to be said, "She's County, you know!", she was tall, eminently healthy and noticeably well-constructed. Home from the sea, she had abandoned the nautical costume of her honeymoon for well-worn, well-tailored tweed. She was far from unattractive in a lovely-skinned, slightly buck-toothed way, and she was also a good listener, letting Anthony's somewhat devious introduction of himself go by without interruption.

So that by twelve-five he had set the stage. He said, "So what it really comes down to is that both Messenger's publishers and his executors—of whom I'm one—are trying to collect enough data to have his book finished." He smiled an apologetic smile. "I do hope I'm being intelligible."

"Oh, absolutely!" Mrs. Kouroudjian was helpfulness itself. "But I frankly don't see how I'll be able to help. Francis didn't know Major

Messenger terribly well, you see. I mean they didn't have one of those deathless friendships sort of thing, if you know what I mean."

"I quite realize that." Anthony smiled. "So all I'm going to bother you with is a few questions. You see, we're having difficulty finding any survivors of the particular war-phase we're interested in——"

He broke off, giving an excellent performance of a man struck by a sudden thought. "I wonder," he said. "Did Messenger himself ever try and get in touch with you?"

"No." She was faintly puzzled. "No, he didn't. He wouldn't have known how to find me, anyway. I never met him, you know."

"Oh, I see." Anthony let himself be downcast for a moment. "Well then, did Messenger ever get in touch with Sir Francis himself? After the war, I mean?"

Mrs. Kouroudjian thought about this. "I don't think so," she said slowly. "Frank used to mention him once in a while, but I'm sure they never did any foregatherin'. If they had, I'd have known about it. Frank told me everythin'."

"May I take it then, Mrs. Kouroudjian, that he talked to you about his war experiences? Particularly Burma?"

She nodded emphatically. "You definitely may. Mostly about Hugo Dalton, of course, and the Dacoits——"

"Now that's very interesting." Anthony mastered a rising excitement. "That's just the operation I was going to ask you about."

"You'll be askin' an expert." She smiled a tender little smile, and Anthony found himself liking her. She said, "Poor Frank! For the first few months after he was invalided out, he couldn't talk about anythin' else . . . Prob'ly because of bein' taken prisoner that time . . ."

"Taken prisoner?" Anthony was all ears. "I didn't know any of Dalton's men were captured."

For the second time in this whole extraordinary case (and again through Sara Pomfret-Kouroudjian) he felt the old familiar tingling which might presage some major discovery. He waited, holding his breath.

And she chose this moment to realize her shortcomings as a hostess! So that it wasn't until she had bustled about and found wine for both of them that he was able to steer her back on course.

He said, "We were talking about some of Dalton's men being taken prisoner· —"

"Oh, yes." She sat on the arm of a chair and sipped from her glass. "All from the 'Black Buck' column—that was Major Messenger's lot; Black Buck was their code name. They were all trapped, just before they got to the wireless station they were tryin' to cancel out. Most of 'em were killed, and the rest captured. They were only prisoners three or four days; but somehow it was always preyin' on poor Frank's mind. I s'pose it must've been because of that bloody Canadian sergeant playin' Judas that way . . ." Again she sipped at her wine, serenely unconscious of the bomb she had dropped.

"This sounds just the sort of thing we want." Anthony kept himself under iron restraint. "A *Canadian* sergeant, did you say? What did he do—betray some plan for escape or something?"

"How did you guess?" Mrs. Kouroudjian regarded him with innocent wonder. "That's exactly what it was! Just to get himself better treatment, he sneaked to the Japs about some scheme that Frank and Major Messenger had worked out for gettin' away. Frightful type, apparently! But, oddly enough, a hell of a good soldier otherwise, Frank said . . ."

Again her voice had drifted off into silence, and again Anthony had to keep himself on a tight rein. "I wonder," he asked placidly, "whether you happen to remember his name?"

She shook her head. "Frightfully sorry, I don't. Matter of fact, I'm not sure Frank ever mentioned it. He used to call the chap 'that bloody Canadian' all the time." She smiled. "Only 'bloody' wasn't exactly what he said, if you know what I mean."

"Quite." Anthony gave a dutiful smile in return. And then, before he could embark on his next line of questioning, was interrupted by the entrance of the bridegroom.

Shaking hands, Anthony thought vaguely of Capulet's daughter and how right she had been about names and what was in them. Because, as did his wife, Anton Kouroudjian looked far more like someone who ought to be called Pomfret. He was also, again like his wife, cheerful and pleasant and helpful. So much so that, having insisted on Anthony staying for lunch, he took himself off immediately after the meal, leaving them to unhampered talk about his predecessor . . .

Anthony stayed another hour. And after it, when he was taking his leave, Sara Kouroudjian smiled at him apologetically.

"Only too glad," she said, in answer to his thanks. "Sorry I couldn't be more helpful——"

"But you were." Anthony's tone was heartfelt. "Extraordinarily helpful, believe me!"

CHAPTER EIGHT

There was a bigger and brighter fire than usual in Lucas's room at Scotland Yard. Which was just as well, for the evening was bitterly cold, with a veil of sleet hissing across the river and slashing at the white-coated windows.

It was six-thirty, and Lucas sat at ease behind his desk while Pike was upright in the smallest guest-chair. They both listened, intently, to Anthony Gethryn, who stood with his travel-cold back to the fire and related the gist of his meeting with Mrs. Anton Kouroudjian.

He reached the point of the luncheon break, and now paused to light the first cigarette of his visit. "What she told me after lunch," he said, "didn't really add anything to what she'd said already, at least not in detail. But one vitally important corroboration did come out of it. She recognized several of the names on Messenger's list as having been mentioned by Pomfret. More than enough of them to confirm definitely my belief that now I *knew* where the heart of this business lay. Or should I say origin?"

Lucas said, "You're sounding a note of triumph, Gethryn. Forgive an ageing Civil Servant if he wonders exactly why . . . Oh, I realize that now you've pin-pointed that 'link' you were looking for; even strengthened it with this Canadian element. But I don't yet understand why you think this really helps us in the down-to-earth business of catching your Smith Brown-Jones . . . Unless, of course," he added, "you've got a lot more up your sleeve."

"I have, Lucas. Not facts necessarily, but certainly conclusions." Anthony caught a small sound from Pike—a sort of ghostly cough. "And what's from you?" he said. "Questions?"

Pike said, "I was wondering, sir, whether you had any more detail

151

about this Canadian sergeant. *Who* he was, for instance. And when he left the service? And where?"

"I haven't." Anthony shook his head. "I don't even know his name yet. Apparently, Pomfret only referred to him in the formalized military idiom, as that copulatory Canadian." He had been smiling but the smile faded now. "And as far as the ex-Lady Pomfret knows, he was listed '*Missing: believed killed.*'"

"Am I understanding you, Gethryn?" Lucas sounded bewildered. "Or have I missed something? I've been definitely under the impression, from the way you were talking, that you'd selected this nameless colonial as the villain of the piece——"

"So I have: he's inescapable!"

"And you're incomprehensible!" Lucas's voice was rising now. "You preface this whole report by saying you're getting somewhere at last——"

"But I didn't say where." Anthony was unruffled. "I couldn't have, because I'm damned if I know——"

Lucas ignored the interruption. "And you come up with this vague, second-hand story about some unknown Canadian who was guilty of some vague act of treachery in some vague operation in Burma. And then, by God, you insist *he's* our unknown killer; when as far as you know he didn't even get out of the war alive!" Lucas surprisingly banged a fist down on the desk. "Upon my soul, I swear you must be losing your grip!"

"You know, Lucas"—Anthony was unmoved—"I suspect you of trying the transatlantic technique of 'needling' me to see what I've got. Either that, or it's not so much a case of my grip slipping as it is of your mentality."

Pike shifted uncomfortably in his chair. He wondered why, at his age and rank, the perennial and indeed almost traditional spats between these two should worry him. He opened his mouth to speak—and then closed it again, swallowing whatever it was he'd been going to say.

He listened instead; and heard Lucas saying, in the over-reasonable tones of the man driven almost beyond endurance:

"But don't you see, Gethryn, that you've *inverted* the only possible murder-motive in this set of circumstances? We're all familiar with the situation in which, following release from a prison-camp and discharge from the service, men will still carry bitter hatred of a fellow prisoner who in some way or another, and to further his own ends, betrayed them to their captors. Sometimes they carry this hatred as far as to conspire to murder (or let's say 'execute') the traitor. It's been a familiar theme in post-war fiction, and here we actually know of at least two real-life cases." He glanced at Pike, who nodded somberly. "Unfortunately—or fortunately if you like—the cabals were far too clever for us, as they generally are in the stories . . . But that's all beside the point I'm trying to make. Which is that while it's almost a commonplace for the injured parties in this sort of mess to murder the man who injured them, it seems to me nothing short of ridiculous to suppose that the man guilty of the treachery would endanger his own neck by setting out to murder the people he'd betrayed!"

Supplying the exclamation mark with a slap of his palm on the desk, Lucas sat back. And then, when Anthony didn't speak, fired his final salvo:

"I *can* conceive a set of circumstances, of course, in which the traitor might try to get rid of the men he'd betrayed. For instance, if he knew they were conspiring to kill him, it's possible he might try to destroy them first. But he wouldn't—he couldn't!—take a leisurely five years about it, cancelling them out one by one, spending all that ingenuity and time to make each death look like an accident. He wouldn't dare! They wouldn't be going to wait that long; and anyway, after the first death or so, he wouldn't be fooling 'em. *They'd* know who was causing the deaths, and it would just make them get after him all the faster!" He sat back again, really finished this time. "It's no good, Gethryn," he said with finality. "This is a time when your theories simply don't work."

Anthony came away from the fireplace and up to the desk and sat on a corner of it. He said mildly, "Is it my turn now? Because if it is, the first thing I'm going to do, my boy, is remind you of the famous dictum to the effect that when the impossible has been eliminated, then whatever remains, however improbable, must be the truth . . . The basic mistake you're making lies in your arbitrary assumption that the only possible motive for this traitor to kill the men he betrayed is fear of his own life and preservation of that life."

Lucas frowned. "If it isn't the only one," he said, "name a few more!"

"I don't think I can," Anthony said. "Not more than one, I mean. But I'm going to give you that; because it's the right one." He stood up now, and paced back and forth in front of the desk as he talked.

"However," he said, "I'm first going to talk about the Canadian, and show that he *has* to be alive and *has* to be my Smith Brown-Jones. It's simple really, but it had better be said. And the simplest way is to start with Adrian Messenger and his actions. The probable motives for those actions we can go into later. What we *know* Messenger did was to go to a friend in the Police and ask him to investigate, quietly, the present condition of ten men; at the same time telling his friend that he was on the track of 'something big.' He himself was then killed in an 'accident' we now know to have been contrived; and subsequently we discovered that the ten men on his list had died, also in contrived 'accidents.' The whole eleven, therefore, must *ipso facto* have been somehow linked, in spite of their geographic and professional and typical disparity. This link was hard to find, but at last we discovered it: the men served together on a specific column in a specific campaign in a specific War-theater. Further, they shared the experience of having been taken prisoner and, during the short period of such imprisonment, *having been betrayed in an escape-plan by one of their own men!*"

Here Anthony paused, looking from one to the other of his audience. "May I take it," he said, "that we all agree betrayal of fellow-prisoners is seed for subsequent murder?"

He was answered by nods, decisive enough. "Very well, then," he said, "with the betrayal, the seed is sown; probably the only murder-seed which could survive the upheaval of return to civilian life." He looked only at Lucas now. "Murder-seed," he said again. "It's there—the only imaginable motive among these *twelve* men for post-war murder. And the seed grows, Lucas. It doesn't matter in whom it grows, or which way it strikes when it's bloomed . . . In other words, *the prisoner-betrayal situation is so impregnated with the possibility of murder that it can't be ignored, no matter in what direction murder strikes!*"

This time, as he stopped, Anthony dropped into the other chair by the desk. Again he looked from one to the other of his listeners—and was surprised when it was Pike who spoke first.

"I see that, sir," said Pike. "The pattern's there, as you might say. But it may not work out quite the way one expects it to."

"Exactly, Pike. Exactly." Anthony beamed on him. "And very nicely put."

But Lucas was another matter. He said sourly, "Forgive me for intruding on this mating of souls, but I'd like to get back to the point at issue. If possible without all these seed-and-bloom hyperbolics. If you remember, Gethryn, this point came down to the question: what possible motives, other than fear of his life and self-preservation, could conceivably inspire your Smith Brown-Jones to a five-year orgy of highly-contrived murder against the eleven men he once betrayed?"

"I'll tell you," said Anthony. "But restrain yourself from throwing things until I've finished . . . The motives are almost the same. Almost, but not quite. They're still fear, and still self-preservation. But what Smith Brown-Jones fears isn't death, and what he wants to preserve isn't merely a continued capacity to breathe . . . So what, you ask, is he afraid of, if it isn't his life? What is it he wants so much to protect? . . . I'll preface the answer by pointing out, first, that it can't be anything in the past, because that's over; and second, that it can't be anything in the present, or he couldn't afford the time he's taking. *Ergo*, it's something in the future . . . You follow me, I hope?"

"Yes indeed." Lucas was acid. "I'd be obliged, though, if you'd tell me where to."

"Into the veiled land of Things-to-Come," said Anthony. "Obviously. But even there the question remains; what does Smith Brown-Jones need so badly to protect? If I wanted to be clever—which God forbid!—I'd say the answer was a matter of three R's; Reputation, Recognition and Retribution. In order to preserve a *future* reputation, S. B.-J. must avoid *future* recognition as an erstwhile traitor, and consequent *future* retribution. Not necessarily retribution in the form of death or punishment, but retribution which would wreck the reputation . . ."

Again it was Pike who put in a word. "Excuse me, sir, but I'd like to make sure I've got your meaning. The way I see it, it's some future *position* in life this man would be concerned about."

Anthony grinned at him. "At the risk of incurring further sarcasm, Pike, let me say three cheers for you! *Position's* a much better word."

Lucas said suddenly, "Well I'll be damned!"—and then actually laughed. He looked at Anthony and shook his head in wonder. "All right, Gethryn," he said. "*All* right! You've done it again!"

"Meaning you're convinced? My dear fellow, I'm delighted."

Lucas laughed again. "You've convinced me of a possibility," he said. "Let's leave it at that for the moment, while I ask if you've done anything yet about tracing your nameless Canadian? Or would you rather I called him Smith Brown-Jones?"

"I'd be flattered if you did . . . And before I came here this evening I got hold of Guy Dennison at the War Office. He's going to supply me with all the information he can as soon as he can."

"So we mark that 'Pending,'" Lucas said. "And turn our attention elsewhere. But where *is* that?"

Pike came out of a chin-rubbing reverie. "It seems to me, sir," he said, "that we haven't reached the end of Mr. Gethryn's chain of reasoning, as you might call it." He looked at Anthony. "Like for instance, what *sort* of position it would be that Smith Brown-Jones is looking forward to."

"You couldn't be nearer the truth, Pike." Anthony smiled at his old friend. "So?"

"So we realize one thing right off." Pike was speaking slowly, picking his words. "It must be a position he's *sure* he's going to get to."

"Exactly." Anthony was approving. "If he weren't completely *certain*, he wouldn't have wasted five years of ingenuity and danger the way he has."

Pike said, "So it can't be any position he'd have to work for. Or gamble on, in any way——"

"Wait!" Lucas interrupted. "If you two are putting on this act for my benefit, it's wasted effort. I once read Logic too. So let's jump. To the only possible conclusion, which is that the future position of Mr. Smith Brown-Jones must be coming to him, in some way, through inheritance. Inheritance of either wealth or rank. Millions or a Dukedom, so to speak."

"Or both, Lucas," said Anthony. "Or both."

"So all we can do," said Lucas, "is mark time until Dennison turns something up?" There was a question in the statement.

156

Pike nodded. "I'm afraid so, sir."

Silence followed, and the clatter of a coal falling in the grate seemed unnaturally loud. And Anthony said at last, "Yes. I suppose you're right . . ."

He felt suddenly tired. Very tired. The sense of triumph had faded completely. He could say a lot more, of course; show them some inescapable conclusions. But what purpose would be served at the moment? They still couldn't do anything; and anyway, the only thing that had to be done, he could do better than they could. Besides, they might not agree it was necessary, or even desirable. They might argue against it, not without reason, and he didn't feel up to argument.

He said again, "Yes. I suppose you're right," and got to his feet and found his overcoat and hat and put them on. He said, "I'll let you know the minute Dennison has anything," and was making for the door when Lucas—suddenly, and completely without precedent—jumped up and came out from behind the desk and shook hands.

"Wonderful job, Gethryn!" he said. "You're outdoing yourself!"

Anthony looked at him in wonder—and suddenly grinned. "Thanks," he said. "As I believe I said, at the beginning of this case, 'Praise from Sir Egbert is praise indeed!'" He opened the door and started out; then paused to look back.

"I hope I'll be saying it at the end," he said.

He was smiling when he left Lucas's room; but the smile didn't last. It left him long before he was downstairs. And by the time he was outside and getting into his car, it had changed to a deep-furrowed frown.

As he drove, much slower than usual because of the sleet-flurries, out into Whitehall and across Parliament Square and into St. James's Park, he pondered whether he'd been right to stop the conference when he had . . . Surely they'd quickly realize—even if they hadn't already!—that the next step in reasoning must show at least the possibility that Smith Brown-Jones, having got rid of the witnesses against him, might very well be planning to eliminate anyone who stood in the way of the inheritance itself? Anyone *or* everyone!

Yes, of course they'd see it. And, at this stage, he reminded himself, it wouldn't really matter if they didn't . . .

So that was that. He dismissed it from his tired mind, and, by the time he had to fight traffic at Hyde Park Corner, was concentrating on the job in front of him. Which was the job whose necessity, he still thought, Lucas and Pike might disagree with him about . . .

But he had to do it. After all, Gleneyre *was* the richest peer in the United Kingdom; and Adrian Messenger *was* connected closely with the family . . . It wasn't logic, of course. But the *chance* was there, underlined by the Messenger-Bruttenholm propinquity . . .

He was past Knightsbridge Tube Station now, and slid neatly between a bus and a lorry, and made the turn into Stukeley Gardens . . .

As he parked outside the house and walked up to his front door, he reflected how lucky it was that Jocelyn Messenger was not only an intimate of the Gleneyres but was actually staying with them. The task of trying successfully to warn a possibly stubborn and certainly incredulous old gentleman against a danger which might very well be imaginary seemed almost impossible without her help. And even with it, he might not be able to carry conviction . . .

He pulled out his keys and opened the door, suddenly conscious again that he was tired, very tired. The whole case seemed to have turned to ashes in his mouth. And it would take a miracle, he felt, to provide the only solvent which would take away the taste. The solvent of *certainty*. Certainty that Smith Brown-Jones' objective was indeed the Gleneyre marquisate. Despite his usual belief in the Chestertonian dictum that the best thing about miracles is that they sometimes happen, he had no faith that this might be one of the times . . .

He was hardly inside the door before White was there to help him off with his coat. He thought longingly of a drink and a hot bath before the phone call to Deyming Abbey. But something—he'll never understand quite what—made him change the sequence. He said to White, "I've got to use the telephone. Find the biggest glass in the house, will you, and bring it to the study, full of the stiffest whisky and soda you can dream up. Ice; but not too much."

He walked along the hall, past the dining-room and the bar, and opened the study-door, and flipped on the lights, and noted with approval that the room was warm, the fire sending out blue and red and golden shimmers. He crossed to the writing-desk and was about to drop into the desk-chair and reach for his address-book when his eye was caught by something on the stool against the wall, beside the desk and under the corner of the bulletin board . . .

Something in the plural. Whoever had cleaned here had eschewed such modernities as a vacuum-cleaner, and moreover had made this room the last in the tour of duty. And had left behind three homely articles. A dustpan and brush; a long-handled carpet-broom . . .

He stared at them—and something stirred unbidden at the back of his mind. Like a signal of warning, faint but not to be denied.

When White came in a minute later, Anthony was staring motionless at a long, narrow strip of paper on the bulletin board; a strip almost directly above the chair which supported the forgotten household tools . . .

White saw them as he set down a tray which bore a Gargantuan drink. Barely controlling a reprehensible military oath, he murmured something which boded ill for the forgetful one, and bent over the chair to gather them up.

And was stopped in the process by his employer's voice. Which said sharply, "Leave 'em where they are . . . And strike a medal for whoever forgot 'em!"

"Sir?" said White. And then, seeing that his employer had picked up the telephone and was dialing, took himself off. He was inured by the stresses of many years to inexplicabilities which in time came to make sense . . .

In Anthony's ear a deep, wireborne voice said, "Allo, allo!"—and he sighed relief. It hadn't after all been too much to expect that Raoul St. Denis should be in. Fatigue had left him and he felt oddly lighthearted. He said, "Polidor Two to Ajax——" and was further heartened by the chuckle which preceded Raoul's next words, *"Le cochon est mort . . ."*

"À bas le cochon!" said Anthony—and heard another chuckle and then, "It is pleasure to hear your voice, Lecoq. I have been thinking that your Jean Blanc-Dubois perhaps had been bumping off you——"

Anthony said, "Not yet. But *I'm* getting closer to him." He was surprised to find that he wasn't tired any more. He said, "You can help me again. If you will——"

It was only thirty minutes later that Raoul arrived, having preferred to visit rather than be visited. Because, as he said, "This *appartement*—this flat—which I occupy is a strictly flea-bag, from which release is always to be welcome."

He was given a chair and a drink, and was congratulated on his apparent freedom from pain. He shrugged and said, "The bones are mended," and looked at Anthony curiously. "How soon is it you tell me how I am to help?"

"At once." Anthony crossed to the chair next the desk and picked up the carpet-broom and came back with it and held it up. "What do you call this?"

"*Un balai.*" Raoul was prompt, if puzzled.

"No, no. I don't mean in French. What is it in English?"

"A brush," Raoul said, more slowly. "A brush for the floor."

"Hah!" Anthony propped the thing against the mantelpiece, and crossed to the bulletin board and ripped off the strip of paper White had seen him studying. And turned to his guest again.

He said, "Once more into the cruel sea, *copain!*" And without question the Frenchman obediently relaxed in his chair, letting his head fall back and closing his eyes . . .

"Now is okay," he said after a moment.

As he had before, Anthony was sitting on the fender-seat. Still studying the strip from the board, he spoke in a slow monotone:

"You have been in the sea for a long time . . . Most of Messenger's talk is over . . . But then he says something else . . . Like this——"

He drew a deep breath and revived his second-hand imitation of Messenger's voice.

In it he said, *"Only one broom . . . Only one broom——"*

He was stopped, abruptly, by a stifled exclamation from Raoul. Who said, without opening his eyes, "No, no! This is not precise. But I now remember! . . . He was saying, *'All the brooms . . . clean . . . sweep . . . only one broom left . . .'"*

It was his turn to be interrupted. Because Anthony said, suddenly and in his own voice, "That's all. And congratulations! Also heartfelt thanks!"

Raoul sat up, his eyes open and questioning. "This is good, hein? This *broom* means more than the *brush?*"

Anthony said, "Yes. A whole lot more. In fact, my friend, in this

160

case it means everything. Think of it with a capital B, and it's a name. It's not only 'George's surname, it's the real name of Smith Brown-Jones. And it's also the name of the family which Smith Brown-Jones is determined to head. Because his goal is to become Marquis of Gleneyre!"

He let this sink in. He said, "I'll give you details later . . . But believe me, St. Denis, *all* the killing this man's done has been done with this one end in view."

"The Marquis of Gleneyre?" Raoul was frowning. "His name is Broom? . . . I feel I have saw somewhere another name than Broom for this family. A name much more long——"

Anthony had started for the desk, but stopped. "Don't worry," he said. "Just an Anglo-Saxon idiosyncrasy. Spelt *Brutt-en-holm.* Pronounced *Broom.*"

He went on to the desk now, and opened the address-book. "Forgive me," he said. "But this is important. As you'll understand when you hear me talking——"

He found the Deyming Abbey number (Greyne 4234) and got the call through surprisingly quickly. He said, "May I speak to Mrs. Jocelyn Messenger—General Gethryn." There were times, and this was one, when the rank was useful.

But he didn't speak to Jocelyn. He couldn't, because she wasn't there. She was, it transpired, staying for a few days with Mrs. Arnold Messenger at Marston Manor; Lady Gleneyre and Lord Saltmarche had also gone on the visit . . .

"H'mm," said Anthony. "I see . . ." He thought fast. "I wonder, may I speak to Lord Gleneyre?"

But he didn't speak to the Marquis. He couldn't, because his lordship, it transpired, was still confined to his room with the heavy cold which had prevented him from accompanying the family . . .

"Oh," said Anthony. "Oh, I see——" and asked a couple more discreet questions and was told that Lord Gleneyre was expected to be up and about again in two or three days.

He hung up and looked around at Raoul. He said, "Well, *he's* safe enough for the moment," and picked up the phone again and dialed Enquiries and was given the number of Marston Manor . . .

And within a couple of minutes was speaking to Jocelyn. "Can you talk?" he said. "Are you alone?"

"Yes." The soft deep voice was sharpened by curiosity. "What is it?"

"Trouble," said Anthony. "Mixed with progress, though . . . Mr. Smith Brown-Jones, *and* his objective, are coming into focus. Get ready for a shock when I tell you what that objective is . . ."

"All right," said the telephone. "Go on!"

"The objective," said Anthony, "is nothing less than the Marquisate of Gleneyre——"

"*What!*" said the telephone. "I—I don't understand! . . . It's *impossible*—Derek's the only heir!"

"Apparently not. Because Smith Brown-Jones *must* be in line. The connection lies in Canada somehow. Ring any bell?"

"*Canada?* . . . No, I don't—— Oh, wait—did I hear something once, about a young brother of Uncle Rory's who emigrated? . . ." Jocelyn's voice trailed into silence.

Anthony said, "Blacksheep or something?"

"Yes—yes, I think so . . . It was a long time ago when I heard it mentioned. Bernard said something one day—and Uncle Rory shut him up . . . I could find out, I suppose. From Aunt Mildred——"

"Better leave it at the moment. I'm afraid you've got too many other things to do——"

"Such as? . . ."

"To start with, give me the answers to several questions. First, when do you all go back to Deyming?"

"The day after tomorrow—Friday."

"*Without arousing suspicion of anything unusual,* can you arrange for you and me to talk privately with Lady Gleneyre some time tomorrow? Probably in the late afternoon, after I've been to Deyming Abbey and seen Gleneyre himself?"

"Yes. Easily."

"Next: again without giving anything away, can you ensure that young Saltmarche has someone with him all day tomorrow, *and doesn't leave the premises?*"

"Ye-es. Yes, I can." Her voice was slower now. "But—but——"

"Just a minute," said Anthony quickly. "Don't let me scare you too much. I'm just being careful. The boy, and his grandfather, are perfectly safe as long as they stay put. You see, Smith Brown-Jones——"

"*P'sst!*" the voice on the telephone was suddenly an urgent whisper. "Somebody coming!" Behind the voice he could hear background footsteps and a murmur of talk.

"Well, I'm awfully glad you rang up——" Jocelyn was loudly social now. "If you hear any more about Isabel, p'raps you'll ring me again in the morning?"

"I will," said Anthony. "And don't worry——"

He hung up, and swiveled in his chair to speak to Raoul——

And found with an odd little shock that the man was now standing within a foot of him. A very big man; who loomed. His coat was open, and his hands were on his hips. His face was expressionless, and something had happened to the once friendly eyes.

He didn't speak, and Anthony said, "Well, that looks after the boy too." He was surprised by the tentative quality in his own tone.

Raoul said, "I wish to be sure I have complete comprehension." His voice was chill as his eyes. "It now is that the Milord Gleneyre and his young *héritier* are dangered by your Smith Brown-Jones? This is correct?"

"Yes. But not immediately." Anthony stood up; and then when the Frenchman still didn't move, leaned against the desk. He said, "While they stay at home, they're perfectly safe. Smith Brown-Jones is far too subtle, much too cautious, to pay murderous visits. And anyway, he's not about to change the pattern he's established; the pattern of death by accident-in-travel."

Raoul was unimpressed. "But this is a man most intelligent. And he is knowing his pattern can in possibility reveal him. So I think that he will of deliberation be changing it."

"Not now." Anthony shook his head. "Not with these two. And certainly not on premises it would be so dangerous for him to enter."

The Frenchman pondered. "It does not seem to me——"

"What's more," cut in Anthony, "I don't believe he'll alter the pattern at all. In the first place, he can't have any idea we're onto him, so there'd be no point in changing a procedure which so far has worked so well. Secondly, and more important, he *must* be planning to make these two deaths seem even more unquestionably accidental than the others. Because if there were even a whisper of murder, the suddenly emerging heir would immediately be suspect Number One!"

"You are most clever." There was an edge to Raoul's voice. "But perhaps you take to yourself too much of responsibility."

"Sorry you think so." Anthony felt anger rising, and warily tried to suppress it. "I wonder what you think I should do. Have a heavy police guard clapped around both houses, starting tonight?" In spite of himself his voice was louder.

"Most exactly that is what I think." Raoul's voice had risen too, but there was a different note somewhere in it; a note that foreshadowed what he said next. "And if it is that which you intend to do, I must give you apologies."

"You don't have to," Anthony said. "Because I'm not going to do anything of the sort. I'm averse, if you follow me, to letting Mr. Smith Brown-Jones know that anyone thinks there's any reason to protect the present Marquis of Gleneyre and his successor."

Raoul stared at him, and frowned. And moved for the first time, turning away and crossing slowly to the garden-windows and staring blankly out of them into darkness.

Anthony moved too. He went back to the fire, and took a cigarette from a box on the mantelpiece and lit it. He looked at Raoul's back and said:

"Both the old man and the boy are perfectly safe for twenty-four hours, *as long as they stay where they are*. And that's been arranged for, as you heard: Gleneyre's in bed with a cold, and the boy won't be allowed out. And within the twenty-four hours I'll have told the Gleneyres the whole story and made provision for the right sort of protection. Protection which won't be apparent; protection which won't warn Smith Brown-Jones we're after him . . ." He paused, giving Raoul a chance to speak.

But no word came, and no movement. He wasn't sure whether or not he was wasting effort, but he went on all the same.

"That's the crux," he said. "We're on the verge of finding out exactly *who* Smith Brown-Jones is, and this knowledge might put us onto *where* he is. But if he's warned that we're after him, we might as well never have found out anything! All he'd have to do would be to stop. Because with all the will and work in the world I doubt if we could pin any of the previous deaths on him. So he'd go free, and then——"

Raoul cut him short, turning to face him. "Okay—okay!" This was

164

the old Raoul again, with the old smile. "The Maître is once more right!" He joined Anthony in front of the fire. "You will have been deducing, of course, that I do not trouble two pennies' worth about Milord Gleneyre and the young inheritor?"

"It *had* occurred to me your worry was about someone else." Anthony smiled. "Someone who happens to be close to young Saltmarche for the time being."

"Indeed yes." Raoul was frowning again; a troubled frown. "Who is there to know better than I know the danger of being close to any *cible,* any target, of Jean Blanc-Dubois!" His fingers drummed on the mantelpiece as he looked down into the fire; and after a moment he said suddenly, "This place where are staying the young boy and the ladies? You know it, perhaps?"

"Marston Manor? I know where it is; I've never happened to be inside it."

"It stands alone? In the middle of country?"

"Hardly. The main gate's at the end of the village street. Right opposite the inn. Why?" Anthony was curious.

"The reason will appear. But first a question: Jean Blanc-Dubois—Smith Brown-Jones—he is a lonely wolf, hein? . . . *Alors*—there would be no harm to your plans if tonight a French visitor should appear in this village? A newspaperman from Paris, who writes for his journal an account of life now on the English countryside? A newspaperman who can without making suspicion discover if perhaps there is any other alone visitor in the locale?"

"No harm at all. And just conceivably the reverse." Anthony smiled. "So go ahead. Want to look up a train?"

"I will drive, I think. I have the auto of my friend in whose flat I stay. A good car; as big almost as the flat, and more comfortable by a wide shot. So there is left a question only of route——"

"Which can easily be settled," said Anthony. And found a map, and had just finished tracing the route when he was struck by an idea. He said:

"You know, St. Denis, this might be very useful. If you could hang round the village till Friday, we could arrange for you to drive the three of 'em back to Deyming. It would save us from having to make too much public fuss about the Gleneyre car. Which, knowing S.

B.-J.'s methods as we do, will have to be thoroughly gone over before we let anyone take any sort of journey in it."

"This is an A-one thought!" Raoul was delighted. "Not only for your plans, but for myself in person. You see, I have lately been in a dog's house with the certain lady. There was an unhappy *rencontre* in the Hotel Alsace; and a picture in your journals which indoubtedly she has been seeing. And through these misevidences, she is now thinking the whole life of Raoul St. Denis is to make *zizi pom-pom* with every young woman of which the chest is more around than a meter!" He shook his head sadly. "A delicate situation. In particular because I have not yet announced myself . . ." He hesitated. "I am, you see, a gone coon. The intention which I have surprises myself——"

Again he stopped, this time looking down and muttering something to himself; something of which only three words were audible, *bourgeois*—and *bien sérieux*. And then he looked up, and laughed. He said, "But you have matters to investigate more serious than my emotions. Forgive, please."

And after that, refusing another drink, he was gone. Anthony closed the front door on him and went back to the study.

He sat, heavily, at the desk. He looked at the telephone with distaste, and sighed, and reached out for it and dialed the number of Lucas's house.

And presently was talking to the man himself. Who listened, and moaned, and said at last, "You mean you want a meeting *tonight!*"

"Sorry," said Anthony. "But it's essential . . ."

At some time in the small hours the weather performed one of those astonishing *volte-face* which seem more frequent in England than anywhere else. So that the next day, which was Thursday, dawned sunny and clear-skied, with air like champagne and no trace even of frost. The change was reflected in the person of Roderick Simon Fortescue Bruttenholm, the Eighteenth Marquis of Gleneyre; not only in his chest and sinus-passages, but in his morale. So much reflected, indeed, that when his valet entered his room at half past nine, bearing an invalid's breakfast, it was to see with horror that his lordship was not only out of bed but fully dressed. And dressed, moreover, in boots, breeches and the ancient tweed hacking-coat which was probably his favorite garment.

"Ah, Pidgeon," said the Marquis. "Lovely mornin', what?"

Pidgeon set down his tray and started expostulation. It was bad enough that his lordship was up: it was unthinkable that his lordship should even contemplate going out!

"Now, none o' that, Pidgeon!" said the Marquis. "None o' that!" It was his habit, whenever he was in residence at Deyming, to ride alone around his land every Thursday, visiting his tenant-farmers. The habit had persisted for nearly sixty years and was very dear to him. So dear that he never allowed even hunting to interfere with it.

Valiantly, Pidgeon tried again, drawing an impressive word-picture of the wrath of the Marchioness should she discover this truancy.

But again he wasn't allowed to finish. "What a wife don't know," said the Marquis, "won't ever hurt her. Now you listen to me, m'boy: I've already phoned the stables. Straker's goin' to saddle old Padbury and sneak him out. I'm goin' to do some sneakin' out too—by the backstairs in the east wing." He chuckled. "I'll come back the same way, and no one'll ever be the wiser."

There were times, and this was one of them, when there would appear in the Marquis's eye a glint which meant there was no gainsaying him. He towered over Pidgeon now, and gave that small and worried man the glint's full benefit.

"And so we come," said the Marquis, "to your part in this operation, Pidgeon. You will remain here. And till I get back you'll deflect all visitors and telephone calls. You'll tell 'em I spent a restless night, but now I'm sleepin' like a baby. Havin' left you orders I'm not to be waked." He smiled down at Pidgeon, but the glint was still there. "That clear, m'boy?"

Pidgeon sighed; and capitulated. "Yes, m'lord," he said—and then won a minor victory by successful insistence upon a heavier sweater to go under the hacking-coat.

He had just peered out into the corridor and announced the coast clear, when the house-phone rang insistently——

He lifted the receiver to hear the orotund tones of his friend the butler. Who announced a telephone call from London: a General Gethryn who wished to speak with his lordship; a General Gethryn who was a close friend of Mrs. Jocelyn Messenger——

167

An eye on his master, Pidgeon performed very creditably. His lordship had passed a restless night but was now sleeping. His lordship had given orders not to be waked——

And while Pidgeon was hearing that General Gethryn quite understood and would call in person at the Abbey this afternoon, Roderick Simon Fortescue Bruttenholm, Eighteenth Marquis of Gleneyre, tiptoed like a schoolboy out of the room and along the corridor . . .

It was a few minutes after one that afternoon when the wind changed, completely boxing the compass, and black clouds began to pile up in the sky.

And by the time that Anthony, an hour later than he had originally intended, was able to leave London and start on the sixty-mile drive to Deyming, the rain had begun. He fought slithering way out of town and then, free from heavy traffic, settled down to a high but steady speed.

For a while he rehearsed in his mind how he would present the case to Gleneyre, wondering how the old man would take to the irksome necessity of being guarded. And then, when he'd decided on an approach, ran over in his head what the day had so far brought . . .

First had been Guy Dennison's surprisingly early, and surprisingly fruitful, phone call from the War Office. Dennison had done him proud, providing the name of the Canadian sergeant, which must be the real name of Smith Brown-Jones! And the name itself was more corroboration than he'd dared to hope for.

Corroboration number one; the Christian name was George. Corroboration number two; the surname was *Brougham*.

From *Bruttenholm* through *Broom* to *Brougham!* Exactly the sort of name-switch an emigrating blacksheep might choose. Such blacksheep, of course, being the young brother of Gleneyre's of whom Jocelyn had spoken; George's father, or possibly grandfather . . .

This had been good; but Dennison had given him yet more. Sergeant George Brougham's original Canadian Army* unit was the

---

* For those interested: Brougham was in India only accidentally, *via* a torpedoed transport, an Egyptian hospital, a snafu'd set of orders.

Duke of Athlone's Light Infantry, with headquarters in Ottawa which would surely be able to correct the omissions and mistakes in the very sketchy records of Dalton's unfortunate Dacoits . . . Mistakes? Well, one mistake certainly. For, according to Dennison, Sergeant Brougham's final entry was *"Missing—Believed Killed."* Which couldn't—which mustn't!—be true . . .

Second on the list of the day's activities was his own phone call to Deyming Abbey. A call which had brought the heartening news that Gleneyre was safely in bed and asleep . . .

Third—and a surprise—had been Jocelyn's phone call from Marston. Not waiting for him to ring her, she had been anxious not only to reassure him that Derek wouldn't leave the premises, but also to convey the results of a talk she'd had with "Aunt Mildred." A talk, she'd assured him, which hadn't raised any suspicion in the old lady's mind; a talk which had brought out the facts that the Canadian blacksheep was *Arthur* Bruttenholm, who in disgrace had cut himself off from the family over fifty years ago, and of whom nothing had since been heard. Nothing, that was, except a rumor that he had changed his name to either *Braham* or *Brougham!* . . .

After this unexpected bonus (which was corroboration number three) had come the toughest job of the case to date: the necessity for convincing not only Lucas but the Commissioner himself that the best and surest and fastest way to get a true line on George Brougham was to arm Seymour with all requisite official papers and put him on the next plane for Canada . . .

At this stage of memory, Anthony found himself about half-way to Deyming. He was still smiling at the thought of Lucas's agonized acceptance of the inevitable, when the drizzling rain turned suddenly into a downpour. He increased the speed of his windscreen wipers; and then, to drown out their infuriating *click-clack,* turned on his dashboard wireless and a news program . . .

There was trouble, it seemed in France . . . There was trouble in occupied Berlin . . . There was trouble—and a lot of it—in Iraq and Egypt and India . . . And with a general strike imminent, there was trouble too at home . . .

Weary of trouble, he was reaching out to the dials when the metallic, over-cultured voice said something which hit him like an iron fist in the solar plexus.

"All England," said the voice, "will be saddened by the news, received only moments ago, of the death in a riding accident of the Marquis of Gleneyre . . ."

In spite of the rainstorm, which for a while took on a violence almost tropic, Anthony covered the last half of his journey much faster than the first. Not only was he driven by an inescapable feeling of guilt; but now he didn't have to take precautions about being seen driving up to the Abbey. Before, it had been at least possible that George-Brougham-Smith-Brown-Jones might be in the neighborhood of Deyming; and also just within the bounds of chance that he might know Anthony Ruthven Gethryn by sight and be aware that upon occasion Anthony Ruthven Gethryn represented Scotland Yard . . .

But with Gleneyre dead—Anthony gritted his teeth—it was a thousand to one the man wasn't within a hundred miles of Deyming . . .

It was half past four, and what with the rain, the storm-clouds and the fading daylight, it was dark with a bronze darkness when the Voisin roared through the park, and reached the drive, and pulled up in front of the Abbey's huge main door.

Parked right in front of him was a long and low and continental-looking limousine. As he got out of the Voisin and ran up the steps, ducking against the rain, Anthony wondered if it could be the car that Raoul St. Denis was driving.

The thought was immediately verified. Because, as he reached the top step, the door was opened from the inside—not by a servant, but by Jocelyn Messenger.

She was pale, and there were lines of strain around her eyes and mouth. She said, "I saw you from the window. They just phoned for you from Scotland Yard. Sir Egbert Lucas. He's holding on——"

He stripped off his coat and followed her to a small, office-like room off the big hall. Where she said, "I'll wait for you," and left him alone with the telephone.

"Lucas here," it said. "You must know about Gleneyre—"

"Just the fact. No detail."

"We had the news a few minutes after you left. There isn't much, but here's what they've got: He was found crushed under his horse at the bottom of a disused gravel-pit. Time of discovery, two-thirty this afternoon. The animal was also dead. Broken back. Estimated time of death between eleven and one. Not having our knowledge, the locals inferred the horse shied, bolted or slipped. No visual witnesses. The gravel-pit's in a lonely spot, hidden by a beech-copse. The whole thing might still be undiscovered if Gleneyre's valet hadn't got nervous. Apparently Gleneyre ignored his doctor's orders and went out this morning——"

"Where'd you get all this?"

"Soon as we heard, I rang Spicer. He's the Medeshire Chief Constable——"

"Did you enlighten him?"

"Enough. With strict admonition not to advertise any suspicion that this might be murder."

"Good! Why did you say '*visual* witnesses' just now? Somebody hear something?"

"Possibly. There's a road that runs by the pit and the beech-copse. Old right-of-way. Very little used except by tourists and sight-seers; mostly on holidays and weekends. But there was a car on it this morning; at about the right time. Two farm-laborers, working round a bend about a quarter of a mile away, saw an Astall-Mostyn drive by about eleven-twenty. Brooklands sports model. Man driving; no passenger. Thing had engine-trouble, kept backfiring. Must have stopped somewhere along the copse, because these fellows heard the engine keep roaring and backfiring. As if the man were tinkering with it, they said. Apparently, the noise went on for about ten minutes; then the car seemed to drive on . . ."

For the first time, Lucas paused; and then said slowly, "Eleven-thirty seems to be about the time Gleneyre always crossed this road on these inspection tours. He invariably took the same route, and it's a joke round the countryside that on Thursdays you could set your watch by him. Thursday was even a forbidden day for Meets of the Boileau, believe it or not . . ."

Anthony said, "Backfires?"

"Yes. But if you're thinking that's a good cover for a rifle or a shotgun, you're up the wrong tree. I asked. No wounds on horse or man. No induced wounds, I mean. Both bodies showed scars from rolling down the side of the pit——"

"Where's Gleneyre's body now?"

"They took it to Greyne. For the Coroner's p-m. They haven't moved the horse yet: it'll take a crane——"

"About eleven-thirty, you said? . . . And they didn't find the old man till over three hours later. It's too long, Lucas. Much too long."

"For tracing the car? Yes, I'm afraid it is. But they're trying——"

"And won't get anywhere." Anthony's voice was savage. "Give this bastard a few hours and it might as well be years!"

"I know how you feel. But I started 'em on something else that might produce results. They're combing the district for news of any recent strangers. Solitary strangers. Male. With emphasis on trans-atlantic possibilities."

"H'mm—good for you! . . . Though I'm afraid it won't produce anything . . . Now, where do I ring if I want reports, or any help?"

"Greyne 7431. Ask for Detective-Inspector Glidden. He may be in Deyming, but they'll relay any call."

"Right." Anthony made a note of name and number. "And thanks very much, Lucas. You've done a noble job . . . Which is a hell of a sight more than I can say for myself," he added bitterly.

And rang off, and got to his feet and went out of the room to find Jocelyn pacing restlessly. A disturbing thought came to him and he said, "Newspapermen! You don't seem to have been invaded yet; but you will be! Trampling hordes!"

"I don't think so." She shook the blonde head. "As soon as we got the news, I telephoned Lord Otterbourne. I've met him once or twice, and he's an old friend of Aunt Mildred's, believe it or not. I asked him what to do to be spared, at least for today. He was awfully nice. He said he'd arrange everything. Not only with his papers, but all the others too. It sounded impossible to me; but it looks as if he'd done it."

"Even in Fleet Street," said Anthony, "dogs sometimes stop eating dogs. And scratch each other's backs instead."

"I didn't consult anyone. I just did it." She sounded anxious. "Was it all right?"

"It was much more than that," Anthony said. "You ought to have a medal." He looked around the big echoing hall. "Can we find some-where else to talk?"

"Of course," she said—and then hesitated. "Would it matter if M. St. Denis was there?"

Anthony shook his head, vaguely noting the formality of this reference to Raoul, and she led him across the hall and into a pleasant room which seemed to combine very comfortably the functions of gun-room and study.

Raoul was standing in front of a blazing log fire, looking bigger than ever in tweeds. He said to Anthony, "I am hoping it is right what I have done. When I have heard of the sad death, I do not wait for you on the telephone but at once make my presence known to Mme. Messenger. And we agree I should drive back the family in my auto——"

Jocelyn cut in. She said to Anthony, "I persuaded Aunt Mildred it was just because we'd be quicker." She hesitated. "But she's awfully shrewd, you know. I think she's beginning to suspect."

"She'll have to know sometime, poor lady." Anthony's tone was heavy. "If you're the one to tell her, please don't attempt to disguise the fact that I'm directly responsible." He looked at Raoul. "I should have paid more attention to you, St. Denis."

Jocelyn said quickly, "But you can't blame yourself, Anthony. You mustn't! Not after telephoning this morning and being told Uncle Rory was safe in bed!"

Anthony gave her a brief and far from happy smile. "You're very kind, but I'm afraid it's not as simple as that." He shook his head. "However . . . Tell me something; did Gleneyre leave openly this morning?"

"No." Jocelyn was emphatic. "It was one of his schoolboy plots, poor darling! Only his valet knew—and Straker in the stables. They feel terrible, poor men—but they shouldn't. There was no stopping Uncle Rory in one of those moods."

As she spoke, she was studying Anthony's face; and now she came close to him and put a hand on his arm and pushed him into a chair. She said, "You sit down while I get you a drink," and crossed to a table at the far end of the room.

From the hearth, Raoul said suddenly, "Forgive if I shove my oar. But there is a troubling thought which I have. About the—the domestical *entourage*." He looked at Jocelyn as she carried a glass to

Anthony. "Here there are many servants; both within the house and to the outside. Is there among them any new addition?"

"No. They've all been here for years." Jocelyn looked at Anthony as she answered. "Except Straker, who only started a few weeks ago. But he's what they call a local; we know all about him."

"You needn't worry on those lines, St. Denis." Anthony took a long pull at his drink. "Put yourself in our man's place, and you'll see why. He's murdering his way to the top of this family; so at this stage it's the one household in the world he *must* keep clear of. With the best and blackest false whiskers in Hollywood, he wouldn't venture inside it!"

Raoul stared; and smiled. "Yes," he said. "Yes, you are most certainly right. It appears that my head is unscrewed." He glanced at Jocelyn. "In it there are too many problems, perhaps . . ."

Somehow, Jocelyn didn't seem to see the glance. She looked at her watch, and was shocked. "I must go up to Aunt Mildred," she said to Anthony. "I won't be long. If there's anything you want, please ring. Or there's a house-phone in the hall." She crossed quickly to the door and was gone.

Both men looked after her; and Raoul said ruefully, "You see? I am not yet out from a dog's house."

Anthony drained his glass. "I'd swap your cage for mine," he said, and stared into the fire.

Raoul regarded him with sympathy. "If you are thinking still you are responsible for milord Gleneyre, you are coming off your rocker! Not only have you heard lies on the telephone this morning, but there is another thing possible. It is that this death is a truthful accident. A very good luck for a very bad man. The—the *coincidence par excellence!*"

"Combining the idiom of two great allies," said Anthony, *"merde du taureau* to you, my friend!" He stood up. "This is murder, like all the others." He set down his empty glass. "Unlike all the others, though, I *might* be in time to prove it."

He started for the door . . .

Rounding the corner of the house at full speed, the fifteenth Viscount Saltmarche plunged into the rhododendron bushes beside the drive and watched the front door with unblinking eyes. The rain beat down on him and on the dark world, and icy trickles ran down his neck between cap and coat-collar as he crouched.

The front door opened and a man came through it, outlined for a moment against the light from inside. He closed the door and ran down the steps and crunched across the gravel toward the stables, head bent against the rain, hands deep in the pockets of his overcoat.

The Viscount Saltmarche summoned his courage and stepped out of the bushes, almost colliding with the oncomer.

"Excuse me, sir," he said. "But aren't you Anthony Gethryn—*the* Anthony Gethryn?"

Anthony looked down at the small and dripping figure. "That's my name," he said. "But I'm not so sure about the italics." He held out his hand. "You must be Saltmarche," he said. He was immensely curious.

His fingers were taken in a small wet grip, very firm. And the boy said, "I—I hope you won't think this is awful cheek, sir—but were you going to the stables?"

Anthony said, "You're quite right," and waited.

The boy said, "Were you going to talk to Straker, sir? About—about Padbury?"

"Padbury?" Anthony was at sea.

"The horse my grandfather was riding when—when——" The young voice wavered suspiciously.

"Oh, yes," said Anthony quickly. "You're right again. Why do you want to know?"

The boy said, "Because Straker hasn't been here very long. He doesn't know Padbury very well yet. Not the way old Hawkins used to; not the way I do even." He hesitated, and gulped. "I—I don't know whether you know horses, sir—but Padbury never put a foot wrong. It just wasn't *possible* for him to shy, or bolt, or even slip! My—my grandfather always used to say that if everyone in the Government had half Padbury's sense, England might still be a first-class power! And he used to say if an H-bomb dropped behind him, all Padbury would do would be close his eyes so as not to see the flash and then tittup off to the nearest shelter so he—I mean my grandfather—could get in out of danger . . ."

At this point, Lord Saltmarche appeared to realize that he was saying more than necessary, and saying it much too fast. He drew a deep breath, and put a tight rein on himself, and tried again. He said:

"I don't think Padbury *did* anything. I think something or—or somebody *made* him take that fall! . . . I don't believe I'm explaining very well——"

Anthony said, "Oh, yes you are. So Padbury was what we used to call a 'patent-safety'; a sort of super-patent-safety——"

The Viscount Saltmarche sighed in relief that here was another horseman. "Yes! That's right! That's exactly right!"

"And so," said Anthony, picking his words, "you feel that your grandfather's death might have been deliberately caused?"

Lord Saltmarche drew another deep breath; a sound with a quickly-mastered quaver in it. "That's it, sir," said Lord Saltmarche. "That's it exactly!"

"And have you mentioned this to anybody else?"

"No, sir . . . I didn't think it would be the best thing. Not after I happened to hear Jocelyn—I mean, Mrs. Messenger—not after I happened to hear her talking on the phone to somebody from Scotland Yard. She said your name two or three times; and then you turned up while she was talking . . ." Here the pleasing countenance of Lord Saltmarche was darkened by a guilty blush. ". . . And then—and then—well, sir, I thought I'd better speak to you before you saw Straker——"

"And you were absolutely right," said Anthony. "Absolutely." He smiled down at the upturned face. "And I'm going to ask you to go on saying nothing." He held the boy's eyes with his own. "Not until we know. Not until I tell you it's all right." He paused to let this sink in. "Get it?"

"Roger! sir."

"Good!" said Anthony. "Now the next thing you can do is tell me how to get to this quarry——"

"It isn't a quarry, sir. Just an old gravel-pit nobody uses any more——"

"This gravel-pit, then. How do I get there by car?"

"It's easy, sir." The boy gave clear and succinct directions.

"Thanks," said Anthony. "That's fine." He turned toward the house. "Let's go back, shall we?"

176

Lord Saltmarche fell valiantly into step. He said, "But—but aren't you going to see Straker, sir?"

"Not necessary." Anthony shook his head. "You saved me the trouble . . ."

They reached the house and ran up the steps and in a moment stood dripping inside the big door. Lord Saltmarche stripped off his cap and coat, but Anthony didn't follow suit. Instead, he looked down at the boy and said, "Do a couple more things for me, will you?"

"If I can, sir." The wide steady eyes looked up at him again.

"First's easy," Anthony said. "Dig Raoul St. Denis out of the gun-room and say I want to see him." He paused. "The second's about you, my friend. I don't want any questions yet; but I do want your word you won't go outside the house again tonight."

"Okay, sir." The boy's eyes were still steady on his, reminding him irresistibly of his own son . . .

It was six-thirty, and Detective-Inspector Glidden of the Mede-shire Police stood on the steps of Deyming Police Station and pre-pared himself for a dash across the road to the *Red Lion* and a quick meal. Looking with distaste at the rain bouncing off the black road, he pulled down his hat, and was buttoning the collar of his Burberry when a big low Voisin, water spraying from its tires, pulled in front of the station.

Two wet and mud-stained men climbed out of it and splashed across the pavement. The first was tall and lean and said to him, "You look as if you might be Inspector Glidden. My name's Gethryn." He waved toward his giant companion. "My friend, M. St. Denis."

Glidden took them into a little office at the back of the station; and Anthony Gethryn identified himself beyond doubt while the big Frenchman stood by the inadequate fire and gently steamed.

Anthony said, "We've just been down in that gravel-pit. Looking at the body of Lord Gleneyre's horse."

"Yes, sir?" Glidden hit a delicately questioning note.

"I came straight here to relieve your mind, Inspector." Anthony sat on a corner of the bare desk. "I had an inescapable feeling you people might be thinking this idea of murder was some hashish-dream of Sir Egbert Lucas's. So I brought you some possible evidence."

"Evidence, sir?" Behind the stolid-yokel expression he'd perfected over the years, Glidden's mind was alert.

Anthony opened his sodden, mud-smeared coat. He groped in pockets and brought out a small white envelope and said, "It's in here," and paused. "But before I show you, Inspector, tell me something: Did you or did you not, until this moment, privately believe the cause of the fall was the horse being startled by the sports-car backfiring?"

Glidden permitted himself a smile. He said, cautiously, "Well, sir, you must admit it seems likely."

Anthony opened the envelope, reaching over the desk and shaking out two hard, crystalline granules onto the faded blotter. He said:

"What would you say those are?" And waited.

Glidden looked at them, and touched them with a tentative finger. They looked as if they might originally have been oyster-white in color but had since been stained, not only with dirt but with something of a pinkish tinge. He said, more cautious than ever, "Some sort of crystals? . . ."

"Oh, yes." Anthony swept them back into the envelope, which he then sealed. "Yes, indeed!" He took a pencil from the desk and wrote on the envelope. He said, "Crystals of rock-salt, Inspector. Removed from the epidermis of a handsome old retired hunter named Padbury, property and favorite hack of Lord Gleneyre." He pushed the envelope across the desk. "The epidermis just above the tail, Inspector. I found more, but the granules were almost dissolved. Where they'd penetrated deeper, the body-heat had melted them before the blood cooled. Witness to where I got those two is M. St. Denis." He pointed to the envelope. "This being a Medeshire case, you'd better file that. But very quietly, if you follow me."

Glidden was frowning. "Rock-salt?" He was out of his depth and showed it. Though now the shining light of a country police-force, his origins were cockney.

Anthony said, "An old trick used by farmers, Glidden. To discourage orchard-robbing young fry. Rock-salt fired from a shotgun instead of shot. Comparatively harmless, and extraordinarily painful."

"So it *was* that sports-car!" Glidden's frown of puzzlement was replaced by another kind.

"Yes. With the backfiring covering the shot." Anthony joined Raoul on the dingy hearth. "A shot," he added slowly, "fired by a man who'd taken elaborate pains, and recently, to find out Gleneyre's habits."

Glidden drove a fist into his palm. "Bronson!" he said. "D. Bronson, from Vancouver." He showed more excitement than he usually allowed himself. "You know the Yard asked us to look for strangers who'd been in the neighborhood recently, sir? Well, the only one we turned up had been gone about a week. But I got all the facts about him. I passed 'em on, with dates, to Superintendent Pike when I phoned the Yard half an hour ago. So I'll give it to you quick. This man was at the Gleneyre Arms here from Wednesday evening two weeks ago till last Monday. He originally reserved his room by phone from Birmingham, the Gainsborough Hotel, for the previous Sunday. But then he phoned again from London, saying business had interfered with his time-table, could he come Wednesday instead?"

At this point, Inspector Glidden stopped abruptly, surprised by a sudden and impolite oath from his distinguished visitor, General Gethryn. He said, uncertainly, "Beg your pardon, sir?"

"Never mind," said Anthony. "Sorry." The oath had been a malediction on the head of Miss Madeleine Bixby, of the staff of Updyke and Wallace, Press Cutting Agents. Because now he could see the whole thing like a schedule. In Birmingham, Mr. George-Brougham-Smith-Brown-Jones, having created for himself the role of D. Bronson from Vancouver, had started for Deyming to plan his campaign against Gleneyre. En route, by some malign fate, he must have seen the paragraphs in *World of Books* about Adrian Messenger's unfinished work: an unsuspected danger he must deal with . . . And if only Madeleine Bixby had been on her toes that Sunday morning, Mr. Smith Brown-Jones might well have met A. R. Gethryn face to face in Messenger's flat . . . And then both Miss Gwendolynne LaDoll and Roderick Simon Fortescue Bruttenholm, Marquis of Gleneyre, would still be alive . . .

Glidden was talking again, and Anthony jerked his mind back to the moment. ". . . got a pretty good description." Glidden was consulting a notebook. "Checked it with the Hotel in Birmingham, too. Bronson was in his forties. Medium height and build. Sedentary type; shuffling walk. Bald-headed; no hair on top of head. No distinguishing facial characteristics; regular features. Some disagreement on eye-color; varying from hazel to brown. Retiring type; very pleasant manner. Represented himself as 'a manufacturer.' Dark, conservative clothes. Hobby—photography . . ."

He hadn't finished, but Anthony stopped him. "Sorry," he said. "But if you're thinking the C.I.D.'s going to be able to find Mr. D. Bronson, I'd better disillusion you——"

Glidden said, "Why shouldn't they, sir? He gave a London address, for forwarding. He definitely took a London train when he left. He can be identified by dozens of people here. Including the vicar who struck up quite a friendship with him——"

"Wait," said Anthony. "This isn't any common-or-garden, four-for-a-shilling murderer, Inspector. This is that ultimate rarity; a completely conscienceless, extremely resourceful, and a brilliantly intelligent killer. You can offer five hundred to one and get no takers that Mr. D. Bronson ceased to exist the minute the London train pulled out of Deyming station. Except for a possible change of headgear, the man who got out at Waterloo was probably wearing Mr. Bronson's clothes, but otherwise looked utterly different. Five years younger in carriage and gait, manner and expression; p'raps with a toupee covering that bald pate——"

Anthony stopped suddenly. "The bald pate," he said, "which, it has just occurred to me, may be naturally thatched again before long."

"A real bright one, eh?" Glidden rubbed his chin. "And I suppose he'd go to some busy hotel he'd never used before——"

"Exactly. And create a character he'd never used before. A character who first goes about the delicate business of buying a second-hand shotgun without registration; then at the right time hires an Astall-Mostyn two-seater." Anthony looked at his watch. "Which car was probably back in London and its own garage a couple of hours before Gleneyre was found."

Raoul spoke for the first time. "And now, of course, our friend is some most different Blanc-Dubois in some most different place——"

"Naturally," said Anthony—and looked at Glidden again. "We'll

180

take ourselves off now, Inspector. You know the death wasn't accidental; and I've given you the potential evidence to file." He moved away from the fireplace. "Evidence," he said, "which is not—repeat *not*—to be aired. Not under any circumstances, Inspector!"

Glidden nodded. "I know, sir." He came out from behind the desk. "Sir Egbert Lucas impressed that on the Chief Constable. Very strongly."

"Good." Anthony looked at the man for a long moment, and liked what he saw. He said, "You may be wondering, so I'll explain. Up to a point anyway. Unless and until we get specific information from Canada, Glidden, our only chance—repeat *only*—of getting this man lies in the fact that *he has no idea we're onto him* . . ."

It was ten-thirty, and the Viscount Saltmarche, enshrouded in a traveling-rug which left no sign of him visible, lay flat on his back on the rear seat of the big French car as it drove out of the park. On the floor beside him, mystified but on his best behavior, lay his Stafford terrier, Firbank.

Lord Saltmarche was possessed by conflicting emotions; a hollow ache in his stomach which had been there since he had first realized he would never see his grandfather again, and a tingling, all-pervading excitement. Here he was, being smuggled—*smuggled!*—up to London in the middle of the night! In a bang-on continental car, driven by his bang-on, his sensational, new friend Raoul St. Denis! Raoul St. Denis, hero of the Atlantic aeroplane wreck! Raoul St. Denis, who'd been something frightfully high up in the French Resistance! Raoul St. Denis, who looked even bigger and tougher than the new Games-master at school!

What was more, Lord Saltmarche thought, he was going to stay with some people (they were called Cameron) he'd never seen before. Which might be pretty interesting, because they were bound to be all right because Jocelyn said so. And anyway, Jocelyn was going to stay there too, which made everything even better! . . .

Altogether, it can be taken that the pleasurable excitement which possessed Lord Saltmarche momentarily outweighed the ache. In fact, there were only two possible flies in this thrilling ointment. First was the *odd* way his old friend Jocelyn behaved to his new friend Raoul; sort of friendly but sort of not, all at the same time; and with too many smiles that didn't seem like real ones. Second was this story they'd given him about *why* he was being smuggled. It was supposed to be because of newspaper-reporters, but he wasn't at all sure they weren't having him on . . .

A hand suddenly lifted the rug from his face, and he saw Jocelyn leaning over from the front seat, looking down at him.

"It's all right now, chum," she said. "You can sit up."

He grinned at her, and wriggled his feet to the floor, and Firbank jumped up onto the seat beside him . . .

It was eleven o'clock, and Anthony was still at Deyming Abbey. As he said in a letter to his wife a couple of days later, he had fallen in love. "And with none of your commoners," he wrote. "With a Marchioness, I'd have you know!"

The Marchioness had sent for him some hour and a half after he and Raoul had returned from the talk with Glidden; by which time he was bathed and fed and in borrowed clothes which were reasonably comfortable. Leaving Raoul and Derek cementing friendship over a game of billiards, he'd been taken upstairs to a pretty sitting-room where Jocelyn had presented him to a diminutive lady in a big wing-chair; a grey-clad, white-haired, immaculate person who'd greeted him with a personal and unfeigned warmth which had plucked painfully at his heart-strings.

She had said, "Jocelyn's warned me not to call you 'General,' Mr. Gethryn. So I won't. Particularly as I'm about to ask you a favor——"

And then she'd smiled at him. A smile which had completed his subjugation.

"I want you to tell me *everything*," she'd said. "Jocelyn says she can't take the responsibility; but I hope you will . . ."

And then she'd turned her head away for a moment, looking into the fire, with the light shining softly on the white hair and striking little magic flashes from the small neat jewels in her small neat ears.

"I've lived a very long time," she said. "But no one's ever thought I was a fool. From many signs—Jocelyn's behavior, the presence of M. St. Denis, your own arrival—I feel I *know* Rory's death wasn't any accident." She turned her head and looked at Anthony again. Her eyes were bright, perhaps partly with unshed tears but certainly with vivid, oddly youthful life.

"You needn't try and soften the blow," she said. "It's not as if I were a child of fifty. I know it won't be long before I'm with him." Again she smiled. "So tell me, please—am I right?"

Anthony drew a deep breath. "Yes," he said.

"He was killed deliberately? Murdered?"

"Yes," said Anthony again . . .

That was how it had started—and the following hour had been a crowded one. He had outlined the whole story for her; the question of Derek's danger had been brought into the open and discussed; Jocelyn had both conceived and carried out her notable idea of enlisting the help of the Camerons.

And now, with the boy and his escort half-way to London and the Camerons' house in Hampstead, Anthony and his hostess were still talking——

". . . And so," said Lady Gleneyre sternly, "let me hear no more of this nonsense about your being responsible. I won't have it! How could you know that at *his* age my Rory was constantly subject to attacks of adolescent self-assertion, bless him! You did everything you could and should have done."

Anthony was standing near her chair, and she reached up a hand to him. He took it, and carried it to his lips without speaking, and was rewarded with a smile.

The smile faded, and she said suddenly, "How much do you know about the Bruttenholms?"

"Not enough, I'm afraid," Anthony said. "A general impression of distinguished history; the inferential knowledge that, if Derek were to die, any direct male descendant of your brother-in-law Arthur Bruttenholm would succeed to the Marquisate. That must be right?" He carefully made a question of the statement.

"Of course it is!" The bright eyes stared at him in surprise. "Rory was the oldest of four brothers. Arthur was the youngest; he got into some awful trouble, somewhere in the nineties, and was lucky to get out of England in time to avoid going to prison. The family believe he started for Canada; but apart from that—except for rumors they didn't even want to hear—nothing's been heard of him since.

The other two boys—Maurice and Evelyn—were killed in the First War, both in 1916. And neither of them had a son."

She stopped, reflectively, and Anthony kept carefully silent, taking a chair to face her. She said:

"If you're right about this terrible man being Arthur's son or grandson, this whole horrible, horrible business must be due to that odd flaw in the Bruttenholm strain. Nowadays I suppose they'd say it was all to do with hormones or genes or one of those new-fangled things; but I say it's in the blood, which is all they mean anyway. If you study the family history you'll find the Bruttenholms were always prolific, especially in the matter of boys; and you'll also find that in every generation they've produced several nice, happy, loving human norms and just a single brilliant one . . . The trouble is, though, that these brilliant exceptions have always been blackguards as well. Invariably! And it looks to me as if this—this *tendency*, I suppose they'd call it—had somehow reached some sort of climax; come to some sort of monstrous head . . ."

She sighed, and was silent—and Anthony got to his feet. He said, "I think you're tired, and it's my fault. I think you ought to go to bed."

She sat very straight and looked up at him. She was very small in the large chair. "If I'm tired it's my business." She reached out a hand and lifted her empty glass from the table beside her. "I think I'll be a devil and have another brandy."

There was no resisting her. Anthony took the glass and poured brandy into it from the decanter and gave it back to her.

"Thank you," she said, and sipped. And then she said, "What I *can't* understand is *how* this man could possibly contrive to do all these terrible things by himself. I'm probably being a silly old woman, but I keep wondering—"

Anthony smiled at her. "You're not the only one," he said. "The same question worried no less a person than Egbert Lucas." He stood up, pacing the hearth as he went on. "You see, there are three important factors that make it not only possible, but comparatively simple, for him to have done all the things he has done; *and* to have done them alone. First is his character. You see, he has almost all the virtues: courage and patience, self-reliance and perseverance, and a whole lot more. But in him there's one big, big flaw—a complete absence of sympathy for other human beings—which amounts

to a megalomaniac insistence on Self as the be-all and end-all . . .
In other circumstances, what he's doing might even be considered
admirable. In wartime, for instance, he'd probably get medals for
it!"

He stopped suddenly, "I'm sorry," he said. "This is no time to
philosophize. So back to fact. The other factors that have worked
for him are those twin eternal verities, Time and Money. Since he's
already taken five years over his appalling plan, he obviously has
the first. Which means, *ipso facto,* that he must have a sufficiency of
the second. Now, Time and Money made it possible for him to work
backwards, removing *future* sources of danger before there was anything for them to be dangerous about. And this method, in turn,
gave him all of the advantages and none of the drawbacks of the
truly psychopathic killer. Because, until forty-eight hours ago, his
motive wasn't showing——"

"But now the situation's reversed, isn't it?" The white head was
tilted as his audience looked up at him. "I mean, *you* have one advantage now. You know his motive and who he is; but he doesn't
know you know!"

Anthony surveyed her with respect. "Exactly," he said. "I'm glad
you grasped that so quickly. Otherwise, all that cloak-and-dagger
stuff with Derek might have worried you."

"I don't think so." She studied him gravely. "Not with you in
charge of things."

"That," said Anthony after a moment, "is probably the nicest, and
most undeserved, compliment I've ever received." He paused. "I
don't know what to say; so I won't say it. I'll just go back to the
real core of your original question: How, *physically,* could George-
Brougham-Smith-Brown-Jones have brought about all his 'accidental'
killings . . . To start with, let me put aside all the 'accidents' in which
death was caused by some mechanical failure or defect in vehicles
like lorries, motor cars, motorcycles, and bicycles. Let's just take it
for granted that, given Time and Money plus an obvious ingenuity
in dealing with machines, our man could have arranged everything
that happened. Will you agree to that?"

"Of course. Particularly because, having Time and Money, he
could always have another try if one didn't come off."

"Exactly!" With every moment Anthony was more entranced. "So let's go on to killings of different type. Francis Pomfret, for instance, was drowned when his sailing-boat, in which he was supposed to be alone, overturned in a squall: I don't have to point out there are a hundred ways Smith Brown-Jones could've fixed this one. I'll merely outline a possibility: himself in some sort of small craft (probably a motorboat) he pretends at the right and unoverlooked moment to be in trouble. Whereupon, the unsuspecting Pomfret goes to his aid, takes him aboard, and meets his death . . ."

Anthony found himself pacing again, and stopped, and went back to the hearth. "Then there's the vet, Robert Moreton," he said. "Moreton 'fell' off a footbridge over the railway line at a small country station. At three in the morning. This is a simple case of ambush; wait, bang and shove. And the same routine, plus a jammed-open lift gate, would account for Dr. Devitt. Wait, bang and shove—and the poor devil's at the bottom of the shaft."

Wondering if he were going too fast, Anthony paused. But as he lit a cigarette and studied his listener, he saw her eyes bright as ever and completely comprehending. He said: "So I'd better come to the two mass-murder horrors; the Highland railway holocaust and the Atlantic plane . . . As for the Scots train, I'm told that an hour's work with a pickaxe under a sleeper on the last hillside curve was all that was necessary. Work, by the way, which could never be traced because, when the train came off the rails, a whole section of the permanent way was ripped apart."

He saw another shiver move the grey-clad shoulders, and went on quickly, afraid she might ask how the killer could have been sure of his victim. He said:

"So we come to the plane. A simple problem for our brilliant megalomaniac. All he has to do is somehow introduce a time-bomb into the baggage. Believe me, I can think of ten ways without any trouble. For instance, a week or so beforehand, he takes a room at some hotel—say the Alsace—which caters largely to coming-and-going Americans. Easily finding out who'll be taking the same plane as Adrian Messenger, he strikes up acquaintance with this person or persons; gets to be on room-visiting terms; then at the right time either (a) substitutes a duplicate piece of baggage he has procured; or (b) contrives to be alone with the acquaintance's baggage long enough to insert his deadly package——"

Again he saw her shiver. He threw his cigarette into the fire and took his chair once more. "And that's all I'm going to say," he said. "I think you'll agree it's enough."

"About the past, more than enough," she said. "We're still left with the future, though. Which spells Derek, doesn't it?"

For the first time Anthony saw fear in her eyes. He found himself on his feet, looking down at her, wanting to comfort her. She held up a hand to him, and he took it in both his own. And smiled at her.

"I could give you a more cheerful spelling," he said. "Seymour——"

He told her about Seymour; who and what and where Seymour was. He said:

"So think about Seymour. Concentrate on him; and pray he comes back from Canada with what we want. Which is enough information to weave a net from; a net for Mr. George-Brougham-Smith-Brown-Jones . . ."

But when Seymour did come back, six days later, one look at him was enough to show Anthony that neither concentration nor prayer had worked.

The meeting was at Scotland Yard; in Lucas's room, with Lucas and George Firth there too. Seymour was tired and dejected. But, true to his training, clear and concise as he reported.

He had been to Ottawa, where were the headquarters of the Duke of Athlone's Light Infantry . . . He had been to Regina, where George Brougham, immediately after his discharge from the army, had sold the big farming properties which had passed to him on the wartime death of his father, William Brougham . . . He had been to Montreal, where (apparently owing to the insistence of his French-Canadian mother) George Brougham had been to school . . . And lastly he had been to Winnipeg, where he had found proof that George Brougham was indeed the grandson of Arthur Brougham, nee Bruttenholm . . .

But for all these activities, all he had to show were the following:

1. A To-Whom-It-May-Concern statement by the Adjutant of the Duke of Athlone's Light Infantry, showing that Sergeant George Brougham had been attached to the British Army Units in India; had served in

Burma with General Dalton's Special force. Originally reported "Missing—Believed Killed," Sergeant Brougham had been seriously wounded, and cared for by friendly Burmese; had finally made his way to Rangoon after cessation of hostilities. Through the Consular Service, he had obtained passage back to Canada, where he had reported to his Regiment and eventually received his discharge six years prior to the date of this Statement.

2. A copy of Sergeant Brougham's discharge-papers.

3. A copy of George Brougham's birth certificate.

4. Photostatic facsimiles of the Deeds of Sale for George Brougham's property.

5. An Affidavit, and copies of tax receipts, from the Regina bank through which George Brougham had conducted all the business of the sales. The Affidavit showed that, after the tax payments, George Brougham had converted the net balance of $97,000 into cash and Bearer Bonds.

6. Three yellowed and barely distinguishable snapshots of George Brougham, at the approximate ages of 5, 7, and 12.

Anthony looked with sympathy at Thomas Gainsford Seymour. "And nothing else at all?" he asked.

"Nothing, sir," Seymour said. "Unless you count one more useless verification I picked up. In Regina, from a girl who knew Brougham in his teens. She said whenever he got excited about anything he used to have a little tic beside his right eye."

"H'mm," said Anthony. "All the same our Nameless Samaritan of the Highlands." He shook his head. "But you're quite right about it being useless. We can hardly parade all the twenty-odd million males in the United Kingdom and excite 'em all to see who tics."

Lucas looked at Seymour. "What about passports?"

"Nothing doing, sir. No passport ever issued in the name of George Brougham."

It was Firth's turn. "Descriptions?" he said. "You must've collected quite a few. How did they boil down?"

"To a no-good norm, sir." Seymour shrugged wearily. "They varied so much, the average was useless."

Anthony smiled grimly. "A speaking likeness, I gather, of any Smith Brown-Jones."

A silence followed, broken at last by Sir Egbert Lucas. Who sighed and said, "Where does this leave us? Will someone please tell me? Or is that asking too much?"

Firth looked at the ceiling; Seymour at the carpet. And Anthony said, "Not from me, it isn't. In latter-day American, the answer is 'behind the eight-ball.' *Anglice*—in a fix. Or, in plain words for the young, back where we started, Lucas; standing in the middle of the stable-yard, wondering which door to shut on what empty stall . . ."

"For God's sake!" Lucas was sour. "Not the Police-function lecture again. I beg of you!"

Firth shifted uneasily in his chair. "I know it's imperative not to advertise," he said. "But do you think we've enough men looking after that Hampstead house?"

Lucas said, "For the time being, yes. They're more a token than anything else. To do Gethryn justice, the way he had the boy taken there makes it impossible for Brougham to know where he is . . . And he wouldn't be trying for him yet, anyway. Too close to the grandfather's death."

Anthony stood up. "That's fine," he said to Lucas. "But you'd better underline *for the time being* in your mind." He crossed to the chair where he'd laid his hat and overcoat and picked them up and made for the door.

And turned on the threshold. "What we've got to remember," he said, "is that our friend Smith Brown-Jones is as much at liberty as he ever was. Which, being interpreted, means free as air!"

He opened the door. "Hardly a comforting thought," he said—and was gone.

CHAPTER NINE

On the most rural side of Hampstead Heath, Wellington Lane is an elm-shaded road which wanders off into a stand of oaks and is lined with a few pleasant houses each in its own half acre or so of ground . . .

Number Seven Wellington Lane was the temporary home of the Camerons, and at eleven o'clock on this night, in one of its five bed-rooms, Christopher Derek Bruttenholm, Nineteenth Marquis of

Gleneyre, was sleeping the deep sleep of a pleasantly exhausted young male who has spent a pleasantly exhausting day among pleasant new friends. At the foot of the bed his old friend Firbank, who had been sleeping too, stirred restlessly.

In the adjoining room Jocelyn Messenger was ready for bed. She was very tired, but sleep was far away and she knew it. So here she was, sitting in a nightgown staring into a dying fire. Her head was full of jumbled thoughts, she was smoking one tasteless cigarette after another and listening to the clanking noises of the old-fashioned steam radiator system which (thank God!) the Camerons had insisted on resuscitating . . .

On the mantelpiece a clock ticked loudly, and every tick seemed to jumble her thoughts even more . . . She knew why they were jumbled, of course. Not because there were so many wild and frightening things to think about; not because she seemed to be living in the middle of an overwritten melodrama; not because a twelve-year-old boy she loved like a small brother was in danger——

Not for any of these sane and valid reasons; but merely because a man had gone away. A man, moreover, with whom she had repeatedly told herself she wanted no more involvement . . .

There was one log left in the basket on the hearth. She put it on the fire, and lit another cigarette, and found herself walking aimlessly around the room, thinking about a talk she'd had with Margaret on the second day after she and Derek had come here a week ago. That was the same day she'd discovered that Raoul was going to Paris, having been recalled for meetings with his Editor. Somehow, without anything having been said, she'd assumed till then that he would either be staying in the house or nearby; that he would always be at hand. Not only as a more than adequate guard for Derek, but possibly—just possibly—as a man who might at some time manage to convince her she wasn't going to be just another scalp in his current collection.

That was what she'd said to Margaret, "a scalp." The whole talk was clear in her mind, without any jumbling. It was just after the Camerons had come back from the meeting she'd arranged for them with Anthony Gethryn, and in their completely different ways each of them had very naturally been alight with interest and excitement. But a little later, when John had left them alone, Margaret had suddenly asked, "Where's Beaucaire?"

So she'd had to explain that Raoul had phoned to say he was off to Paris, and Margaret had said, "I don't wonder!" and that had started everything.

In five minutes Margaret had extracted the whole story from her; a story she'd ended with the line about not being just another current scalp.

"If you're thinking of that pneumatic siren from Sicily, you're crazy!" Margaret had eyed her with scorn. "I'd rather have an egg without salt than a man without a Past!"

"How do I know she was Past?" She hadn't known whether to laugh or be angry. "And then there's that Ballerina——"

"A press picture!" Margaret had been even more scornful. "He'd probably never seen her before and never will again. What's the man supposed to do when he isn't with you? Go around in a yashmak, ringing a leper's bell?"

Jocelyn laughed, remembering the tone as well as the words. She hadn't laughed at the time—but she did now, although a trifle ruefully.

She stopped suddenly, as from behind the communicating door to Derek's room she heard scratching and a muffled whine. She crossed to the door and opened it, and Firbank came out, wagging his whip of a tail and looking up at her with an apologetic but unmistakable tilt of the head.

Jocelyn sighed. She glanced into the other room and saw Derek fast asleep and closed the door quietly. She looked down at Firbank, and sighed again and picked up her robe from the end of the bed and in a moment was out of her room and making for the stairs. As she passed the study door, she could hear John and Margaret talking, and thought for a moment of looking in on them. But another whine from Firbank dissuaded her, and she took him quickly down and into the drawing-room. She unbolted the french windows and opened them and he shot out past her, heading for his favorite bush.

She pulled the windows shut and stood by them, waiting and looking out. A knifing nor'easter had broken up the clouds and cold moonlight flooded the garden, criss-crossing it with jet-black, ever-shifting bars of shadow from swaying trees and shrubs.

His mission accomplished, Firbank was trotting sedately back toward her when a large and long-furred feline emerged from a patch of darkness; a feline which in one frozen instant both saw and was seen, and in the next had been transformed to a grey streak heading for the nearest wall. With Firbank in hot and ominously silent pursuit . . .

"Oh, *no!*" Jocelyn pulled open the window and ran out onto the lawn; where the wind tore at her, cutting like a razor and tossing away her frenzied shouts of, "Firbank—*Firbank!*" as the cat flowed up and over the four-foot wall and disappeared, Firbank following with a grim and clumsy scramble . . .

She was half-way to the wall herself before she realized the futility of the chase and stopped in her tracks. She said, "Oh, d-damn!" and realized she was so cold that her teeth were chattering. Not too much troubled over Firbank's defection—during the week he had twice before made temporary exodus and come back both times in short order and good repair—she turned and started back for the house and warmth . . .

And had only taken three steps when from the tail of her eye she saw movement near the big elm at the far corner of the house. She stopped again, gripped by a sudden terror which held her motionless. With the hindsight which fear often brings, she knew the movement she'd seen hadn't been any tossing branch or shifting shadow. It had been the movement of a man's figure, stepping out of moonlight into the darkness surrounding the tree . . .

Her heart thudded in her throat, and she had to fight for breath. She wondered wildly how the intruder had managed to get past the Scotland Yard men who were watching the house from both sides: two in the empty garage on Marlborough Road; two in Wellington Lane itself, apparent night-watchmen over a spurious excavation in the street. She wondered whether they could hear her if she screamed; and then realized that any scream, even if she could force one, would be lost in the roar of the wind . . .

She stole a look at the elm, and found herself calculating distances . . .

From the elm to the drawing-room windows; from where she stood to the drawing-room windows . . .

She thought, *If only it was dark!*

And then dark it was, as a patch of the heavy cloud-wrack hid the moon. She found herself running—and then, as one of her slippers flew off and she stumbled and almost fell, realized with a fresh pang of horror that she was too late. Now the dark figure loomed gigantic between her and the windows——

The cloud-wrack scudded clear of the moon and she could see again . . .

As it had before, that night in Adrian's flat, a surge of relief, mingling with other emotions, left her furiously angry.

"*You!*" she said. "I might've known it! Are you going to make a habit of frightening me nearly to death!"

He came close to her in a stride. He said: "I am most sorry. I had no intent to scare out your wits——"

"You nearly succeeded, though." Although she wasn't conscious of cold any more, she pulled the robe closer around her. "May I suggest the morning might be a better time to drop in? By the *front* door?" Not waiting for any answer, she started past him.

But he moved, blocking the way. He seemed bigger than ever. He said, "Again I am most sorry. But your suggestion has for me no appeal."

She started to say something; just what, she'll never know. Because he came closer still—and she found herself, in utter astonishment, lifted from the ground like a child. There was an arm around her shoulders and another beneath her knees; arms which made no more of her weight than if she'd been a sackful of feathers.

She gasped. "Put me *down!*"

He turned to the french windows, pushing them open with his foot. "In a small moment," he said. "But as *I* want—and where *I* want . . ."

He carried her into the room, kicking the windows closed behind him. The steel arms still made nothing of her . . .

For the first time since she could remember, she felt *little!*

An extraordinary sensation—sweet and impossible and terribly, permanently exciting . . .

It was seventy-two hours later, and a hundred and twenty miles away, that the American guest registered as John Ducross of Duluth entered the bar-lounge of the Royal Crest Hotel in Manchester.

Mr. Ducross was a well set up, athletic-looking person somewhere in his thirties. Of quietly sporting type, he carried a light overcoat on his arm, wore grey flannels, a black sports shirt and a checked tweed jacket. The bar wasn't full, and Mr. Ducross went to his usual corner, cheerily hailing Jock the bartender and being greeted with the special smile which Jock reserved for his favored customers; a ranking Mr. Ducross had achieved in the comparatively short time of his ten-day stay at the hotel.

Mr. Ducross dropped his coat on a nearby chair and pulled off his hat, revealing a well-shaped head on which indeterminately brownish hair was closely clipped in the strictest of crew cuts.

Having ordered two big scotches ("the lady'll be along in a minute") Mr. Ducross settled himself on a bar stool, informed Jock that he had just been to the welterweight championship fight ("best five rounds I've seen over here") and reached for the newspaper some previous customer had left on the next stool.

It was open to a center sheet containing sporting news, and Mr. Ducross was casually running his eye over this when his attention suddenly focused upon a paragraph in the column headed, "Straight from the Horse's Mouth"; a column, it appeared, coming from the pen of someone who lurked behind the playful pseudonym of *Archie Stop-watch* . . .

> THE GLENEYRE STRING: Since the tragic death of Lord Gleneyre, speculation has been rife concerning the future of his magnificent string of both flat horses and 'chasers . . . It is rumored they may be sold, but frankly I don't give the story much credence . . . A statement from Lady Gleneyre herself is the only way to really clear up the situation, because even Major "Bobby" Rattigan, the well-known trainer for the stable, has no information. He has, however, promised to inform me of the decision of the Marchioness as soon as she and the young Marquis return after Christmas from their stay at the family seat in Scotland . . .

Having read through the paragraph, Mr. Ducross read it again. And then, concealing elation, laid the paper aside. He picked up his glass and drained it in a silent toast to Mr. Stop-watch, who at one

194

lucky stroke had saved him from any more of those tedious daily searchings through every conceivable type of news periodical. He caught Jock's eye and signalled for another drink and was half through it when the expected companion joined him.

Since she is of no more importance to this narrative than (save as an aid to health) she was to Mr. Ducross, it is enough to say that she was a handsome and most suitably constructed brunette who had met and surrendered to Mr. Ducross two days before, and fondly envisaged an association which at worst would last several months. She came up beside Mr. Ducross, dropped a quick kiss on his ear and slid onto the next stool. And then, before she'd even tasted her drink, began to prattle about plans for the forthcoming weekend.

"Sorry, doll." Mr. Ducross cut her short in his breezy way. "But I can't make it." He explained mendaciously that he had received that very afternoon a cablegram from Minnesota which made it impossible for him to extend his pleasant stay in Manchester for more than another twenty-four hours.

"Oh, *Jackie!*" The lady was genuinely close to tears. "Where are you *going?*" She achieved an idea, and clutched at him. "Couldn't I come along?"

Mr. Ducross shook his cropped head sadly. "Sorry, chick," he said. "Couldn't use a dame on a trip like this. It's a sorta scoutin' expedition, if you get me. Might or might not turn into real business." And he added, abandoning this undeniable veracity, "Just a little swing around the south counties."

And then he said, "So we'll make a real night of it tonight, huh?" He dropped a hand on her firm thigh and patted. He let the hand lie there—until after a moment he raised it to rub at a twitching little muscle beside his right eye . . .

There were storm-clouds gathering at Scotland Yard. In no less a place than the big, many-windowed room of the Commissioner himself; and on the morning after Mr. Ducross of Duluth had left Manchester, becoming in the process Mr. Martin Crawford from Calgary, Alberta.

There was a conference in the Commissioner's room. What Americans (and nowadays some Englishmen) would call a high-level conference. Extremely high-level. So high-level that, as Anthony said afterwards, "Knighthood was in flower, and there wasn't at any time a real, honest-to-God policeman within earshot."

There were four men present. The Commissioner himself, who was Lieutenant-General Sir Duncan Outram, K.C.M.G.; his Assistant-Commissioner in charge of criminal investigation, who was Sir Egbert Lucas, K.B.E.; a personage from the Home Office, who was Sir Ronald Aston-Phipps, K.C.V.O.; and Anthony Ruthven Gethryn, who was Anthony Ruthven Gethryn.

Anthony had met the Commissioner several times, and rather liked him. He had met Aston-Phipps once, and didn't like him at all; a feeling, he imagined, which coincided exactly with that of Aston-Phipps toward himself. So he grinned at Lucas, shook hands with the Commissioner, and returned Aston-Phipp's frigid nod with one still more arctic. And took the chair he was given, and waited.

But not for long. Whatever his faults, the Commissioner was never a bush-beater. "This amazin' Gleneyre business," he said. "Lucas and I have been discussin' the whole thing with the Home Office. First with the Home Secretary himself; later with Sir Ronald here, whom he appointed to act directly for him. They've both read that full report you gave Lucas. The Home Secretary, by the way, asked me to convey his personal congratulations on a brilliant bit of work."

"Nice of him." Anthony looked at Aston-Phipps. "You don't agree, perhaps?"

The acquiline nose of Sir Ronald Aston-Phipps was conveniently constructed for looking down; and now he looked down it. "Very able," he said. "Highly ingenious. Questions arise, of course. Mainly the anomaly of why this man George Brougham, *if* he is such a master of what you term 'natural disguise,' should trouble to murder eleven men, none of whom have seen him for several years, in order to prevent them from recognizing himself or his photographs should he become a prominent figure in the Peerage?"

"Obvious, isn't it?" Anthony raised an eyebrow. "The eleven men he killed were men he'd campaigned with and then betrayed. Men who wouldn't forget him in a hurry. Men who knew him *as himself*, not when he was playing a role. To have any sort of life after achieving the Marquisate, he would have to *be* himself. *Ergo*, he'd be in danger of recognition from any or all of the eleven. *Ergo,* he must get rid of them. Q.E.D." He kept his eyes on Aston-Phipps. "I imagine you were also going to ask why we plainly don't expect Brougham to indulge in another holocaust of 'accidental' deaths to get rid of the people who've known him here over the past five years . . . If you were, the answer's the same, but conversely. Having *never* been himself over that period, he won't be much concerned over possible later recognition. The most anyone could do would be to see a chance likeness."

"That is valid." Aston-Phipps stopped looking down his nose to shoot Anthony a glance of acid dislike. "One has no more questions."

Lucas shifted in his chair. "So perhaps," he said, "we can now get down to the real purpose of this meeting?"

"Yes, yes." The Commissioner gave him an approving nod. "Gethryn, what we're really here to discuss is the pressin' question of permanent guards for young Gleneyre. That is, of course, until we've got our hands on the killer."

Anthony braced himself. "Nothing to do with me," he said. "The decision rests with the family; and the work's purely a police job."

Lucas and the Commissioner exchanged glances. And the Commissioner said, "I've heard from Lady Gleneyre, Gethryn." He took a single sheet of notepaper from a drawer in the desk. "Here's what she says: 'Dear Sir Duncan Outram, Thank you for your letter. Will you please consult with General Gethryn about all arrangements regarding Derek. I am sure he will consent to act for me, and you may accept whatever he says as representing what I wish. Please forgive any delay in receiving this . . .' And that's all except for the signature." He put the letter away and raised his eyes to Anthony's again.

Lucas was looking at Anthony too. He said, "For the moment, let's leave aside the question of whether or not you already knew this decision of Lady Gleneyre's——"

"Yes, let's." Anthony was expressionless.

"And let's assume," Lucas went on, "that now you will give us any help you can——"

"No." Anthony was definite. "No, I won't. Because in my opinion the boy shouldn't have any official guard at all. Not even so much as your token quartette in Hampstead." He met stares and ignored

197

them. "Not even if you put your best and lightest-shod and most un-copperlike coppers on the job. To be wholly effective, they'd first have to be numerous; and second, they'd have to be close to the boy at all times. And if they were numerous enough, and close enough, they'd inevitably be obvious. And if they were obvious, their inevitable effect would be to destroy our single advantage over the man we're after. Because their very existence would warn him we were onto him and his scheme."

This drew more stares, and deeper frowns. And Lucas said slowly:

"But what's the alternative? To get Lady Gleneyre to keep the boy hidden, while we go on with the intensified search for Brougham? Is that all we can do?"

Anthony regarded him. "You tell me."

Aston-Phipps said, "But all this may take many months. And then, very possibly, come to nothing." He turned fish eyes from Lucas to the Commissioner. "One doesn't like it. One doesn't like it at all. It seems to me that we are losing sight of the main issue. Which is surely that a young Englishman, a peer of the realm, is threatened with death by murder. Our duty is clear, therefore. We must at all costs prevent the crime. At all costs."

Anthony was lighting a cigarette. "If that's all you want," he said, "it's very simple."

Again they stared at him, and Aston-Phipps said, "Really? Might one enquire precisely what method you have in mind?"

"Certainly." Anthony took his time. "Give the Press a full statement of *everything* we know. Even ask for public help in locating Brougham." He paused again. "With his whole scheme known by the whole world, he'd have to abandon it. For many a long year, if not for ever."

"We-ell," began Aston-Phipps, and was swamped by the Commissioner's violent, "Dammit, Gethryn, that'd only drive the fella deeper into the bushes. What we want's to flush him into the open! Give us a plan for *that*."

"By all means." Anthony was deceptively bland. "How would this do? Keep young Gleneyre *really* hidden—and publish the disturbing news he's got pneumonia. Issue bulletins—and top them off with an obituary. Follow this with a fake, confined-to-the-family funeral, and wait a few weeks . . . If the whole thing were staged right, I'd guarantee that George Brougham-Bruttenholm would walk up to the front door in person. Hat in one hand, birth certificate in the other."

He sat back, surveying his audience and their new expressions; Lucas troubled, Aston-Phipps increasing his resemblance to an aristocratic cod by letting his mouth fall open, and the Commissioner agog.

Aston-Phipps recovered first. "Ingenious," he murmured. "Smacks of chicanery, perhaps, but highly ingenious."

"It's brilliant!" The Commissioner crashed a fist down on his desk. "*Brilliant!* I don't see how it could fail." He glared happily at Anthony. "Why the devil didn't you put this up before?" He rubbed his hands. "We do this right, and we've got him!"

"Oh yes," said Anthony. "Yes indeed . . . However, a question remains. Rather a large one. What're you going to do with him after that?"

"What the devil d'you mean *now?*" Under stress, Duncan Outram was becoming more and more the old soldier, less and less the policeman. "We'll arrest him. And send him to trial. And hang him!"

"The arresting part's all right, I suppose." Anthony shrugged. "But I'm afraid that's as far as you'd get." He pointed at Lucas. "Look at your Assistant-Commissioner, Sir Duncan. He knows what I mean."

Lucas nodded gloomily, but Aston-Phipps said, "Which is?"

"That there is no case against the man." Anthony spaced his words. "Because we have no *proof*. If the D.P.P.* would consent to prosecute, I'll eat all my wife's hats. We know what Brougham's doing, and why he's doing it, but our knowledge is based only on *probability*. We haven't a shred of honest-to-God *evidence* against him. We haven't even any real *evidence* that any of the deaths weren't accidents after all——"

"Now wait a minute!" Duncan Outram pounded his desk again, his white eyebrows bristling. "You may be right about all the others, but what about Gleneyre? What about that rock-salt? Eh? What about that, sir! That's evidence of intent to murder, if I ever saw any! And if we used that scheme of yours and flushed this fella into the open, we'd not only have that against him, we could confront him with all the people in Deyming who met him while he was

* Director of Public Prosecutions.

callin' himself Bronson! I'll wager someone'd recognize him, whatever he'd done to himself. They'd be bound to—bound to——"

He ran out of breath, coughing as he inhaled. And Anthony slid neatly in. "Certainly I found rock-salt in the horse's rump," he said. "And certainly it was from a shotgun charge. But can we prove who fired the gun? Or even that the charge was intended for this particular pair of equine buttocks?" He shook his head. "We can't. And so if we did grab Brougham and did find someone to identify him as Bronson, all he'd have to do would be to admit that he was. I can hear him . . . *'Sure I stayed in Deyming under the name of Bronson. A man can call himself anything he likes, as long as he doesn't use the name to break any laws . . . Why did I do it? Because I wanted a quiet look at the ancestral estates without getting in anybody's hair, and Brougham sounds a little too near Bruttenholm . . . Sure I'd shaved my head. No law against that, is there? Specially if you've had a scalp infection . . . Why did I walk and talk differently? Why did I seem older? I didn't know I did; it must have been that bellyache I got from the Medeshire water . . .'"*

Anthony checked himself. "I could go on," he said, "*ad libitum et nauseam.* But I'll spare you. After I've reminded you that Mr. D. Bronson left Deyming a full week before Gleneyre's death, I think I've given you enough." He stood up and crossed to the desk and dropped his cigarette into an ashtray.

"We've got to face it," he said. "Until and unless, by luck or by judgment, we can collect some concrete *evidence,* no case lies against Brougham. As things stand now, there isn't a judge who wouldn't have to sum up for his acquittal or a jury who'd dare to say guilty . . . Too bad in this instance; but a good thing really, I suppose. Our conception of justice would certainly be hell-bound if we started hanging people on a basis of pure probability, however arithmetically massive that probability might be."

He stopped, and grinned apologetically. "I should have organ-music," he said, and went back to his chair and waited for someone to say something.

But no one did. They were waiting for him, and he had to go on.

He said, "You know our real trouble, don't you? We're up against something new. A man I didn't believe existed outside sensational fiction, where he's a master-mind generally called something like *Dr.*

X, or *The Professor*." He looked around at them. "But now we have him with us in reality," he said slowly. "A mass murderer who never makes mistakes!"

He was somber. "A man," he added, "whose shadow grows all the time longer and more terrifying . . ."

He shrugged. "End of message," he said. "Anybody any ideas?"

Sir Duncan Outram and Sir Egbert Lucas exchanged a glance in silence. But Sir Ronald Aston-Phipps cleared his throat.

"Yes," he said; and took the stage . . .

And he had the center of a different stage two hours later, as he neared the end of lunch with the Home Secretary himself and another personage who was of considerable importance at the Foreign Office.

Aston-Phipps was in the middle of his report on the morning's meeting at Scotland Yard. "And at this point," he was saying, "one feels it necessary to state that there is no doubt Gethryn's analysis was completely right. However much one may disapprove of the man himself as didactic, intolerant and offensive, one is forced to admit he brings brilliance to this type of problem. His conclusions, in fact, cannot be ignored."

The Home Secretary pulled thoughtfully at his ragged moustache. "Do I gather," he said, "that these conclusions stop us from providing police guards for the young Marquis! Even though he seems in imminent danger of—h'm-ha—assassination?"

"That is so," said Aston-Phipps. "But there are other factors which one was about to outline. Factors which mitigate the perils of the situation. Factors which one must admit one introduced oneself; in the form of suggested procedure." He made an arch of his finger-tips and surveyed his audience over them. "A procedure which was agreed to by the police from their viewpoint, and by Gethryn from the viewpoint of Lady Gleneyre."

He paused, not ineffectively. "You see," he said, "one was personally convinced that the necessary discovery of evidence against George Brougham must be only a matter of time. One felt that our police, with their painstaking persistence, must inevitably unearth what was required; if only they could be given a long enough period in which to work unhampered by any pressure inherent in the threat to young Gleneyre. And such a period seemed to be attainable when one discovered from Gethryn that it was the intention of Lady Gleneyre to leave England, with her grandson, immediately after Christmas. On a visit, I might add, of some months' duration."

"This 'agreed procedure' you were talking about," said the man from the Foreign Office. "Couldn't we hear what it is? And also where you think the F.O. comes in?"

"I was about to reach that point." Aston-Phipps regarded his questioner with an icy stare. "The procedure tentatively agreed upon was that, immediately after the Gleneyre's departure, and thenceforward, special steps should be taken to investigate very fully the passports and visas of all men with American or Canadian backgrounds who attempt to leave the country. Regardless of where they are going, or why."

"Ah, yes," said the man from the Foreign Office. "Now I see what you're after. And you would need our help, of course." He pondered. "With certain minor reservations, I think I could promise it."

"One moment, please." Again the Home Secretary was tugging at his moustache. "I'm afraid you're going too fast for me." He looked at Aston-Phipps. "Could you give a little more detail?"

"With pleasure," said Aston-Phipps sourly. "The advocated procedure is based upon two facts. First, that no passport has ever been issued to George Brougham in that name. Second, that our very stringent post-war travel regulations make it impossible for *anyone* to leave England without showing a passport, duly visaed." He arched the finger-tips again. "Now bearing these facts in mind, you will realize that a thorough investigation into the passport backgrounds of all American or Canadian males wishing to leave England, *after* the Gleneyres' departure has been announced, cannot fail to produce admirable results."

"It can't, eh? Why can't it?" There was more tugging at the ragged moustache.

Aston-Phipps controlled a sigh. "Let me elucidate. If George Brougham does *not* try to leave England in pursuit of the Gleneyres, everything is happily in *status quo*, with no danger to the young Marquis while the police continue their work. And if George Brougham *does* try to leave England, he will inevitably be stopped by the passport investigation. Which will not only expose him as George Brougham, but will also enable us to control his movements *without* revealing to him that we have any knowledge of his murderous activities."

He paused briefly for emphasis. He said, "To clarify this, one should point out that there are only three possible ways in which Brougham can originally have entered England. He must (a) have legally changed his patronymic before his journey and therefore have carried a *legitimate* passport in the new name; or (b) have carried a *stolen* and altered passport; or (c) have carried a forged, a *spurious* passport . . . Now, to take these in order of probability: in case (c) or case (b), the procedure would be that Brougham is arrested, tried on the appropriate 'illegal entry' charge, and sentenced to at least a year's imprisonment. In case (a), which one feels highly improbable, he cannot be charged with any infraction of law; but it nevertheless should not be difficult to keep him in England. By a simple prolongation of bureaucratic processes heightened by deliberately created confusion over the name-change . . ."

He'd been about to go on, but didn't have to. The Home Secretary was smiling now, the moustache bristling untouched. "Yes! Yes, of course!" said the Home Secretary. "I see it all now. Clever. Very clever!" He looked at his other guest for confirmation.

"Yes," said the man from the Foreign Office. "I suppose so . . . Except that it seems to leave one loophole. Rather a dangerous one; the time between now, and the Gleneyres' departure." He looked at Aston-Phipps. "You said 'immediately after Christmas,' and that leaves over a week."

Aston-Phipps nodded. "One raised this point oneself," he said. "But it seems certain there is no real danger. In the first place, it is almost impossible that Brougham should know the boy's present whereabouts. In the second place, the police seem entirely satisfied with Gethryn's assurance that adequate personal protection will be covering this period."

"H'mm," the Home Secretary was thoughtful. "Are you satisfied yourself?" he asked. "Do *you* place this much reliance on Gethryn?"

Again there came a nod from Aston-Phipps. This time a nod which contrived to be both reluctant and decisive at the same time.

"Yes," he said, and left it at that.

"Splendid!" The Home Secretary's smile was back again. "It looks as if everything were settled." He regarded Aston-Phipps with grateful benevolence. "And I have to congratulate you on a brilliant piece of work!"

"Oh, please," said Aston-Phipps. "One merely does one's best . . ."

The Home Secretary's luncheon ended at half past two. And by that time, in his room on the other side of Whitehall, Sir Egbert Lucas had just finished giving his own report of the morning's meeting to an audience of one. Who also happened to be the first professional policeman to hear of it.

"An insufferable type, this Aston-Phipps," said Lucas. "But you'll have to admit there's a head on his shoulders." He studied Pike, and Pike's expression. "What're you looking like that for, man? It's a workable plan, and you know it!"

Pike went on rubbing at his lantern jaw. He didn't look any happier. "Oh, it's *workable* all right," he said. "As far as it goes."

"Meaning that's not very far? Personally, I thought it was reasonably comprehensive."

"No, sir." Pike shook a gloomy head. "Full of holes as one of those Swiss cheeses. How do we know our man or his passport is going to look American or Canadian? How do we know he doesn't look as German as Hitler?" He stood up and began to pace the room. "If it comes to that, how do we know he even looks like a man!"

"Oh, come now, Pike!" Lucas showed signs of irritation. "You must be in a bad way to worry about transvestitism at this stage! Aston-Phipps at least gave us a better idea than any we'd had ourselves. Better than any of Gethryn's, too. All Gethryn did this morning was put up brilliant schemes and then knock 'em down again."

Pike started to say something, but thought better of it. He went on pacing unhappily.

Lucas said, "Look at it this way: even if the idea isn't completely holeproof, it does cover a lot of ground. So we'll have to act on it. And if we keep on digging hard enough we might get something sooner than you think. Especially if we concentrate on that sportscar. All we need's a little luck, and we're due for some, God knows."

Pike stopped pacing. He leaned on the desk and looked across it at Lucas. He said, "There's something you haven't told me, sir. How did Mr. Gethryn take this scheme? How did he react to it?"

Lucas thought about this. "About the way I did," he said. "He seemed to think it was a good idea. He certainly didn't raise any objections."

"I just can't understand it, sir." Pike shook his head. "You mean he just *took* it? No argument? No comments even?"

"No argument, certainly. And no comment really—except to say it was a sound scheme and might give us the time we certainly wanted." Lucas was suddenly smitten by a memory. "Oh, there was something else—but it doesn't amount to anything. A remark he made to Outram. Something about this being an extraordinary criminal but unfortunately we had no extraordinary powers——"

"Ha!" Pike came to life. "Could you remember the exact words, sir?"

"Why should I? It was just a casual remark——" Sudden comprehension dawned in Lucas's eyes. He stared at Pike and said, "You're absolutely right, and I must be losing my grip! What he said was that the *police* didn't have extraordinary powers!"

Pike smiled. "That sounds more like Mr. Gethryn, sir." The smile faded and he rubbed at his long chin again.

"I'd give a lot," he said, "to know what's up that sleeve of his . . ."

CHAPTER TEN

On the evening of the sixth day after he had left Manchester, Mr. Martin Crawford of Calgary returned from Scotland, and made his way to London.

The day of his arrival being the twenty-second of December, the town was filled to bursting point, and he was lucky to get a room in a small hotel off the Marylebone Road. Where he underwent another name-change, appearing on the register as Leslie Schoonmaker of Niagara Falls, New York.

Over a solitary dinner, Mr. Schoonmaker pondered his position . . .

So this guy who wrote as "Archie Stop-watch" had been wrong,

*and neither the old woman nor the boy had been in Scotland at all.
So what? It didn't matter. In fact, it was maybe all to the good.
Because unless some exceptional opportunity had popped up, the
time was 'way too early to do anything . . . When he came to think,
he was surprised at himself for having even considered it. After five
years, this was no time to start getting impatient. And anyway there
was still plenty of money . . .*

He checked the money that night. In his hotel room, with the door
locked and the blinds down. He stripped, and from around his lean
and muscular midriff unbuckled the oilskin-covered belt, and eased
out its contents . . .

And found, as he'd known he would, that the balance he'd been
carrying in his head was completely accurate . . .

An ingenious adapter to circumstance, Mr. Schoonmaker managed
in this way and that to spend a reasonably pleasant Christmas, his
only concession to the more serious side of life being a diurnal visit
to some Public Library (he varied them from day to day) where
he would carefully scan all the society columns in all the newspapers.

It was the twenty-eighth of December before this devotion to his
work was rewarded by the *London Post*, and there was an oddly
coincidental prelude to the discovery.

Because on the front page of the *Post*, just as he was about to
turn it over in search of the society news, a name caught his eye.
It was the name *Messenger*, and it was in an item low on the page.
Under the head, "PLANE DISASTER BRINGS ROMANCE," was a report of
the hitherto unpublicized wedding, on Christmas Eve and by Special License, of M. Raoul St. Denis to Mrs. Jocelyn Messenger, widowed sister-in-law of the late Adrian Messenger . . .

Mr. Schoonmaker didn't trouble to read the rest. Smiling faintly
to himself at the memory of how nearly this Frenchman had ruined
one of his more difficult jobs, he turned to the center pages—

And there it was, staring him in the face:

> . . . The Dowager Marchioness of Gleneyre, accompanied by
> the young Marquis, left yesterday for the United States. After
> a short visit to relatives in New York, they will proceed to
> California for a protracted stay of six months or more at Lake

Messenger, the fabled mountain estate left to the Marchioness
by multi-millionaire Hiram Messenger . . .

This time, there seemed no doubt of authenticity. But, to make
assurance doubly sure, Mr. Schoonmaker consulted other journals.
And found the same information in all of them . . .

Twenty-four hours later, Mr. Leslie Schoonmaker of Niagara Falls,
New York, had ceased to exist; but a Mr. Don McTaggart of New
Brunswick, Nova Scotia, was on his way to Cornwall . . .

And, on the night of the fifth of January, a nameless and invisible
passenger left for France aboard the trawler *Trewythyn Belle*. The
comparative (though inordinately expensive) simplicity of this un-
authorized departure from England would doubtless have horrified
Sir Ronald Aston-Phipps and his like. But Cornwall will always be
Cornwall, and among Cornishmen will always be found certain sea
captains who indulge in the freest of all free-trade systems.

Ostensibly going about her normal business of fishing, the *Trewythyn Belle* was actually bound this night for the coast of Brittany,
where her crew would engage in certain nocturnal (and untaxable)
activities; on this particular occasion the simple barter of whisky for
brandy . . .

So that, at three o'clock in the morning, the passenger was trudg-
ing along a country road not far from Morlaix. He was now, if anyone
had chanced to ask him, one Gaspard Lecroix, a French-Canadian
seaman making his way to Cherbourg after a visit to friends in
St. Brieuc. From cap to boots, from his rolling walk to his clanging,
metallic, Montreal French, Gaspard Lecroix looked and sounded
and behaved exactly as should any man of his adopted name, na-
tionality and profession . . .

By autobus, by train, by lifts from friendly wagon drivers, he made
easy and unquestioned way to Cherbourg.

And Luck smiled on him. Instead of the two or three weeks he
had prepared himself for, it was only three days before he was able
to obtain exactly the sort of passage to America that he wanted.
This was a steward's berth on a Scandinavian passenger-carrying

freighter, and it was attained just the way the five-year-old reverse experience had told him it would be; open-handed expenditure in certain dockside bistros; selection of the right man to approach; eventual introduction to a genially venal and not too inquisitive Purser . . .

Luck went on smiling. The S. S. *Brünnhilde* was clean, well-found, and—so far at least as the steward's labors were concerned—more than sufficiently manned.

She sailed on January the twelfth . . .

She made Los Angeles harbor on February the twenty-third, and like all her kind docked at San Pedro.

On the afternoon of February the twenty-fourth, Gaspard Lecroix, in company with several shipmates, made ready for a trip ashore. Freshly bathed, dressed in the cleaner of his two outfits, and with his travel-grown beard handsomely brushed, Gaspard Lecroix kept his nerves under admirable control as the group left the ship.

But nervous he was. So nervous that it wasn't until after the second drink in the first Wilmington bar that he could really believe entry to these security-girt United States could be so casually, so completely simple. Beyond the most cursory examination by a Customs' man, no one had so much as looked at him or his companions. And what was more—he smiled to himself—although no pass had been necessary to leave the dockyard, he had carefully been provided with one he must show to get back!

He paid for another round of drinks, and took himself off, obviously bound for Long Beach and the imaginary female whose unimaginable charms he had been extolling for the last ten days of the voyage.

He found a taxi, and was driven to Long Beach.

He stopped the cab at the Municipal Auditorium, and found himself a bus to Los Angeles, and an hour later was decanted into the tawdry, dismal anonymity of Main Street.

Gaspard Lecroix was already a character of the past. But the following hours of shopping were destined to bring into the world one Benjamin J. Knight of Chicago, free-lance photographer of the flora and fauna of his native continent . . .

That winter, like all California winters, was unusual. November, December and early January had been cold and wet; but now, nearing the end of February, the usual freak heat-wave, which had struck the southern half of the state some six weeks before, still persisted.

So that it was a sunny, seventy-eight degree afternoon when Benjamin J. Knight turned off Highway 30 some five miles east of San Bernardino and headed for the mountains, and the little settlement of Tomahawk.

Tomahawk is five thousand feet up the southern side of Mount Lobo, perching on a heavily wooded plateau, which, in its turn, is some thousand feet below Lake Messenger. The road up to Tomahawk from the Yucaipa Valley is a steep, none-too-wide and (for people driving it the first time) apparently endless corkscrew. But the second-hand jeep which Benjamin J. Knight of Chicago had purchased in Los Angeles on the previous evening made light of the tortuous miles. The jeep had been expensive, but its owner didn't regret having paid the price; its rubber was good, and its engine better, and now that it was filled with all the gear of an itinerant, bohemian, flora-and-fauna photographer, it made a most convincing background for Benjamin J. Knight himself.

Benjamin J. Knight wore a checked lumberjack shirt, wrinkled denims and those rough-hide shoes known latterly as safari boots. Bearded, bare-headed and genial, he was a figure which in some parts of the country might have stood out like an ulcerous thumb, but in this part of California melted into the landscape like a tiger in the jungle . . .

It was about three-thirty when he drove up onto the plateau and came through the towering sugar pines into Tomahawk itself. Even at this height, the westering sun shone pleasantly warm from an almost indigo sky, and the air was clean and sharp like champagne.

He stopped the jeep on the outskirts of the village and walked through the trees to a sheer and precipitous edge. He looked down the brown-grey mountain flank to the green valley and saw a city like an ant-castle, six thousand feet below. He turned his back to the precipice and looked up the brown-green ascents to a snow-topped peak four thousand feet above.

He filled his lungs with pine-scented air and went back to the jeep and drove slowly into Tomahawk; past the little church, past the post-office-cum-general store, past the Trading-Post saloon and "eatery," past a double row of steep-roofed little houses, and came at last to the Wolf's Head Motel.

Since there was no snow this year, there were no skiers, which meant that he had no difficulty in renting a double cottage for an indefinite stay, and even less in obtaining permission to use the extra bedroom as a darkroom.

He was settled in by four-thirty, and spent the rest of the day making Tomahawk acquainted with Benjamin ("just call me Ben") J. Knight, world-traveler, photographer-at-large and the best of good company.

He started on his first scouting expedition early the next morning, taking with him a convincing selection of equipment. Armed with the local knowledge he'd absorbed the night before, he drove up the winding mountain road until, after a couple of miles, he saw another tree-covered plateau to his left and found the sign-post he was expecting. It had two arms, one pointing straight ahead, "TO BRIDLE-PATH AND SKI-LIFT—2 MI."; the other indicating a narrow dirt road through the trees, "LAKE MESSENGER—1 MI."

He didn't take the dirt road, but drove on and up, for perhaps another mile, until he was some five hundred feet higher. Here he stopped the jeep, and picked up the new binoculars from the seat beside him, and put them to his eyes and slowly began to sweep the whole of the mountainside above him.

He was checking on last night's information. Checking carefully. And he saw nothing that didn't jell with what he'd been told, for above the timberline there was no sign of man or his work except the gaunt skeleton of the ski-lift and the closed and deserted hut at its base.

He turned around and knelt on the seat and now scanned, even more slowly, what he could see below him, paying particular and minute attention to the Lake Messenger plateau. Here the trees towered thick and green, with even less sign of man and his work. Except for a thin steady stream of smoke which carved a dark exclamation point against the blue. A stream of smoke which must come from a chimney.

And then, to clinch every detail of the map he had drawn in his head, he saw a glitter through the trees; the unmistakable glitter of sunshine on water.

He slid behind the wheel again, and put the binoculars away. He started his engine, and turned the jeep, and drove back to the sign-post and this time took the dirt road and headed through the trees.

In half a mile, the road dipped suddenly in front of him, and he had his first sight of the lake. It was shaped like a capital L, lying on its side, with the long arm transverse to the way he was going and the shorter arm almost straight ahead. Edging the shore was a rough stone wall, marking the boundary of the property for as far as he could see.

What really surprised him about the lake was its size. In spite of what he'd been told, he hadn't envisaged anything as big as this. The long arm of the L must be, he thought, over a mile lengthwise and nearly half a mile across.

He stopped the jeep; and now he sat for several minutes just taking in the scene. The water shone deeply blue, its surface sparkling in the sun, and except for the throb of his engine and the occasional squawking of a jay there was no sound at all.

And, except for the thin black column of smoke, there was still no sign of habitation. From where he sat, the tree-covered hillside above the far shore obscured the house. But, running over his mental map again, he realized that it must be visible across the shorter arm of the L. He drove on, following the road to the right as it skirted the wall, and passing from the shade of the pines to the bare tracery of a stand of birches.

The birches, in their turn, gave way to a grove of giant cedars, and he parked the jeep inconspicuously in their shade. He took the binoculars with him, and walked on. And after a couple of minutes found that his map hadn't failed him.

Directly across the water were a boathouse and landing-stage of weathered log. Above them, well-tended terraces rose like a series of giant steps to the house itself, a huge and rambling structure which must have been an eyesore fifty years ago but had somehow contrived over the decades to adapt itself until it seemed a reasonable part of the landscape.

He kept well back in the grove and sat on an outcropping of rock and put the binoculars to his eyes again.

The whole hillside jumped into three-dimensional life, and he became aware of activity on one of the higher terraces. There was a tennis court there, and on it a fast singles game was in progress. It was a mixed single, between a tall woman with silver-blonde hair and a giant of a man, who, for all his size, was quick as a cat on his feet. Watching them were a small, neat white-haired woman in a deck-chair, and a dark-haired boy of fifteen or so who stood beside her.

Behind the glasses, he frowned. The old lady must be the Marchioness herself; the players, very possibly, were the Frenchman St. Denis and his new wife. But for dark-haired fifteen-year-olds there was no niche in his mind.

He was still watching, and still frowning, when the game ended with an overhead smash from the man—and, at the same time, a fifth figure came out of the house and ran down the steps toward the court—

Another boy; shorter, more squarely-built, two or three years younger. A boy whose close-cropped hair shone gold in the sunlight. A boy he'd seen before, four months ago and seven thousand miles away, astride a neat grey pony. A boy who had said, "My name's Bruttenholm—Derek Bruttenholm."

A boy who was now the nineteenth Marquis of Gleneyre . . .

The tennis had finished at noon, with a doubles set in which Derek Bruttenholm and the big Frenchman had played the silver-blonde and the unknown dark boy. By twelve-fifteen, all four players, and the Marchioness, had climbed the steps and vanished into the house. And since then, although it was now two-thirty, the watcher had seen no further sign of them. No further sign of life, indeed, except for the puttering figure of a gardener.

At three o'clock the watcher stretched, and put down the binoculars, and treated himself to a cigarette. He had a little trouble lighting it, because the wind which had sprung up gently a couple of hours ago was strengthening.

At three-fifteen, with even the gardener gone from sight, he decided to call it a day. He got stiffly to his feet and struck back through the cedars to the jeep. He sat in it, and found the packages of sandwiches he'd brought and devoured them hungrily, washing them down with nips from a big flask.

While he ate, he put his mind to work. He had run the quarry to its earth, and now only two problems remained. Only two problems, out of the hundreds which had faced him five years ago! They weren't simple, of course, but they certainly weren't insurmountable. How to get said quarry out of its earth and vulnerable; then, when this had been done, what method to use for the quarry's final disposal?

He sat for a long time, with the wind soughing and creaking in the trees around him. He sat until he was startled by the sudden crackling fall of a dead bough somewhere behind him and the outraged squawking of a family of jays.

He decided it was time to move. Neither problem was going to be settled sitting here. There was a lot of work ahead. A lot more scouting, to collect a lot more knowledge. Knowledge of how the household lived; of how and when and why any of them came out from the house and its grounds . . .

He started the car and bumped back to the dirt road. He had reached the top of the rise, the same point from which he had first seen the lake, when something made him stop the jeep and turn for a last look at the terrain——

A last look which took his breath away. A last look which, even in the first instant of awareness, offered a possible solution to both problems!

There was a sailboat on the lake. A sleek little fourteen-footer, heeling way over as she turned out from the short arm of the L and scudded before the wind under the deft handling of her crew of one . . .

He grabbed for the binoculars, although even before he had them to his eyes, he knew. But he had to make sure there was no one else aboard.

There wasn't. There was only the nineteenth Marquis of Gleneyre . . .

He put the glasses down, noting with surprise that his hand was shaking. He had the same strange, ineluctable sensation which had seized him twice before in the past five years, that some sort of Providence was on his side. Although he knew it was ridiculous, he found himself contemplating an instant attempt. In his mind he could see the whole thing. The hardy stranger who braves the February waters for a swim. The apparent seizure of cramp. The cries for help. The boy bringing the boat close into the wind beside the drowning man——

He saw it all, even while he knew he mustn't do it *now*. Not yet!

He picked up the glasses again, and put them to his eyes a fraction of a second before his ear caught the wind-borne *putt-putt-putt* of an outboard motor. And he saw, coming out from the boathouse, an auxiliary-motored dinghy with the dark boy at the tiller.

He dropped the glasses onto the seat, his hand still shaking. He forced himself to turn his back to the lake and slip the jeep into gear and drive on. His head was whirling, and the muscle by his right eye was throbbing violently. For the first time in five years he allowed himself to forget the role of the moment, his mind filled to overflowing with the potentialities of the sailboat and the lake. Potentialities which were crying aloud to be used, to be turned into fact. Potentialities which, the more he thought of them, became more and more proof of that guiding Providence . . .

Without really noticing it, he came to the sign-post and automatically turned right on the main road and drove on, down toward Tomahawk, his mind now worrying at an objection thrust up by memory.

Pomfret! Pomfret had died in a sailing accident, and another sailing accident would violate the one inviolable rule he had made for himself at the beginning—*Never repeat!* . . .

But it wouldn't really be a repeat, because it wouldn't *show*. It couldn't. In the eyes of the world, there was no conceivable connection between Francis Pomfret and Derek Bruttenholm. And anyway, Pomfret had died years ago, thousands of miles away . . .

And here it was—a gift. He'd have to do it this way. He *would* do it this way. So simple. So easy. All he had to do was wait. Haunt the lake, and wait. Wait until the time when the other boy wasn't along. Or, if absolutely necessary, arrange somehow for the other boy to be elsewhere. On the long arm of the lake, near the far end, would be the place. With no one to see. No one ever able even to guess. Just like Pomfret. Just the overturned boat. Just the——

With a sick and sudden jolt he came back from plans of the future to facts of the instant, perilous present.

He was driving too fast. He was passing a road-sign marked with the S which means dangerous curve. He was coming into the first bend of the S, with a white guard-rail on his right outlining the edge of a frightful drop. In a sick flash he remembered having passed it on his way up, safely on the other side; even remembered talk of it last night. Jackman's Fall, and the drop was six hundred feet into a rock-strewn crevice called Jackman's Gorge.

He clung to the wheel, and braked as hard as he dared, and swayed somehow around the first loop—and saw disaster staring him in the face. A stationary car was half blocking the narrow road; heading uphill, its rear end stuck out across the road, jacked up and with two men bending over it, working on the left hind wheel——

He stood on the brakes now, with all his weight. And swung the wheel with a racing-driver's quick one-two——

And somehow made it—in a bedlam of dust and screaming rubber, and shouting voices, and a roaring circular skid which ended with the jeep pulled up behind the other car, bare inches from its lifted rear . . .

And somehow, with tremendous effort, he forced himself back into the shell of Benjamin J. Knight; the shell he should never have left.

So it was Ben Knight who dealt with the situation, and the ominous converging upon the jeep of the two men he might so easily have killed. Obviously Mexican, they were dressed alike in nondescript overalls and big, dusty-black sombreros. The burly one was glowering and silent, the little wizened one enraged and voluble, pouring out execrations in a weird mixture of Spanish and English.

It says much for the personality of Mr. Knight, best of good fellows, that within a matter of minutes the atmosphere had changed completely. So completely that now he and his new friends stood around the new friends' old car, passing Mr. Knight's big flask from hand to hand.

Before the flask was empty, the new friends had not only been told all about Mr. Knight and his profession, but had also confided to Mr. Knight their own reason for being on Mount Lobo. Having noticed a leather case on the front seat of their car, Mr. Knight had made a genial jest about fellow-photographers—and the little Mexican, more and more voluble as the flask went around and around, had winked at Mr. Knight, and pointed up toward the top of Mount Lobo, and opened the case to show a geiger-counter . . .

Farewells over and the flask empty, Mr. Knight drove slowly down to Tomahawk. Every once in a while he put up a hand and rubbed gently at a spot beside his right eye . . .

He had to wait. For another three days. Three days which seemed the longest of his life.

On the first day there was no wind at all, so that his watch on the lake, this time from deep in the pines at the far end, was fruitless. There was no boat; no sign of any human, anywhere.

On the second day, a fitful breeze sprang up late in the morning, and the boy sailed again. He was again alone in the fourteen-footer, but again was accompanied by the *putt-putting* dinghy, which this time carried not only the dark boy, but a dark and handsome woman who might be his mother.

The third day was windless. Utterly windless, and even warmer. So warm that the date might have been the first of August rather than of March . . .

But the fourth day—the fourth day was different. He sensed it when he waked at seven. He knew it when, at eight-thirty, he went out for breakfast and saw the pine tops in gentle movement, and felt a strengthening breeze . . .

He was at the lake by nine, in his new place among the pines. He parked the jeep with its nose toward the road and took the binoculars from their case and sat with his back to a pine-trunk and watched the other end of the lake, where the short arm of the L turned toward the invisible boathouse.

He waited again, while the hot sun filtered down through the great trees, and the wind increased. It was a different wind today, blowing up from the valley behind him; a wind hot from the desert instead of cold from the peaks.

He didn't mind waiting. Because he knew. Because with every

minute his certainty increased that this was the day. And the time. And the place . . .

And then at last he saw the sail, as the sleek little craft nosed out into his view and, beating against the wind, began to tack up the lake toward him.

He slid behind his tree, keeping the glasses to his eyes, and raking the sailboat with them, first on the port tack then on the starboard, and repeating this until she was close . . .

There was no doubt. There was only the boy. Only Derek Bruttenholm. Only the nineteenth Marquis of Gleneyre.

With a deft, canvas-slapping turn, the boat went about and headed away down the lake, cutting through the blue water before the wind. And there was still no sign nor sound of the dinghy.

He stood up and went back to the jeep. Taking his time, he stripped off sweatshirt, trousers and shoes and dropped them into the back seat, with the binoculars.

Naked except for his trunks, he started toward the shore. He could see the boy turning his craft again at the far end of the lake.

There was still no dinghy, and he knew it wasn't coming. Knew it as surely as he'd known since waking that this was the day.

The white sail bright in the sun, the boat was tacking up toward him. He stood watching it, keeping in the shadow of the trees and moving along so that he'd be near it in its final turn.

The time came, and he walked out of the trees and down to the shore and knew the boy had seen him. He waded into the water up to his knees and raised a hand and shouted, "Okay if I take a dip?"

On his last port tack now, the boy raised an answering hand and a light young voice came clear across the water. "Go ahead——"

The water was cold. But not so cold as he'd feared. By the time he'd swum fifty yards in a fast crawl, it was just another element. Another element in which he was completely at home.

Looking after the sail as it scudded away, he swam lazily on and was perhaps a hundred and fifty yards out when, treading water, he saw the sailboat putting about again, not nearly so close to the far shore as before.

So much the better, he thought. So much the quicker. His breath came short, and he could feel the pulse throbbing in his right temple.

He took himself in hand, and began to swim around in circles, varying strokes, duck-diving once in a while, generally disporting himself.

The zig-zagging white sail drew closer. This was the moment.

He gave a sharp, agonized cry and flailed at the water like a man in the throes of cramp. He let himself sink, waving a wildly clutching hand above the surface . . .

He surfaced again—and screamed—and saw the boat, on short tacks now, surging toward him.

He let himself sink again—and again came thrashing to the surface —and there was the boat, right beside him, hauled neatly into the wind with the boy leaning over the gunwale, an arm outstretched.

With a masterly show of desperation, he clutched at the hand and the gunwale; and let the boy use strength to help him; and finally tumbled aboard and lay in a sprawling, gasping, convincing heap.

Sheet and tiller in one hand, the boy leaned over him, saying something he didn't trouble himself to hear.

The boy's throat was only inches above him, and coming to his knees in one convulsive thrust, he reached for it with both hands——

And stopped in mid-movement as the doors of the locker under the decked-in bow flew suddenly open and he saw a man lying in the locker, the doors framing his head and shoulders. A man with a lean face and grey temples and cold eyes of strangely vivid green. A man who had a gun resting easily on his right palm. A man who said, with deliberate and icy calmness:

"Mr. George Brougham, I believe?"

Something—everything!—exploded inside his head . . . He threw his whole weight at the boy's legs, sending him flying in a tangled heap in front of the locker. And in the same movement he came to his feet and dived overside and struck out for the shore——

And swam as if every fiend in hell was after him. Swam with a mounting fear of the bullets which must surely start humming around his head.

But no bullets came. And underwater his feet touched the shelving beach, and he stood up, thigh-deep, and began to splash at a fevered run toward dry land and the trees and the jeep, risking one backward glance and seeing the gleaming sail scudding away from him, already half down the length of the lake.

So they must be going to send someone after him. But he still had a chance. He was nearer the jeep than they were to the boathouse.

His lungs laboring, his heart-beats thudding in his ears, he ran for the trees—and a man stepped out of them, right in his path.

A big man; a giant of a man. The Frenchman who must be St. Denis.

He put down his head, and dropped his left shoulder, and charged . . .

But the Frenchman wasn't there at the end of the charge. There was only a foot which caught him across the shins and tripped him so that he fell face down into the soft loam.

And there was an iron knee in his back. And iron hands that clamped around his wrists and pulled them up with insulting ease until they touched his shoulder blades and he was helpless.

A deep voice said, *"Alors, copain!"* and he was jerked to his feet with a searing pain down his shoulders, and found himself being propelled along the shore, away from the jeep and all hope of safety.

He went quietly for a few paces, bent double and stumbling more than he had to, his mind working furiously. He saw a big rock a few paces ahead, and knew what he was going to try.

He groaned. "My arms," he gasped. "My arms!" and let his legs buckle—and threw all his weight against his captor's knees.

It worked. The Frenchman fell headlong over the rock, relinquishing the wrist-grip and shouting in pain; a barrage of oaths from which the words *jambe* and *rompu* stood out clear . . .

He was free. He wheeled and ran back into the trees, swinging to his right and making for the jeep, throwing one look behind him to see that the Frenchman was still down. It didn't occur to him that the Frenchman had fallen too easily; that escape from the iron clutch had been far too simple a matter . . .

Hope pumping life into him, he burst through the trees and came in sight of the jeep——

And stopped dead.

There was a man standing by the jeep. A little man in nondescript overalls and a big, dusty-black sombrero. The wizened little Mexican of Jackman's Fall.

There was no time to wonder; no time to ask questions; no time to waste. He charged—and caught the little man in the midriff with

219

a shoulder which carried all his hundred and seventy pounds plus the impetus of his speed.

The little man reeled back, falling with a rushing, sliding crackle onto a carpet of pine needles. And groaned—and lay still in a twisted heap . . .

The jeep roared into life and screamed away in low gear, throwing up from its wheels a screen of dirt and pine-cones as it raced for the gateway in the wall and the lakeside road beyond . . .

George Brougham was gone—so possessed by the fever of flight that there was no room in his mind for even the suspicion that he was being herded . . .

The little man got briskly to his feet. His sombrero lay on the ground, and without it he didn't look like a Mexican at all. Showing no sign of any hurt, he stood where he was, pulling back the cuff of his left shirt-sleeve and keeping his eyes fixed upon his watch.

Another man—his burly and sombreroed companion—emerged from behind a huge pine-trunk only fifteen feet away. And, at the same moment, Raoul St. Denis came running through the trees from the shore, showing no more sign of injury than the little man himself.

The little man heard them both, but kept his eyes on the watch, his head cocked as he listened to the receding sound of the jeep. Now it was on the road and in high gear, racing for the far end of the lake and the turn which led up to the highway.

"Un minute," said the little man, and, when the others came up to him and shot questions at him in French, cut them short.

"Ç'a va!" he said, and raised his hand for silence. *"Écoutez!"* he told them, and went on listening himself, his eyes still on his watch.

The sound of the jeep was faint now: it had come to the turn and was climbing to the highway.

"Deux minutes!" said the little man . . .

And then, after sixty endless seconds in which the sound faded completely, *"Trois minutes!"*

They went on listening.

"Quatre min——" said the little man, and stopped.

There was no need to listen any more . . .

CHAPTER ELEVEN

It was the tenth of March and a pale sun shone over London, gilding all Westminster and the wind-ruffled surface of the Thames; shining into the riverside windows of New Scotland Yard.

Among them were those of Sir Egbert Lucas, and behind them Lucas himself was concluding a conference with Pike and George Firth.

They had reached the last item on the agenda, headed simply "Gleneyre," when with fateful timing a secretary announced two visitors—"Mr. Gethryn, sir, and a friend . . ."

Lucas stared. And frowned. He said, "Show 'em in," and in they came; Anthony first, with Raoul towering behind him.

There were brief greetings—and introductions for Raoul—and a shuffling of chairs.

And then an uncomfortable silence, with Lucas frigid, Firth non-committal, and only Pike offering anything like a smile.

Anthony studied them. "Do I detect a flavor of Coventry in the air?" he asked mildly. "A trace of cold shoulder?"

He winked at Pike, and looked from Lucas to Firth. "I'm surprised at you both," he said. "Why the sub-zero welcome? If you haven't been able to find me, it's because I've been abroad."

"I know," said Lucas. "How was it in Switzerland, by the way?"

"Fine." Anthony was bland. "Very Swiss. Of course, I was only there for a few hours, and a couple of months ago at that."

"Hah?" Lucas tried to repress surprise. "But I thought——"

"I know you did," said Anthony. "It's a habit you should conquer, my dear fellow—especially in your position. Actually, Alan and I only stopped in Montreux overnight, to pick up his mother. We were all in California before the New Year." He glanced at Raoul. "St. Denis and his wife joined us a few days later," he said. "With some friends of his."

"*California!*" said Lucas, and Firth sat forward on his chair, and Pike mastered a chuckle.

"Yes." Anthony was blander than ever. "We were staying with Lady Gleneyre."

He stood up suddenly. "I'm sorry," he said. "I know I shouldn't be playing the fool. But in the first place this atmosphere always has a bad effect on me; and secondly I was annoyed by this assumption that I'd walked out on you." He looked at them. "Didn't anyone realize wild horses couldn't have dragged me off the Gleneyre case?"

Lucas smiled, thinly. "I have to admit that was Pike's contention," he said. "But mine is that you might at least have communicated with us."

"And have a pack of Aston-Phippses baying on my heels!" Anthony shook his head. "No, Lucas! When I told Outram that George Brougham was an extraordinary criminal, and the police didn't have the extraordinary powers necessary to deal with him, I was implying he'd have to be dealt with by some person or persons who weren't bound by any book of rules."

He paused, sitting on a corner of the desk. He said, "People like me and St. Denis, for instance. Men free to set a trap that would catch the man *flagrante delicto.*" He paused. "So we set it, using the one irresistible bait. The boy. The boy whose death was going to make all those other sixty-seven murders worthwhile for Mr. Brougham . . . Don't look so horrified, Lucas. Derek wasn't in real danger at any time. We had a corps of guards, small but elite. Myself, and St. Denis, and those friends of his I believe I've mentioned already." He glanced at Raoul.

Who said, "Yes. Some old acquaintances from the Maquis." He shrugged. "Deplorable persons, perhaps, but high in efficiency."

Glaring, Lucas opened his mouth to speak, but Anthony cut in first.

"It didn't take Brougham long to arrive," he said. "Passport or no passport, he turned up on our mountain-top at the end of February. We dangled the bait in front of him for a day or two; and a week ago he grabbed for it."

"You mean he made an actual attempt on young Gleneyre's life!" Lucas was incredulous. "In front of witnesses?"

"Oh, yes." Anthony nodded. "Myself for one; St. Denis for another——"

"But where is he? What did you do with him?" Lucas was on his feet now, Olympian calm forgotten. "Did you get the police? Was he arrested? What's *happened* to him?"

It was Raoul's turn to interrupt. He said, "Here *I* must put a word. This man was in my hands, but somehow pulls his getaway." He was apologetic. "And from my friends too." He shook his head sadly. "What you would call a slippy customer. Very slippy!"

Wild-eyed, Lucas ran a hand through his hair. "Are you trying to tell me he *escaped!*"

"Take it easy," said Anthony. "Preserve absolute calm." He had pulled a wallet from his pocket, and now, from the wallet, took a newspaper cutting.

"Read this," he said—and laid it down in front of Lucas, squarely in the middle of the blotter.

As one man, Pike and Firth came to their feet, moving around the desk to stand one on each side of Lucas.

They read the cutting with him. It was from a California paper, the *San Bernardino Herald-Chronicle*. It was dated March the third, and it ran:

STRANGE DEATH ON MOUNT LOBO
Jackman's Gorge Claims New Victim

His jeep crashing through the guard-rail at Jackman's Fall on Mount Lobo, a man identified as Benjamin J. Knight of Chicago hurtled to his death in Jackman's Gorge yesterday.

A photographer of wild-life, Knight was staying at the Wolf's Head Motel in Tomahawk, where he had proved very popular among the winter residents.

The man's broken body, nude except for a pair of swim-trunks and a money-belt containing more than $3,000, was thrown clear of the car, the wreckage of which had burst into flames.

The mystery angle suggested by the almost nude condition of the body is heightened by the statement of a Tomahawk boy who told police he heard an explosion before the sounds of the car crashing down the rocky precipice.

Under the direction of Lieutenant Hagmeyer, Sheriff's officers are investigating. At present, however, they do not place too much credence in the boy's statement, feeling that the accident was probably caused by excessive speed, combined with a possible tire blowout . . .

Lucas finished reading. He looked up, staring at Anthony. "I suppose——" he said.

"Yes." Anthony nodded. "For Benjamin J. Knight, read George Brougham."

It was Raoul who broke the silence which followed. He said, "So his death is through explosive accident——" He was philosophic. "What you would call, I think, a justice poetic . . ."

ABOUT THE AUTHOR

Philip MacDonald, grandson of the Scottish poet and novelist George MacDonald, was born and educated in Britain. He wrote numerous novels, suspense stories and film scripts, most notably the classic *Rebecca*.